Aailaine dropped her bow as some of the Shadows lunged at her. She picked up the blade and stood to face the onslaught, silently hoping she had inherited some of her mother's natural ability. Now in her hands, she could feel the hum of sero that ran through the hilt and she jerked the sword, causing the electricity to shoot out over the blade. The Shadows stepped back at this, and Aailaine smiled savagely.

"Alright." She smiled as she swung the blade and killed some of the Shadows that stood near her. She continued to slice and dodge them as best she could, being especially aware of the shifting werecats. However, she found that she was still being overwhelmed by their sheer numbers and her strength was failing her. Even though she managed to wield sword with a level of proficiency, her swings were clumsy, and very few of them connected. She glanced at the never-ending hoard and prayed for the moon to come out from behind the clouds.

Legends of A'sthy Series

Shroud

Legends of A'sthy

Shroud

Yasmina Iro

*To my eighth-grade teacher
Who never gave up on me.*

*To Elliot Strauss,
For helping me get here.*

*To John Edward Panlaqui,
Who taught me to do what makes me happy.*

EXLA

VONN

LINGAR SMI

COATLLI

REDAN

TOLSAN   YOLT

SLALAN

ANCEO

LIS YST

LIKHA

HIRIE

YOTLRI

GIREYR

RIBI LANES

IMASLO

RISCK IMYD

YAREL

HEL

MIXOH

TORORA

SWARI LANES

SASSRANE

LANOL

DIXAD

Prologue

Now, listen closely to me, for here is the tale told throughout the ages.

In the beginning, there was nothing but chaos. If there was land in that time, it was not visible or habitable. Nothing but the insufferable Darkness existed in those days. It covered the whole world and moved with a life of its own. No one is sure where it came from, or how it came to be. Perhaps it had always existed, or perhaps it was placed there by beings unknown.

From that Darkness, a single being of light was born. Its skin was as white as freshly fallen snow, and its long robe shone with the light of a million stars. It lifted its eyes to the dark heavens and its name was Orassul.

Orassul wandered through the Darkness surrounding it but could find nothing. The Darkness was everywhere and concealed everything, making it difficult to navigate. This made Orassul feel lonely and one day it tried to rise above the Darkness to see what else existed. Breaking through the veil, Orassul found the sun and the stars and was awed by the light. Having finally seen light for the first time in its existence, Orassul knew that it never wanted to return to being inside the Darkness. Using power granted to it by beings unknown, Orassul broke through the dark veil and allowed the light of the sun to hit the world. Upon hitting the world for the first time, the sun revealed the stunning blue green oceans and the green canopy of trees in the forest. All of A'sthy was revealed when the sun's light pierced and scattered the Darkness.

Orassul wandered these lands for many a cycle, studying the land it had revealed. Soon however, it grew lonely again, as no living soul was to be found. Only nature and her wonders greeted it, and it grew sad.

One day, as Orassul sat in the plains of Dochel, it occurred to it that maybe it could create someone to end the loneliness. Orassul began to pick up weeds from the surrounding area, twinning them together. Once enough had been gathered, Orassul blew on the weeds gently and revealed the first male elf: a graceful creature of the flora, with a slight green tint to his skin. The elf revered Orassul with awe and the Creator was delighted. Excitedly, it began to gather flowers and twinned them together as it had done with the weeds. Orassul created a female elf, her skin as colorful as the flowers that had created her. Orassul asked the elves what they wanted to do and both elves left the open plains to make their way to the forest, where they and their children would stand guard for all eternity.

Orassul then collected piles of giant boulders and smaller yet sturdy rocks. Orassul hit both piles lightly with its hand, and from the shattered remains were born the first dwarves. Small and sturdy, they were truly creatures of the stone. The Creator asked them what they would like to do as well. The dwarves looked about them and saw the mountains that rose above the land. They asked if they could learn to speak to the stone and Orassul sent them gladly. Next, Orassul created the beasts to roam with its creations: the bear and wolf that walk the ground, the dragons and birds that own the skies, the whales and fish that inherit the sea, and the insects and tiny creatures that live in the shadows of those larger.

Soon the land was filled with all manner of beast and creature. The races changed and moved about, giving rise to most of the races we know today. The gnomes and trolls, who preferred wide-open skies to their mountain heritage, and the fairies and nymphs, who longed to leave the green forest of Hirie. And so, the world became filled with all kinds of creatures, even those we could not even imagine.

Watching the world change and become full of life pleased Orassul greatly and it was happy for a time. But soon, Orassul felt as if something was missing. Even as it celebrated with the dwarves, dined with the fairies and listened to the stories of the spindly, Orassul still felt alone.

Orassul wandered into Exla, walking along the shores of that inner sea. Orassul ran the mud through its fingers, allowing it to fall and be washed into the unknown depths of the water. An idea came to it, and it began to use the mud to make a creature unlike any other on A'sthy. Out of the sand and water of Exla's shores, Orassul gave life to the first of your kind, the humans.

As Orassul finished giving life to humans, it sent the humans across the land bridge that connected Exla to the rest of the world, and humans mingled with the other races, living side by side with their predecessors. Orassul, however, never left the shores of Exla and over many cycles, the land became shrouded in a mist and clouds are always seen over that land, even on the clearest day. Many believe that Orassul sleeps there, tired from the effort to create humans, which took many cycles to complete.

But, worry not, dear child. Orassul will wake if A'sthy has need of it and the Creator will soon walk among us again.

Yasmina Iro

Tolsan
Where Life Continues

Chapter 1

"Aailaine! Get up Aailaine!"

A pair of eyes as silver as moonlight snapped open as the door was closed, drifting away from the land of dreams. Groaning, the girl slowly sat up, pushing her long, disheveled hair out of her face. The orange glow of the lamp on the wall offered a soft light and her hair reflected that small light around the room, creating an aura of colors. Aailaine sighed and watched the flame flicker before pulling herself out of bed and walking into her wash closet. As she removed her gown, she stepped into the shallow stone basin and dumped a bucket of lukewarm water over her head. Shivering, she quickly reached for a small green cloth and washed away the sleep, refreshing herself. Finished with washing, she carefully began to brush her hair, styling it in a single fishtail braid over her left shoulder with a plain clip.

Once her hair was styled, she left the wash closet and dressed, pulling on her dark brown trousers and fastening the dull grey shirt. After slipping on her sturdy black boots, she dropped a small amulet over her head. Aailaine carefully made her little bed, being sure to fold her bedding at the foot. She sat on the mattress and glanced over the walls of her room. The few possessions she had disappeared into the dark corners and the amulet around her neck helped to reflect the soft light of the lamp. Aailaine picked up the amulet and turned it over in her hands, inspecting it. The eye-shaped amulet had a single white sapphire set in silver and a mo'qire coiled around it, protecting the gem from harm. Aailaine sighed heavily as she tucked the gem in her shirt and started to roll up her sleeves just as her door opened.

"Aaila-, oh, you're up. Well, get going." The small figure quickly shuffled out of the doorway and Aailaine followed. The dwarf was about a meter tall, and his disheveled brown beard was riddled with grey. His bald dome seemed shiny in the dull light of the Elddess lamps as he limped his way down the steps from Aailaine's room and back into the main hall. His once blue tunic was now dark with stains and the leather belt around his waist was worn from use. The dwarf collapsed into his large chair and inspected the food on the stone table in front of him as he took a swig from a jug. The small table had three wooden baskets: one with bread, one with dried meat, and the third with small pieces of cheese. Aailaine carefully stepped down into the main room and sat on a stool opposite him. Helping herself to the other jug in the center of the table and reaching for a small loaf of bread and cheese from the baskets, she leaned back and began eating her meager food.

"Do you know what I'm doing today, Rfkr?" Her voice was quiet and melodic, and she looked away as she spoke, playing with the food in her hands. The dwarf sighed, and sunk deeper into his chair, sliding his bare feet on the stone floor. He remained quiet and Aailaine resigned, taking more bites of the bread. Rfkr lifted his eyes from his beard to glance at the girl and sighed again, straightening up in his chair. He reached across the table and quickly ate some of the dried meat before speaking.

"I think gardening again, but don't count on it." Aailaine's face lit up and she quickly finished her food. She lightly kissed the dwarf's cheek, who grunted, and she quickly left the little home. As she stepped out, she made sure to lock the door behind her before climbing up the ladder to escape from their small crevice in the mountain and stepping onto the busy streets of Mathydar. In front of her, both man and dwarf walked to and fro in the large cavern, eager to reach their individual destinations. The ceiling of the cave was lost to the darkness above her and the crest of the Nivim clan reflected brightly on the armor of the dwarven soldiers who passed, greeting her with a lively, "*Fingge!*"

Aailaine greeted them with a warm smile and a slight wave before heading toward the edge of the city. She walked briskly past the other travelers, at times having to crawl through the small dwarven passageways. The city was an intense stone maze of small spaces containing dwellings and large caverns filled with public buildings, and Aailaine knew the city by heart.

Climbing up the side of a cavern wall using small-carved footholds, she finally reached her destination: a small door built into the side of the mountain. Standing on the narrow ledge beneath the Elddess lamp, which casted the soft glow of twilight, she knocked on the door and stated her name. A moment passed, and the door slid open, grinding a rut into the loose gravel as it went. She swiftly walked inside to be greeted by another dwarf sitting on a stool next to a desk, a small stack of papers in her hand. The desk was covered with several stacks of paper and baskets, all neatly arranged on the stone surface. The dwarf herself was well built, her muscles all too visible with her black short trousers and sleeveless tunic that split down the sides, showing her tanned skin. Her red hair was pulled into a high ponytail and a few frays hung in her face, which she ignored.

"Ah, *Keoi,* Aailaine. Let's see...gardening again? Hm, that's the third time this week. Guess it's just as good, with autumn just starting." The dwarf began to file through the papers in her hand and desk as Aailaine patiently waited. She looked up toward the ceiling, her eyes tracing the outlines of the various details carved into the stone there. A pack of the yeitre were carved with explicit detail as they ran around the room. The mo'qire flew among them, the dragon's wings keeping its serpent body afloat. Soon she found herself roaming alongside the wolves, getting lost in the design. Aailaine jumped when the dwarf exclaimed, pulling out a single piece of paper.

"Here you are, your plots for the day." Aailaine bowed her head and accepted the paper. "And here's your basket with tags should anything be ready to be harvested. Remember to mark it."

"I will. *Nao Fei,* Hvidr." Accepting her basket and tags, Aailaine began for the back of the dwelling where a set of stairs waited to carry her to the world outside. As Aailaine left, the female dwarf watched her go before she settled into her stacks of papers again, nudging the many baskets with her foot.

Chapter 2

Aailaine knelt on the cool earth, weaving her hand into the soil so she could grip the weed by the roots. Ripping it away, she tossed it into the pile of weeds she had already uprooted. Once the pile stood large enough, she would dump it over the edge of the narrow cliff she knelt on. She looked over to the edge, where the grass ended and became smooth stone. Soon the stone ended as well, and the empty expanse of sky filled the space. She looked up to see the cloudy blue sky tinged with slight pinks and oranges and she knew the sun was setting on the other side of the mountains. She briefly considered waiting until after the sun set to return to the mountains, but she knew Hvidr would question her absence. It had been quite some time since Aailaine had been lucky enough to see the night sky and she longed to see the sky filled with stars again.

As soon as the pile allowed, she walked over to the edge as she tossed the pile of weeds. As she watched the plants plummet down the side of the mountain, she wished she could follow. It seemed a cruel twist of fate; the weeds, which didn't wish to leave their mountain home, would safely tumble to the ground far below, no worse off than they had been. However, if she, who desperately wanted to leave, took the same journey, she would be lucky if it did not claim her life.

Sighing deeply, Aailaine turned to resume the tedious task of tending to the plot. As none of the harvest was ready to be picked, Aailaine quickly watered the plants before gathering her things and making her way to the path that would take her back into her mountain prison. Before stepping into the dimly lit passage, she turned to look over the darkening sky one last time and fancied that she saw a white bird soaring in the distance. The bird flew majestically and seemed to tease Aailaine with its freedom, gaily weaving a path between the mountain peaks. Aailaine slowly turned her eyes away and returned into the cold embrace of the stone.

Aailaine made her way back to the room where Hvidr waited patiently for her. The dwarf accepted the girl's empty basket and paper without a word and quickly did her paperwork. Aailaine waited to see if she would be dismissed for the day, but Hvidr remained silent, filing papers and making marks here and there. She coughed softly to catch the dwarf's attention and Hvidr only paused for a moment to look up at her.

"You may go. You're gardening again tomorrow, so be sure to be on time." Aailaine nodded and headed for the door. "Aailaine."

"*Oiihead*, Hvidr?"

"Tomorrow you get paid, so bring your own bag to receive it." The dwarf eyed her carefully. "We don't want an incident like last time."

"*Oiihead,* Hvidr." Aailaine nodded her acknowledgment and walked out into the cavern, the door sealing behind her. The cavern was nearly empty now and only a few dwarves moved within its walls. Aailaine looked over the expanse for a moment, sitting on the edge of the ledge. The public buildings with their glittering purple veins running through the stone and their high walkways filled the expanse of the cavern. From their tall archways dangled colorful gems, like drops of water on a spider's web. Even from where she sat, she could make out some of the symbols that labeled the buildings. The symbols glowed slightly in the stone, pulsing as if they were alive. The crevices in the floor and walls of the cavern glowed softly with the light of the Elddess lamps.

She watched as some beings crawled out of their neighborhood crevices and others returned to theirs, which reminded her she needed to get home as well. Aailaine carefully climbed down the side of the wall and landed safely on the stone floor. As she turned to head home, she noticed that some warriors of the Nivim clan were making their way to her.

"*Uodoushe*, Aailaine." Their leader hailed her, and she bowed her head as they approached, marching in rhythm with each other. Their training was reflected in their movements; the perfect march, their weapons held at the ready and their eyes ever gazing around for trouble.

"*Fa okad ang*, Yovuik." The young dwarven lord stopped his troupe in front of her and the warriors clanged their weapons against their shields, as was custom. Yovuik removed his helm and shook his dark brown braids free from their confines. His beard was short and trimmed and he stroked it with his free hand as he spoke.

"I have new warriors with me that will soon brave the Dark Tunnels. They wished to meet the human who braved the Tunnels with me." Aailaine blushed softly as the young dwarves encircled her to examine her stature. She herself had gotten lost in the Tunnels underneath Yoltnir after an earthquake separated her from her hunting party and she ran into the young lord on his way out. Yovuik had challenged her to a hunting game and promised to show her the way out if she won. She quickly proved herself quite a match and he declared her victor from exhaustion.

"If it had not been for you, Yovuik, I would still remain in those Tunnels." Aailaine bowed her head again. "But I'm afraid I must leave. Rfkr waits for me and I should return to him."

"Rfkr?" One of the warriors squeaked and the rest seemed excited. "*The* Rfkr?"

"Is he truly four meters tall?"

"Can yo-"

"*Oiihead,* that Rfkr. And *ika,* what a ridiculous question." Yovuik shook his head at their questions. "We will not keep her from him any longer. *Goad Sheeideong,* Aailaine."

The lord replaced his helm and lead his party off, heading for their faraway city of Yoltnir. Aailaine, after watching them go, quickly returned to her own crevice in Mathydar. Unlike most home crevices in the city, her home with Rfkr was the only dwelling and it allowed them the utmost privacy. She slid down into their hole and let herself in to find Rfkr asleep on his chair. Rfkr's stained blue tunic had been changed to a cleaner green one, and in his hand, he held an empty bottle of smibi, the rice wine he occasionally brewed.

Aailaine carefully lifted the bottle from his hands and left it outside their door for the night crew to retrieve. She considered waking him, but decided against it, content to sit on her stool and eat more of the food. She had to pick large areas of mold off the remaining bread and the cheese basket sat empty. The meats seemed the safest choice to eat, so Aailaine stuck to those.

As she drank and ate, her eyes fell upon the gleaming armor that stood in the corner of the main room. The colors and emblem of the Nivim clan embraced the metal and even in the still room, the scarf seemed to billow in some unknown wind. In his youth, Rfkr was a decorated warrior who had traveled outside the Tolsan, gaining recognition in every corner of the land for his acts against the Shadows. When he returned to the mountains, the Nivim buried him with honors and it was said that his space in the stone was sung by some of the best Hongekako in the Tolsan. Some said he even travelled to Exla and met Orassul, which he always vehemently denied. One of his companions had been Aailaine's mother, although Rfkr claimed he didn't remember her well. Most of the time when Aailaine asked about her, Rfkr would grunt and complain about how Kleia dumped her child on him.

"Kleia," Aailaine whispered, lifting her amulet from beneath her shirt and looking it over. The old dwarf had mentioned that Kleia was not her full or real name, but it was the only name she had to call her mother by, as even Rfkr claimed to not know her real name. From what Rfkr had described in one of his better moods, her mother was a fierce woman, able to wield any weapon put in her hands as if it belonged there. She was a Teieimoko and was more determined than most to drive the Shadows from A'sthy. No one really knew what drove her, but it was obvious that she was a force that could not be stopped. It seemed nothing could tear her down, and it came as a great shock when Rfkr found her dying on his doorstep, the young girl in her arms.

Rfkr groaned, sitting up in his chair slightly and looking for the bottle that had been in his hand. He glanced up at Aailaine, who nodded her head toward the door.

"Finished a fresh batch," he groaned, standing from his chair. He gathered the old food and set the baskets on their doorstep along with another empty bottle. "The Viwl are celebrating some event or other and want some wine. I'll be gone all day tomorrow so make sure you wake up on time. I made extra for you, alright?"

"*Nao Fei*, Rfkr." Aailaine accepted his explanation and quickly finished her food. Rfkr grunted and limped his way to their small storage area and checked the cupboards there. Pulling out some more of the smibi and bread, he made his way to his room and decidedly shut his door. Aailaine picked herself up from her stool and placed it in the corner next to Rfkr's old armor. She grabbed a bottle of smibi and began undressing as she made her way to her room, placing the dirty garments in a basket filled with soiled wear. From a clean basket she pulled a fresh blue gown and made her bed ready for sleep, placing the wine on the floor next to her bed to drink in the morning. As she lay down to sleep under the soft glow of the Elddess lamp, she watched the reflections off her hair dance across the stone ceiling and let the colorful shapes lull her into a deep sleep.

Chapter 3

Aailaine hummed to herself as she carefully harvested the fresh vegetables and marked them with her tags. The harvest was good for both human and dwarf plots and Aailaine was filled with relief. Whenever one race had a better harvest than the other, the Tolsan would become a sight of political turmoil, with the races crying foul against the other. It was usually left to the Covern to then ignore the plot markings and distribute the harvest equally, so that no one got more than the other. Although it was still early into the fall, the slightest indication of an uneven harvest could cause turmoil beneath the quiet mountains.

Finished with her current plot, Aailaine lifted the heavy baskets and turned to make her way to the next plot marked on her map. However, sitting on the path was a large white akhby, its glittering scales giving off a blinding light. Its horns were long and curved forward, ready to spear anything that got too close and its body was long and curled on top of each layer, hiding its limbs. Its eyes were a deep grey and as it watched her, its clubbed tail twitched like a cat ready to pounce. It seemed to study her for a moment before speaking, its voice rumbling through Aailaine's mind like a mountain stream.

< Hello, little one. > The voice was unmistakably female, and a small bit of Aailaine's fear left her. She tried her best to relax her muscles and mind, preparing herself to flee if needed. She knew she couldn't get back into the mountain, as the dragon blocked that path,

but she knew at least one plot was below hers, and she would take her chances with jumping to that plot. Aailaine's heart jumped again when the dragon resumed speaking. < It seems my sudden appearance has unsettled you. Rest assured, I mean you no harm. >

"I do not mean to offend, but please forgive me if I do not believe you." Aailaine spoke loudly, although the rushed beating of her heart disagreed with her confident tone. The dragon laughed, the sound echoing through her entire being. Although it was no physical attack, the mental push caused Aailaine to take a step back and almost drop her baskets.

< You fear me so greatly. I suppose it is understood, though. I am quite intimidating in this form. > As she spoke, the dragon began to undergo a metamorphosis. Her giant form shrunk as her claws receded into hands and her tail slid back into her body. Aailaine's eyes grew wider and wider as the majestic beast transformed into a woman, her silver hair flowing down past her waist. Her smaller wings folded into a long tunic and she stretched her arms, as if inspecting them.

She looked up and began to take a step toward Aailaine, who quickly stepped back. However, Aailaine failed to notice the edge of the grass and slipped on the smooth stone, teetering off the edge and the baskets falling from her. She closed her eyes, preparing herself to land as she began to fall back off the cliff, when she felt a scaled hand grab her arm and yank her back up. Aailaine then found herself very close to the giant dragon woman. The woman, after pulling Aailaine up, took a few steps back.

"It seems you still are afraid of me, even though I look like this." The woman gave Aailaine a strange look, before sighing and taking a few more steps back. The woman turned her gaze to the sky, watching the clouds roll by for a moment. "It can't be helped, I suppose. How long have you lived here, little one?"

"I have lived here for seventeen cycles." Aailaine answered, gathering herself mentally before standing. Whatever this woman was, she had just saved her from falling, so if nothing else, Aailaine felt that had earned the being her attention.

"And is that your age?"

"No. I have twenty-one cycles."

"Ah, time passes too quickly in these mountains. It seems like it was only yesterday..." The woman spoke softly, bringing her eye back down to Aailaine. "You've grown to be so beautiful."

"Um...thank you." Aailaine's eyes drifted to the edge of the cliff as she spoke, worrying for the condition of the food she had harvested. The woman followed Aailaine's gaze and she giggled softly.

"Remember this life, Aailaine." Aailaine snapped her gaze back to the woman. "Don't forget these precious cycles. I will return shortly to visit again."

"Wha-" Aailaine started to speak when a voice rang up the side of mountain.

"Aye, Aailaine, *Or kodad uab*?" Aailaine knelt on the edge of the cliff, glancing down at the dwarf below, who called up to her. "Aailaine!"

"*Rea kodad uab*, Jozzick! I slipped and almost fell. Is the food alright?" Aailaine waved down to grab the dwarf's attention, who sighed deeply, obviously relieved.

"*Oiihead*, the food is a little bruised but fine." He smiled up at her, motioning inside the mountain. "If you're alright, I'll wait for you inside."

"*Nao Fei!*" Aailaine shouted down as Jozzick waved just as a large gust started up behind her.

"*Ika heia!*" The dwarf's voice rang up behind her as Aailaine turned to face the dragon woman again, but the path was empty. Another large gust blew through the plot and Aailaine looked up to see a white shape disappear over the mountain's peak. The dragon's clubbed tail waved as it disappeared over the peak and Aailaine thought she noticed a dark shape follow it.

"What just happened...?" Aailaine whispered to herself, her eyes glued to peak the dragon disappeared over. "That dragon knew me. Maybe..."

"Aailaine!" Jozzick's voice brought Aailaine out of her thoughts and she shook her head to clear it. As she made her way into the mountain to meet up with Jozzick, she began to wonder what the appearance of the woman meant.

Chapter 4

"Ah, Aailaine, that's quite a harvest. So early, too, maybe it's a sign." The she-dwarf accepted Aailaine's full baskets and paper without much question. Aailaine shook her head and waited for the dwarf to finish filing her report. As she waited for her pay, she decided to test her luck.

"Um, Hvidr, can I ask you something?"

"Ask away." Hvidr never looked up from her work as she spoke. A wave of uncertainty passed over Aailaine, but her curiosity got the better of her.

"Is it possible to see akhby this deep in the Tolsan?" At this, Hvidr stopped working and looked at Aailaine suspiciously. Aailaine, uncomfortable under her gaze, began to stroke her index finger with her thumb. "I'm just curious."

"Did they speak to you?" Hvidr asked, ignoring Aailaine's last statement. Aailaine nodded, deciding not to lie to her. She chanced a glance at Hvidr, who stared at her a bit longer before turning back to her work. Relieved that the moment had passed, but puzzled by the dwarf's reaction, Aailaine remained silent as Hvidr finished calculating her pay. She soon finished her work and handed Aailaine a strip of paper.

"*Nao Fei*, Hvidr." Aailaine bowed her head as she offered her thanks, but Hvidr merely waved her off. Aailaine took her leave and returned to main cavern. A lot more people were out and about now, so Aailaine knew she needed to be careful about her path. She needed to reach the deep-dweller Commune, which stood in the heart of Mathydar, in the city's largest cavern. However, the quickest route would be by far the busiest, filled with both deep-dwellers and dwarves alike. She had no interest in being around that many people, so she decided to take the longer but more deserted path.

As she crawled and walked her way through various tunnels, she became aware of the whispers that followed her presence. She had grown used to the whispers over the cycles, but they still bothered her. When she had been a child, no one ever cared that she looked different, but as she and her friends grew into their later cycles, one by one the friends began to disappear. Aailaine tried many different ways to hide her strange features, going as far as cutting off all her hair. However, it never made a difference and soon Rfkr was Aailaine's only company.

Soon, Aailaine reached the center of Mathydar and quickly made her way to the deep-dweller Commune. The large building was packed with people and Aailaine paused, considering whether or not her pay was worth waiting for. She took a glance at the paper, and nearly dropped it in her surprise. The pay was made out for almost three times her normal pay and she had to do a double take to make sure she hadn't misread the amount.

Aailaine silently thanked the dwarf and stepped into line. Living was hard with it just being her and her dwarven caretaker. Rfkr was an old adventurer and a Meiouko, and didn't have many work opportunities, so they mostly lived off Aailaine's pay. Her work was usually limited to half the week- only four or five days, leaving her without pay for the remaining five or six days.

"Next! Oh...it's you." Aailaine's spirits instantly dropped when she reached the front of the line. The teller almost seemed ready to dismiss her but waved her over with a look of disdain. The entire room grew silent as she made her way to the front and handed the teller her pay slip. She could feel her ears growing red as the crowd continued to stare and talk in whispers.

"Aailaine, yes, it seems as if quite the bonus has come through. If I didn't recognize Hvidr's handwriting, I'd say you wrote this yourself." Aailaine scowled at the accusation but didn't respond. The man behind the window reached into a drawer behind him and began to count the money. He put the money in a small pouch and handed it to her, a small smirk on his face. "Please, continue your service to the deep-dweller community."

Aailaine took the pouch cautiously and began to leave the room. Once she stood outside the building, she produced a pouch of her own and slid the pouch with her pay inside, leaving the string that would open it hanging out. Carefully, she pulled the string and the outer pouch bulged and smoke ebbed from its stitching. Aailaine sighed as she opened the larger pouch; once again, her pay pouch had been lined with smoke powder, with the hope that it would jet into her face when she opened it.

Waving away the last bit of the smoke, she checked the amount in the bag. As if the smoke prank hadn't been enough, the teller also shorted her pay, although if she hadn't been expecting it she wouldn't have noticed, as only a couple of silver pieces were missing. She sighed and stood, sealing the two bags and beginning her slow trek home.

"I'm home." Aailaine whispered, speaking to the empty dwelling. She made her way to her room and, kneeling next to the bed, she reached underneath and pulled out her quiver. Attached to the quiver was a leather bag, which she carefully removed. Inside the bag were two smaller drawstring pouches. She opened the larger of the two and carefully removed her pay from the trapped pouch and into her savings. Once her money was safely stored, she pulled out the smaller pouch and opened it, removing one single white emerald. White and translucent stones were a rarity and Aailaine was fortunate to have so many. She happened to be well known within the Stryn clan, the dwarven clan based in Mathydar, because she had saved the now-leader from a wild totiriel who had found its way into the city. The large mountain ram was about to trample the young lord when Aailaine took down the ram before it reached him. As thanks, he now allowed her to have first pick when white and translucent stones were found, and in return she provided them with the smibi that Rfkr made, which was made with rice from Dochel. Dochel rice was a rare treat in the mountains, making Rfkr's smibi heavily valued.

Aailaine put away her stones and made her way back to the main room. She pulled down another bottle of smibi, before tidying up the small space, sighing deeply. She began sipping the wine as she walked back to her room and, kicking off her boots, collapsed on her bed. She looked up at the Elddess lamp that cast its soft glow over her room. She finished drinking the small bottle and dropped it on the floor, watching it roll away on the smooth stone.

<Orassul, please hear me, > Aailaine silently prayed. < I know the life I have here isn't the worst it could be, but if you see fit to, can

you let me leave? I want to see the world that my mother and Rfkr knew and then maybe the deep-dwellers would accept me too. But, I really want to see the world outside. >

Aailaine found her thoughts once again returning to the dragon woman and she slowly sat up, undoing her braid. She considered for a moment asking Rfkr once he returned but shook her head.

"He would probably just ignore my questions again." Aailaine fell back into her bed, burying her face into her pillow. "And that's assuming he knows something. But Hvidr seemed to know..."

"Maybe I'll try to find her later." Aailaine looked up once more at the Elddess lamp and slowly drifted into sleep, leaving the cares of her world behind her.

Chapter 5

Aailaine awoke to find the city in chaos.

Hvidr burst into her room as Aailaine woke up violently and the dwarf quickly yanked her out of the bed. Before she could even ask what was happening, Hvidr pulled her quiver from underneath the bed. She glanced around for a bow, but upon not finding one, looked at Aailaine questioningly.

"It got broken a couple of months ago by some people harassing me." Aailaine admitted, sliding on the boots Hvidr had tossed her way. "I've been saving up to buy a new one. But how did you even know-"

Hvidr promptly began to curse as Aailaine fixed her hair and fasten the quiver around her waist. "...*guofi Hebu kodad ritye*! I'm sorry, but we don't really have time for this. Let's hope Rfkr has a replacement for you."

"Hvidr, what's going on?" Aailaine tried to pull away from Hvidr's grip as she pulled her out of the house, but the dwarf's grip was strong. Hvidr picked up the war hammer she had left by the door and fastened it to her back. It was at that moment Aailaine noticed the armored breastplate Hvidr was wearing, bearing the insignia of the Nivim clan.

"The Shadows are attacking Mathydar, and while the main of my clan is on their way, there are too few of us here to fend them off for long. All thanks to the Stryn and their stupid rules." Hvidr admitted, rushing Aailaine out of the crevice as another group of dwarves rushed past them, heading toward the western side of the city. "We could've had a decent force here if not for them. We need to find Rfkr and get you out of here."

"The...the Shadows?" A wave of fear washed over Aailaine. The Shadows were twisted beings, only shreds of their former selves. They attacked and preyed on the other races of A'sthy, instilling terror and fear with their very name. Aailaine desperately wished her bow hadn't been broken as she followed Hvidr through the chaotic city. While the few soldiers quickly moved to the west side of the city, other dwarves and deep dwellers alike scurried into their homes.

Hvidr led Aailaine toward the heart of the city, weaving their way through the caverns and tunnels, taking shelter in a crevice or abandoned dwelling anytime someone other than a Nivim dwarf passed. Aailaine began to question why, but Hvidr always silenced her words. Eventually the dome of the Threrayrt came into view, the gem room shining brilliantly despite the chaos beneath it. Lying in the street beneath it was the crumpled form of a familiar figure.

"Rfkr!" Aailaine stepped from behind Hvidr and ran forward, taking the old dwarf into her arms. Blood began to soak into her shirt and trousers as tears poured down her cheeks. Rfkr sank into her embrace, no longer able to support himself. "Why are you here? You should've been in Slalan; you said so!"

"The Viwl were the ones who sent the warning. The Shadows were coming, had to make sure you were safe..." He was bleeding from several different wounds, and even Aailaine knew he wouldn't survive until help arrived. Rfkr coughed and pointed toward the large brown pack that he had been attempting to move, covered in his blood. Hvidr went to inspect the pack as giant tears rolled down

Aailaine's face. The old dwarf meant more to her than any father ever could and yet she could do nothing to save him.

"Rfkr...." Aailaine's voice came out choked as she tried to stop crying over the old dwarf's body, closing her eyes to try and stop the tears. The old dwarf groaned and coughed more blood before sighing deeply. Aailaine opened her eyes to see a slight smile on Rfkr's face before he met her gaze, a strong determination in his eyes.

"You have to be strong now, Aailaine. I have fulfilled the task your mother asked of me, and I have lived a fuller life than most. Don't cry over an old miser like me." Rfkr looked past Aailaine to Hvidr, who nodded and handed him his sword. Aailaine looked at the blade in surprise as Hvidr handed it to Rfkr; she hadn't noticed that Hvidr had grabbed it as they ran out of the dwelling.

"You're a liar, you know that?" Hvidr punched Rfkr's shoulder lightly, and he returned the favor, hitting her with the hilt of his sword. "At least have your blade with you before you try to fight."

"Why, when I think I did just fine without it." The old dwarf laughed as he lifted his sword, smiling at the two women. "Now go Hvidr, take Aailaine out of here. I'll see if I can't take more of those Shadow *heiirmeia* with me."

"C'mon Aailaine. We don't have much time." Hvidr shoved the bloody pack into Aailaine's hands. Aailaine carefully slung the pack on her back and glanced at Rfkr once last time. The dwarf's eyes were surprisingly full of vigor, although he kept shaking his head, holding on to life as hard as he could.

"*Rea kodad beirz*, Rfkr." Aailaine turned and ran to catch up with Hvidr, who began toward a tunnel Aailaine had never noticed.

After Aailaine entered, Hvidr pulled a switch, blocking the entrance with a giant rock.

"That should buy us a little bit of time." Hvidr placed her hand on the giant stone and lingered on the rock for a moment. Aailaine thought she might be holding back tears as Hvidr's hand slowly dropped away. Breathing deeply and straightening herself, the dwarf turned and took the lead. Aailaine followed closely, tracking their progress by counting the Elddess lamps they passed. The dark spaces between the lanterns caused Aailaine to become filled with fear and she stayed very close to her dwarven guide. All the while she lead, Hvidr spoke to herself softly and tossed her war hammer between her two hands. Although Aailaine was curious to know what Hvidr was saying, she remained silent.

After the twelfth lantern, the dwarf paused, leaning against the wall. She slowly lowered herself to the ground and sat against it. "We'll rest here for a moment. We should be far enough ahead that we could afford a small break."

Aailaine remained standing, staring into the darkness from whence they came. Hvidr watched her for a moment and then took a swig from the container she had on her person. She offered some to Aailaine, who refused.

"Take this time to unpack that." Hvidr motioned to the pack Aailaine carried. "That pack should have everything you're going to need to face what's ahead of you."

Aailaine finally sat down and spread the pack before her as Hvidr pulled out her ponytail and closed her eyes, her long red hair shielding her face. The largest item was a large black bow, with silver runes that danced and pulsed down its length. Aailaine traced the runes with her finger, and the shapes grew brighter with her touch. The bowstring was made from twisting the hair from a black totiriel. As she plucked it, a residual "twang" resounded through the tunnel and Hvidr sighed.

Tears welled up in her eyes as she examined the rest of the contents. With the bow were two large pouches: a pouch of money, more than twice the amount she had saved up, and a pouch of various jewels. The jewels were of great quality and she could sell each of them for a high price. Among the money and jewels were a few scattered bottles of smibi, easily a season's worth.

"Hm, I suppose that's enough of a rest." Hvidr stood, stretching her limbs. She redid her hair, tucking in the loose strands and began to start off again when Aailaine caught her arm.

"No, I want answers. Explain to me where you're taking me, or who the dragon woman I saw earlier was." Aailaine stared at her, the tears still flowing from her eyes. "I need to know why Rfkr died."

Hvidr raised an eyebrow and twisting her arm, easily broke free of Aailaine's grip. After repacking Rfkr's gifts and tossing the large pack in the girl's lap, she grabbed Aailaine's shirt and angrily pulled her close. With their faces close enough to kiss, Aailaine noticed the tears in Hvidr's eyes that she refused to let flow.

"If you value the life of Rfkr and everyone else who is dying for that life of yours, you *will* keep going." Hvidr's voice was deep and full of anger as she softly spoke to Aailaine. Compared to the dwarf's unnerving tone, Aailaine wished Hvidr would've just raised her voice and yelled at her. "To be honest, I don't know why any of this is happening, but I value that stubborn fool's life enough to do this last thing for him."

Hvidr made as if to drag her on the ground until with a heavy sigh, Aailaine stood. She slid the bow into her quiver and slung the bloody pack over her shoulder and resumed counting the lamps as she walked behind the female dwarf.

After the thirtieth lamp, Aailaine's patience had reached its end and her curiousity was getting the best of her. Crossing her arms, she sighed as she walked behind Hvidr. "Can't we at least talk while we walk? You have to know something."

"It's not much." Hvidr admitted, not missing a step. The anger had faded from her voice, but she still sounded annoyed with Aailaine's pestering. "If you really want answers, wait until we reach the trolls."

"Trolls?!" Aailaine nearly tripped on her own feet in surprise. "I thought you were trying to save my life, not kill me!"

"Hmph, shows how well deep-dweller education has failed you." Hvidr scoffed, shaking her head. "At least I can fill you on that."

"Nowadays, few beings even believe in the existence of deep-dwellers outside of these mountains. The deep-dwellers cut off all ties to outside races, so other races grew to believe that we wiped them out during the Tolsan Conflict. The trolls I'm taking you to, however, were close with Rfkr and are aware of your upbringing. They won't harm you." Hvidr paused, taking another swig of her drink. This time when she offered Aailaine some, the girl accepted, realizing with disappointment that it was only water. "Most other trolls won't even realize you're a deep-dweller. If anything, they'll probably think you as a plainsfolk, especially with your complexion."

"What even am I?" Aailaine asked timidly, handing Hvidr back her water.

"I don't know, but you're not from Tolsan. Your mother brought you here to hide you from the outside world, that dragon woman arriving shortly after her death. I don't know any more than that." Hvidr sighed, staring into her water before putting it away. "Rfkr is... was the one with all the answers, and he was supposed to be the one to bring you to the trolls if anything happened. However, that task now falls to me."

"Did all the dwarves know? Is that why you all were so kind to me?" Aailaine stopped in her tracks, staring at her feet. Hvidr paused to look back at her and sighed with annoyance again.

"No, only Rfkr and I knew. I only know because I insisted on him telling me. As a whole, we may tend to not like other races, but we don't forget our debts. You saved the SkiRyldes of the Stryn and helped the Viwl Hongekako when the stone wouldn't listen. You even proved yourself a warrior to my clan." Hvidr started walking again. "You earned our respect and kindness and so it was given."

Aailaine began to mull over what Hvidr said as she walked quickly to catch up to the she-dwarf. She knew so little of the woman Rfkr had called Kleia, and even less about the dragon woman. "Hvidr, did you know my mother?"

"No, I never even saw her." Hvidr shrugged. "Rfkr told me what I needed to know in case it fell to me to take you and as fate would have it, it has. I do know that when she died, she was encased in a sapphire tomb deep in the Fourth Crypt. She's one of the few to actually have their body there."

"Wait, the Fourth Crypt? Was she not human? Why not the deep-dweller Crypt? Why did Rfkr-" Hvidr huffed, shooting Aailaine another glance, causing the girl to pause in her questions.

"You know that the Fourth Crypt is for those the dwarves hold in high enough regard to be buried in a jeweled tomb. Your mother was highly enough regarded in these mountains to have one made for her, although no one thought she would ever inhabit it." Hvidr sighed, glancing into the oncoming darkness as Aailaine mumbled. "I don't know why Rfkr never took you to see her, but I think he didn't want to remember her as anything other than the woman he knew. When he used to talk about her-"

"Rfkr used to talk?! About Kleia?!"

"He wasn't always a bitter old man, Aailaine."

Aailaine wasn't satisfied with the answer but gave up her interrogation. At least now she knew where her mother was buried and she vowed to return to Mathydar to visit her mother's tomb.

Aailaine followed silently behind Hvidr as they continued to pass the twilight lamps. After what seemed like an eternity, the moon's soft light appeared in their path and a cool breeze brushed against her face. Hvidr's pace picked up as they neared the exit, and the silver light stung Aailaine's poor eyes as she stumbled out into the open air. Hvidr merely rubbed her eyes and continued walking into the cool autumn air of the plains. Aailaine attempted to follow, her eyes barely open as they tried to adjust to the soft moonlight.

"Hvidr! Hvidr wait!" she called out, rubbing her eyes again. Hvidr seemed to pay her no heed and continued getting further and further away from her. "Hvidr, I can't-"

Her sentence was cut short as her half-blinded eyes caused her to run into a tree. She rubbed her stubborn eyes for a final time and managed to open them fully. That's when she noticed her tree was wearing a long kilt and was covered in hair instead bark. Startled, Aailaine stumbled back and tripped, landing on her backside.

That's when Aailaine realized her tree was actually a troll.

Dochel
Where the journey begins

Chapter 6

It stood almost twice her height and was covered in thick red curls from the crown of its head down to its large, bare feet. The only clothing it wore was a white kilt around it's waist, which glowed in the bright moonlight. Its small green eyes seemed to study her for moment before offering her a hand. Slowly, she took it and in a quick fluid motion, it yanked her to her feet. When it spoke, it reminded her of the sound of two smooth stones being rubbed together.

"Come. The white one and your companion await you." He turned from her and began to walk through the open plains, off the beaten path. Aailaine began to argue, but after realizing she had no idea as to what the correct path was, bit her tongue and ran to catch up with her new guide.

After walking a short way, they reached a small clearing where the grass had been cut and one could see the soil beneath. More trolls similar to the one who led her sat or stood around a blazing fire, watching its tongues lick at the heavens. As they grew closer, Aailaine recognized Hvidr among them, a sapling among the trees.

"Well, at least they found you." Hvidr bowed to the group and turned to face Aailaine's troll. "I leave her in your hands and in the hands of Sirix, as was decided many a cycle ago."

"Go with caution, Hvidr. While the Shadows may leave Mathydar once they learn she is no longer there, that will not make the city safe," the troll warned, placing his large hand on Hvidr's head. Hvidr nodded and ducked under his touch. "Also let us apologize for the fate of Rfkr."

"I am aware, but I must return to my home." Hvidr looked down at the ground before glancing at Aailaine. "As for Rfkr, his soul has finally found the rest he sought, and his body will be preserved in the stone."

"Then go and go with haste." Hvidr looked at Aailaine and nodded at her as she passed, leaving to return beneath the mountains. Once Hvidr vanished from sight, the troll returned his attention to Aailaine and motioned her forward. "Here you will find the answers you seek."

Aailaine slowly walked forward and made her way toward the center of the circle. As she neared the fire, she realized that her earlier observation was incorrect. The other trolls weren't looking at the fire, but rather something close to the fire. It was the dragon woman, now clothed in a shorter white robe, and upon seeing Aailaine, she bowed to the trolls and walked to meet her. The sleeves of the dress hung way past her hands and hid them from sight. Her huge wings were still visible this time, but her large tail hid her feet, and Aailaine couldn't tell whether she actually walked or glided.

"So, you made it safely, although since Hvidr is the one that brought you, I'm guessing Rfkr was not so fortunate." Aailaine struggled to hold back tears as she shook her head. The woman laid one of her scaly hands on Aailaine's shoulders and looked at her with sympathy. "He was a good person and lived a full life. I...I'm sure he died with no regrets. I must apologize for not introducing myself earlier, as I had hoped we had more time.

"I am Sirix, and I was Kleia's Vuiej. Come, follow me." Sirix led Aailaine to a small tent and opened the flap to allow Aailaine in. Aailaine paused, eyeing Sirix with wonder. "Do not worry. The trolls will alert us of any danger should it come our way."

Aailaine carefully ducked her way into the tent and sat down in the furthest corner. Sirix followed her and lit a lamp to light the dark space before sitting with her back to the flap. Aailaine squinted at the harsh light of the lamp, which was brighter than the dull light of the Elddess. After she finished settling and sticking her tail out the opening, Sirix turned to face Aailaine, who waited patiently.

"I'm sure you have many questions, Aailaine, but some of them I can't answer for you. Most importantly, you need to understand what happened tonight." Sirix sighed, gathering herself before she began her explanation. "First of all, I'm sure you know about the Shadows?"

Sirix smiled a bit when Aailaine nodded but the smile quickly faded. "Their leader we call Irdrin, although it is merely a name we have given to them. They are a remnant of the old chaotic Darkness that used to cover the land, and their only goal is to cover this land with that Darkness once more now that Orassul sleeps.

"However, it was prophesized that a person would be born who could journey through the mist that covers Exla, the resting place of Orassul, and restore their Light to our world." Sirix paused, her gaze growing serious. The pause in her speech caused Aailaine to squirm, adjusting her quiver and reseating herself. Sirix's grey eyes seemed to pierce down to her very soul, as if judging her worth. "When you were born, the elves said that you were that one. The Shadows attacking Mathydar were looking for you."

"So, Rfkr died.... because of me?" Aailaine's voice quivered as she spoke, and the tears threatened to flow again.

"Do not blame yourself for his death, Aailaine. Rfkr knew the risk when he agreed with Kleia's wish to hide you with him." Sirix carefully touched Aailaine's shoulder before withdrawing once again. "I was meant to come get you to get you started on your journey to Exla but the Shadows-"

"Wait, I...I'm supposed to go to Exla?!" Aailaine interrupted the dragon woman, her voice shaking with disbelief. "But how? That's too much to ask of me! And I may be skilled with a bow, but I can't make it across A'sthy by myself."

"Calm down, Aailaine." Sirix raised her hand to stop Aailaine. "You don't have to do anything; it was Kleia's wish that you have a choice. But realize this; even if you refuse, Irdrin will hunt you for the rest of your life. They are aware that you can lead to their downfall and they will not allow you to exist peacefully."

Aailaine sat silently, mulling over what Sirix said. Sirix's words sounded so surreal; it seemed unbelievable that she was the one who was supposed to awaken Orassul. However, if she refused, she could never go back to having a normal life. Rfkr was gone, so she really had nowhere to go back to anyway. "But how? I don't even know what I'm supposed to do."

"That is why I am here to help you. You must go to Hirie to retrieve an artifact from the elves there. That artifact will allow you to awaken Orassul when you reach Exla," Sirix offered, smiling. "You will have to find someone to travel with you on your own however. I cannot, as I have other things I must do on my own accord to ensure your success.

"But as I said, Aailaine, you do have a choice. I will give you the night to think it over." Sirix stood, and Aailaine stood as well. "This tent is yours; rest here for the night and gather your thoughts. In the morning, I will return with fresh clothes for you."

"*Nao fei.*" Aailaine looked at her blood-soaked clothes and pack and wished she had one of gowns with her. Sirix smiled softly.

"*Ika heia. Ikaded fuo,* Aailaine." With that, Sirix left, leaving Aailaine alone with her thoughts. Aailaine's mind drifted to her time with Rfkr and how even though he seemed uncaring, he was always there when she needed him. Aailaine pulled the bow out of the quiver to examine the beautiful craftsmanship. A small paper tumbled out of the quiver and Aailaine quickly grabbed it. She opened it to read it and as she did, her eyes shone with tears.

Aailaine,

I know that there's a chance that I won't be around when it comes time for your journey, whether Irdrin attacks Mathydar or I die of old age before Sirix comes for you. But I want you to have everything in this pack. The bow was an old gift from your mother to you and it has been sung and enchanted by the elves themselves. The power within the bow is strong and will serve to amplify your own abilities as they manifest. Use it well and make Kleia proud.

The money and jewels are my gift to you. They are from the days I travelled with Kleia and Sirix. I realize that you may hate me for withholding this money, especially with the meager existence we had, but please understand that these gifts will be far more valuable during your journey. The life of a traveler is hard and it's not easy to make money, so please accept these gifts and spend it wisely.

The wine is just a little going away present. I know how much you've grown to love this wine over the cycles, and while I'm sure the dwarves shall miss it, it will serve to remind you of home. Your journey will be rough and at times you'll miss these mountains with their walls of stone and glowing jewels. The smibi, this wine, will serve as the cure for your inevitable homesickness. On the reverse of this letter is how to make this wine. If you can, be sure to procure some rice from a Dochel merchant and make yourself more.

This may all be a lot for you to take in. You grew up being shunned because of your appearance and I know you just wanted to be normal, but this journey, it is important. It could save everyone from the tyranny of the Shadows. You could be the one to restore peace to our world and live the normal life you always wanted. To be accepted by the same community that shunned and harassed you.

So please, for this old dwarf, strongly consider accepting. I would like to see you live happily, not so sad and withdrawn. I'm sure Kleia would feel the same if she were here. Although if she were, she herself would've ensured that no one harassed you. She was a strong, proud woman who cared very much for you. I wish I could've done more to protect you, but I couldn't risk upsetting the SkiRyldes or the Commune.

Please understand; I wanted to do so much more for you. I know that I haven't always shown how much I cared for you, at times I have even acted with disdain, but that's because that's just who I've become. This long life has made me bitter and I took that out on you. I

have always cared much for you Aailaine, and I wish for you to be
happy and free.

Odo kodad ashe dikang iktad.

Rfkr

Aailaine wiped away the tears before they could drip onto the paper and she carefully refolded the note and slid it into her private pouch. She added her money to the money Rfkr gave her and slid both the new pouch and the pouch with the sellable jewels into her leather bag attached to her quiver. She carefully folded the bloodied pack and placed it outside the tent. The letter was all she needed to finalize her resolve; if for nothing else, she would do it for Rfkr and Kleia.

< Rfkr, > Aailaine silently called out to her caretaker as she lay down to sleep. < I'll make this the peaceful world you and my mother longed to see. >

Chapter 7

"Um...Aailaine? Aailaine, it's time to wake." A soft voice roused Aailaine, and she sat up slowly, rubbing the sleep from her eyes. She ran her fingers through the cool earth and stood, stretching out her sore limbs. She looked at the opening of the tent to find that a bucket and washcloth had been left for her, as well as a small bundle of clothing. Sluggishly, she undid her rumpled braid and undressed from her filthy clothing, dumping the cold water over herself. She shivered, reaching for the cloth and washing herself down as quickly as she could.

As she waited to dry, she inspected the clothing brought for her. The green shirt was short-sleeved, a gold band encircling the sleeve. The neckline was v-shaped and loose, making the shirt more breathable. A pair of brown knee-length pants lay underneath the shirt. They laced up the side, allowing her to adjust how tightly they fit. And finally, there was a pair of sturdy leather boots; at first they appeared similar to her old boots, until she noticed that the leather felt different.

As Aailaine began to dress, she noticed a smaller stack of clothing underneath that she had missed. In the smaller bundle was a pair of brown gloves with a green band around the ends. The right-handed glove covered all her fingers except her pinkie and ring finger whereas the left glove only covered her thumb. As she pulled them on, she realized that the gloves were to protect her fingers from cutting on the bowstring.

The last article of clothing was a half-skirt, which sat low on her hips. It was a lighter green than her shirt and sat just right so that it would protect her skin from the quiver's strap. She quickly set the skirt and attached her quiver to her waist.

She picked up the black bow from the ground and, removing a single arrow, drew it back carefully. The bow's belly and back bent, allowing the nocks to move ever so slightly. The fletching touched her lips and the soft feathers moved under her breath. She closed her eyes as she held the arrow ready, breathing carefully.

For a moment, everything around Aailaine disappeared and she could feel the runes pulsing on the grip underneath her hand. She could feel the bow and arrow as if they were extensions of her own body rather than foreign objects. The bow breathed with her, bending and moving with her as she drew in breath and released it.

"Aai-" Sirix's voice surprised Aailaine and in her surprise she released the arrow. Sirix moved her head slightly and the arrow went flying by her. Aailaine stepped out of the tent as Sirix turned, and both women watched as the arrow buried itself deep inside a pole the trolls had set up to mark their land.

"Well, I see being without a bow has not dampened your talent," Sirix remarked, turning to Aailaine, who sighed with relief before looking at the dragon woman. Sirix still watched the girl with her unnerving gaze, although Aailaine thought she noticed a touch of warmness. "Have you made your decision, Aailaine?"

Aailaine paused, reaching for her amulet. Upon realizing she had failed to put it back on, she rushed back into the tent and grabbed the amulet. Its pure white stone shone in the bright morning light and the mo'qire seemed to wink its red eyes at her. Sirix's eyes widened as Aailaine slipped the cord over her head, but she said nothing as Aailaine turned to face her.

"I…I'll do it, Sirix. I'll go to Exla." Aailaine spoke softly but with conviction. Sirix smiled softly and placed her scaly hands on Aailaine's shoulder.

"Then I thank you, Aailaine, on behalf of the world you will save." Sirix smiled brightly, squeezing Aailaine's shoulders. "As I said last night, you will need to make it to the forests of Hirie and visit the elves. However, I would suggest you stop in Lanol, get a large pack if you can, and find a guide. There are plenty of beings that travel around a lot and know about the world."

"You can likely find one who would be willing to help you. So, walk straight from this camp and follow that road. However, you still must be careful." Sirix pointed Aailaine toward the beaten path in the grass. "As I'm sure Hvidr told you, not many races know of deep-dwellers. It would be a dead giveaway to anyone who means to do you harm if you mention you're from the Tolsan. Say you are from a family of plainsfolk that lived with these trolls. It's a common occurrence in the plains."

Sirix smiled and handed Aailaine a piece of paper. Written on it were several different names and Aailaine looked at her questioningly. Sirix laughed slightly, running her finger down the paper.

"Here is a list of last names you can use as your own, all of which are from plainsfolk origin." Sirix explained, her laughter fading. "Choose one you like and use it when you introduce yourself or buy anything. Remember, never tell anyone your true origins."

Aailaine nodded and tucked the paper away just as a huge gust of wind forced her to take a couple of steps back. When she turned to face Sirix again, the dragon woman was gone. A large shadow passed over her and she watched as Sirix finished shifting and flew toward the peaks of the Tolsan. Aailaine was a little disappointed to see her leave so quickly; she had wanted to ask Sirix more about her mother. As her Vuiej, Aailaine had hoped that the dragon woman would be more willing to talk about Kleia than Rfkr had been.

She watched until she could see no more, then turned back to see a woman her height looking at her. The woman's skin was a light caramel and her dark hair was pulled into a neat bun.

"If you are ready, we have some food for you to take with you on your journey." The woman spoke softly, handing Aailaine a large backpack. "It is our gift, our way of thanking you for accepting this quest."

Aailaine graciously accepted the food and settled the pack on her back. She began to walk past the woman, who spoke again. "Also, we...we would be honored if you would eat with us before you left."

"I...I would like that." As Aailaine followed the woman, she took a chance to look around. In the darkness and confusion of the night, she had failed to get a good look around the farm, but now she noticed the fields that seemed to stretch indefinitely, as well as some pens she assumed were for animal keeping. They passed several wooden huts, some obviously too small for the trolls, and Aailaine assumed that humans, like the woman who led her, must have lived in them. It also seemed that the human huts were square in shape, while the troll homes were more rounded. The one structure that stuck out the most was a long cabin, easily seven meters long and it was this building that the woman led her to.

The woman held open the door and Aailaine stepped inside to find the group of trolls that she had seen the night before seated around a large feast, along with a scattered number of humans that appeared similar to the woman who had brought her to the hall. On its walls hung colored mats of every hue and pelts of animals that Aailaine didn't recognize. The table sat about a meter off the ground and all present knelt on pillows next to the table. The pillows seemed to be the same height for almost all the guests, with the exception of a troll and a human who sat at the head of the table. Aailaine recognized the troll as the one that had found her the night before and assumed he must be the head of the farm.

The man next to the troll waved her over and the woman gently nudged her. Slowly and nervously, Aailaine made her way to her seat and set her belongings on the floor behind her. She carefully knelt on the pillow and was surprised by how firm it was.

"We hold this feast in celebration of the great harvest we're due to have this cycle, as well to celebrate Aailaine, the one who will save us all." The head troll spoke and the male plainsfolk lifted up a bowl filled with a sweet-smelling drink, which he offered to Aailaine. Aailaine brought the bowl to her lips gingerly, taking in the scent of the drink. When the first drop reached her lips, she recognized it as a wine, although it was very different from smibi. As she sipped from the bowl, the man began to speak.

"Let us thoroughly enjoy this feast given to us by Orassul and enjoy the company we have." Aailaine passed the bowl to the troll to her right, who took a sip as well. Once the bowl had made a complete circle around the group, the host began to feast. Aailaine ate little, merely nibbling on the food before her. The man next to her took notice and spoke to her softly.

"Does something trouble you, Aailaine? Is this too foreign for you?" He touched her gingerly, and Aailaine looked up from her food at him. His green eyes watched her with concern and she sighed, glancing down again. "I'm sure we have something more similar to what you're used to."

"No, the food is just fine. It's just...I've never been treated with so much kindness by humans. Where..." Aailaine paused, thinking back to her home in the mountains. "Where I come from, I was ostracized by the other humans because of how strange I look. It's...strange to be so accepted instead of judged."

"It's something you get used to when you live in the plains. The humans you knew were very close-minded." The man smiled at her and heaped a larger portion of food onto her plate. The woman next to him hit his shoulder, lightly chastising him. Aailaine watched him as he shook her off and looked up to the roof of the dwelling. "Out here, especially since many people travel through the plains, you often see many strange people wandering around. I'm sure as you travel around, you will see stranger than what we see here on our little farm."

"So, most humans won't really judge you for how you look here, or in most places, I'd imagine." Aailaine smiled and began to eat the food offered to her. Inside, she felt warmth that threatened to overflow.

Chapter 8

Aailaine wondered at the size and layout of the city; dwarven cities were spread out, split among several large and small caverns. But Lanol was just spread out over a lot of ground with a tall wall surrounding it. There was a plethora of people entering and leaving the city and the buildings were tall rectangles with rounded corners. Their rounded roofs were covered with green tiles and seemed to sparkle like gems in the morning light. Strange boxes that carried people across the city hung from wires in the sky, swinging back and forth slightly as they moved toward their destinations. In the distance Aailaine could barely make out the shape of a tall, cylindrical building, with what had seemed like birds circling around it.

When she first tried to enter the city, she wondered if they would let her in, as the Teieimokos at the entrance stopped her and asked to examine her pack. The merchant who had given her a ride was allowed in without a hassle, as all she carried was food to be sold. Aailaine conceded, quickly thanking the merchant and jumping off the mechanical sled they rode. The Teieimoko's akhby sat near them, curled up and watching all the travelers that waited to get inside the city. Their colorful yellow and purple scales shimmered in the light and their narrow eyes seemed to pierce through every person they watched. Despite meeting Sirix, their presence still unnerved Aailaine, and she couldn't help but feel uncomfortable as she waited to get clearance into the city. After examining her packs and accepting her explanation for the bow, they allowed her in, much to her relief. The air off the Swari Lanes made the morning cool and pleasant but promised a hot and humid afternoon.

After walking in the gate, Aailaine once again stopped and wondered at the city. Up close, the buildings were impossibly massive, filled with wonders she couldn't even fathom. The streets were more crowded than any city in the Tolsan, people walking so close together that it seemed to be just an endless flow of movement. Merchants called from their stalls, endlessly trying to grab the attention of the moving throng. A shadow passed above Aailaine and she looked up to see a box pass above her, swaying in the wind as she watched it drift toward one of the large buildings.

"Um," she stopped in front one of the many shops, gaining the attention of an assistant who was showing off its wares. He smiled at her brightly as she got closer and put down the bandages he had been holding.

"How can I help you today, miss?" His voice was cheerful and helpful and Aailaine dared to meet his gaze as she spoke.

"Could you tell me where I could get a larger pack?"

"You must be new to Lanol, but your accent is unfamiliar to me." He gave her a confused smile as he waited to service her. "Where are you from, miss?"

"Um, my name is Aailaine Danend, my family lived with a group of trolls near the mountains." Aailaine smiled nervously. She had practiced introducing herself several times on her way to Lanol, making sure she could do so comfortably. The assistant nodded, waiting for her to continue. "I'm on my way to Hirie. I received a letter from an elf there who was a close friend to my parents. I'm hoping to buy a bigger pack to consolidate my luggage."

"Ah, it is a great honor to be called into Hirie. Your parents are lucky to have made a friend there." The shopkeeper smiled and pulled out a map of the city. He placed it on the table nearby and waved Aailaine over, motioning for her to look. "Follow this road and turn left here. It's a side street and there are several merchants that sell various pouches and backpacks. But if you want a chance for a good price, go to this guy. He doesn't usually have much, but he usually carries big packs. Merchants often buy from him, so he tends to be a bit of a haggler. If you're good, you can get one for a good price."

"Ah, thank you." Aailaine bowed to the shopkeeper and began to leave when he called after her.

"Miss! Wait!" He had rolled up the map and handed it to her. He laughed as she slowly accepted it. "Lanol is a big city, so a lot of people stop here first to ask for directions or to buy the essentials. It's our practice to give away maps to newcomers. Don't forget to come back if you need anything else."

"Th-Thank you." Aailaine bowed and following the map, she soon reached the side street filled with merchants selling various packs, all with different sizes and colored leather. She stood, looking awe-struck at the various merchandise until several people bumped into her trying to get into the narrow street. She shook herself from her stupor and made her way to the merchant that had been suggested. He was busy with another customer when she arrived, so she amused herself by examining the various bags.

As she had been told, he had various large bags, but many were bigger than she needed. He only had a few that were about the right size, and they were all brightly colored. She took this moment to glance at the other stalls, but their wares were all much bigger than what this merchant carried.

"Excuse me miss, can I help you?" The merchant, done with his previous customer, called her over and she moved to him nervously. He was a short, thin man, and he held his hands in anticipation of making a sale. He didn't seem like a swindler, so Aailaine ventured a bit closer to his stall.

"Um, yes, I was looking for a slightly bigger pack than this, one that has pockets, so that I can consolidate all my bags." She showed him the pack with food she had received from the trolls and the merchant seemed to think for a moment before looking through his wares.

"Well, dressed as you are, I would assume a brightly colored pack is out of the question. I thought I had a few dark ones, where are they..." Aailaine waited patiently as the man looked through his wares. Her mind began to wander to Sirix's instructions on trying to find someone to travel with her. Based on what she had learned, mostly merchants, werecats and Teieimokos travelled freely throughout A'sthy. Merchants were unlikely to help, due to the business nature of their travels, and she was unsure how safe she felt around an unknown Teieimoko and their Vuiej. That left werecats, who were shape-shifters, and rarely walked around in their original forms. Finding one in such a huge city would be a hard task, and she wasn't sure how rude it would be to ask around.

"Hmm, this isn't good." Aailaine jumped to attention as the merchant murmured, pulling out a bright blue pack of the right size. "It seems I'm sold out of all the dark ones in this size. However, I'm a local merchant who lives in the city, and my wife is the one who makes all these bags. If you like, I could have her make one for you tonight and give it to you tomorrow. It would be similar to this one, which has several pockets on the inside, so you can store money or other small valuables. All the pockets close, so you don't have to worry about the contents spilling out if the bag is jostled."

Aailaine inspected the pack as the merchant held it open for her and nodded as she stood back up. "How much would it be?"

"Well, I usually sell packs this size for eighty gold pieces, but I'll give it to you for sixty. Thirty now, and thirty in the morning." He smiled as Aailaine considered the price. It was more than she wanted to spend, considering what she had, and she was about to walk away when she remembered the jewels. She quickly reached into her leather pouch and pulled out some of them, showing them to the merchant.

"Will any of these cover the full price?" The merchant's face lit up as he examined the glittering gems. He gave Aailaine a confused look and returned his gaze to the gems when Aailaine didn't withdraw her hand. Carefully, he reached to take three of the larger ones from her hand when a voice from behind her spoke.

"C'mon now, don't you think that's a bit much?" A tanned hand reached around Aailaine's shoulder, picking up the large sapphire and dropping it in the merchant's hand. She turned to see a handsome young man with tanned skin and raven hair standing behind her, his cat-like tail and ears twitching. "There, that should cover the original price and little extra. Fair enough if you ask me, especially since she's not getting the bag right now."

The merchant seemed ready to argue, but the werecat leaned closer to him. He spoke softly enough that Aailaine could not hear, but the merchant sighed with defeat and pocketed the gem. He turned and wrote down the order on a slip of paper before signing it and motioning for Aailaine to sign as well and giving her a copy of the slip. Her business concluded, she turned back to the stranger and bowed.

"Thank you very much." He laughed as he stood her up and placed one hand on his hips.

"It's no problem, miss. It seemed like you could use some help. He's not a bad guy but putting that many gems in front of anyone would be tempting." He smiled, his blue eyes flashing, as he extended his other hand. "I'm Iasi Tonath. And you are?"

"Aailaine, Aailaine Danend." She took it and he gave it a hardy shake before releasing her and she took this as a chance to look him over. He was wearing a tight blue top that barely served to cover his well-defined chest and midsection. Across his shoulders was a low-sitting shrug decorated with various gold symbols and around his waist was a gold chain with many golden charms dangling from it. He wore black shorts with a small pouch hanging off them and from there knee length boots served to cover the rest of his legs.

"Well, be careful doing that. You shouldn't show all your cards at once." With that, he started to walk away. Quick to stop him, she grabbed his shrug and he stopped mid-step. He carefully turned to face her, lifting up an eyebrow in surprise. "Was there something else you wanted?"

"Um," she looked away, unsure of what to say. She started to feel childish, so she released his shrug and he faced her properly. She started rubbing her forefinger with her thumb as she spoke. "I've never really been in this city before, so I don't really know my way around well. You seem well versed in the city, so would...you mind helping me?"

Iasi smiled and folded his arms around his chest, looking her up and down. For a moment, she thought he might refuse, but then he locked her arm with his and started walking, almost dragging her along.

"I would love to, Aia." As he led her back out onto the main streets of Lanol, she started to wonder whether or not she had made a wise choice. However, as he led her around and helped her buy various things and haggle with the merchants, she decided he wasn't a bad person, even if he was a bit strange.

Chapter 9

Sirix watched from a distance as Aailaine followed Iasi into a small shop. She was glad to see that Aailaine had made it into the city safely and had her followed at a discreet distance. Iasi's sudden and timely appearance unnerved her, and she didn't like the air he gave off. She had hoped Aailaine would choose a Teieimoko as her guide, but the girl seemed to be content with the werecat. The fact he was in the city at all made her more nervous; being an akhby herself, she knew that the akhby at the gate should've seen the Darkness that followed him, hiding in the shadows of people and buildings whenever he turned to look at it. The Darkness only followed people who were already infected, or people it purposely wanted to infect. If the werecat were either one, he was too dangerous to allow around Aailaine.

"Anywhere else, Aia?" Sirix quickly hid as the pair stepped out of the shop again and Aailaine quickly stowed away the arrows she had bought. He paused with his hands on his hips and his tail waved from side to side. Aailaine seemed to be thinking before pulling out the map.

"I want to sell some of the jewels my caretaker gave me. I feel more comfortable carrying around money and I can avoid what happened earlier." Aailaine said at last and Iasi nodded, looking at the map with her. "How about here?"

"No, he's a thief. He'll buy it from you at a third of the price and resell it in another city for twice." Iasi seemed to study the map for a moment, trying to locate a different shop. After a moment, he sighed, running his hand through his hair before speaking. "In all honesty, your best choice is either going to the Guild or the Spire."

"What's the Spire?"

"The Spire is the gnome registry. Anyone who wants to offer a gnome craft in the city has to be registered there. They also do money exchanges there." Iasi nodded toward a tall tower in the distance. "A lot of people bring in spare parts and valuables to be sold and then the Spire sells them to the gnomes and their apprentices for a cheaper price for use in their creations."

"Sounds good. Why would the Guild want them?" Aailaine queried and the werecat gave her a surprised look. Even from her hiding spot, Sirix couldn't help but sigh. The Tolsan was cut off from the rest of the world and turned out to be a mixed blessing; while it did manage to hide Aailaine's presence for seventeen cycles, the mountain teachings left a giant hole in her education, especially since the deep-dwellers knew very little of the outside world. If the dwarves had taught her, her education would have been more complete, but human and dwarven political relations are always tense. If Rfkr had pushed, he could've had her in a dwarven school, but even Sirix knew it would've weakened relations between deep-dwellers and dwarves. Sirix returned to listening as Aailaine apologized for not knowing.

"It's okay, I guess you didn't leave the farm much though." Iasi chuckled as she nodded furiously. "Well, regardless of breed, all dragons have hoards. A lot of akhby tend to like gems for their hoards, which is hard for their Teieimoko since gems only come from the Tolsan. They pay greatly for gems, since helping an akhby build its hoard helps improve relations between them and their Teieimoko.

Also, sometimes other Vuiej like gems, so a Guild is always willing to buy."

"Oh?"

"Yea, so they'll pay what the gem is worth, sometimes more, if one of the Vuiej stationed in this city likes that particular kind of gem." Iasi added and Aailaine seemed to be mulling over her choices. The werecat stretched, this time folding his arms behind his head while leaning on his tail slightly. His ear twitched, and he shot his gaze over to where Sirix stood in the shadows of the next building. He appeared puzzled by her shadow and seemed ready to walk over. Sirix's tail twitched as he unfolded and took a step in her direction.

"I think the Guild then. The dwarves practically gave these to us and I'd like to use them to help out the city and it sounds like the Teieimokos could use them the most." Aailaine finally announced, looking up at him. At her voice, he jumped as if struck and turned to face her, forcing a smile. She watched him for a moment and turned to peer where he had been facing. "What is it, Iasi?"

"Hm? Oh, it's nothing, thought I saw a cat or something." He glanced out of his eye toward Sirix again and continued to smile at Aailaine. Sirix allowed herself to relax in her hiding spot. She would've fled if he had gotten too close, as she couldn't risk Aailaine seeing her. Alternatively, she wanted to get a good look at Iasi, to determine the purpose of the Darkness that followed him. "I'm sure the Teieimokos and their Vuiej will be extremely grateful."

"Then let's-"

"Wait." Iasi quickly pulled Aailaine into a thin alleyway as two guards turned around a corner. At first, Sirix could not see the reason for his actions and thought that he meant to harm Aailaine. She started to step out of her hiding place, when she noticed that the guards had their helms on, despite the heat of the day. Wearing full armor in this humid heat could kill a man, and yet the two guards walked on unaffected. Sirix pressed herself against the building and held her breath. They stopped near where she stood and began to converse among themselves.

"The Teieimoko said that woman came in this morning, but we haven't seen her at all." The first guard whined, adjusting the helm on his head. At this distance, Sirix could see their red glowing eyes, as well as the Darkness that seeped between the pieces of armor, only to retreat back in. The strong stench filled her nostrils and she fought the urge to spill her stomach. "We've been through almost the entire city already. And I want to take this stupid armor off, it's uncomfortable."

"Do that and you're as good as dead." The other laughed, glancing off in the direction of the Guild, with an akhby circling above its point. "Perhaps they lied to us. She's one of them, right?"

"Why would they lie? With this armor and that sorcerer's spell, we should look and smell like humans. It's probably the stupid armor, isn't it too hot to be wearing this?"

"I suppose." The guards began pondering over their situation. Sirix had no doubt that they were Shadows that either sought herself or Aailaine. Visiting Aailaine in the mountains had given Irdrin the last clue he needed to find Aailaine there, and there was a good chance he was still tracking her to find the girl. "Perhaps they were mistaken."

"Perhaps. Anyway, let's go check the Spire. She might be there." The guards started off down another street, and Iasi slowly came out of the spot where he hid with Aailaine, careful to make sure that they were gone. Once he was sure it was safe, he waved Aailaine out, and she stumbled out into the open street.

"Were those...?"

"Yea, they were. I don't know who they're looking for or how they're able to walk around, but it's best to get off the streets." He turned to face her and gave her a reassuring glance. "Let's go to the Guild and then find you a place to stay for the night. I don't think it's safe to be out right now."

As they walked from sight, Sirix quickly and silently made her way out of the city, leaping over the wall without any guards noticing her. Once the city was out of sight, she let out a deep sigh and a low giggle started from her lips. Soon it became a full laugh, which spilled forth as she shed her human guise, wriggling her long body. She laughed for quite a time, finally stopping as she watched the sun set slowly in the south.

< Perhaps, that werecat is not as bad as he seems. > Sirix hummed, curling up in the evening sun to sleep. She allowed her eyes to slowly drift shut, and her snores echoed across the plains.

However, her slumber didn't last long as she heard a tapping noise near her back. At first, she attempted to ignore the distraction, deciding it was just some plains creature that had gotten too close. However, the tapping grew louder and more insistent and she was forced to acknowledge it. Annoyed and ready to pounce, she slowly uncurled herself and turned to face the disturbance.

Much to her surprise, rather than a creature, she found a small child, purposely tapping a rock with a stick while staring at her.

The large, dark cloak she wore made her small frame look even smaller, hiding many of the girl's features.

"About time you woke up. It took forever for me to find you, which is a good thing I suppose." The child's voice was rich with wisdom beyond her apparent age and she tossed away the stick before crossing her arms across her tiny chest. "Don't you have work to be doing instead of napping here?"

<Who are you child, and why do you bother me?> Sirix turned fully to face the disturbance, trying to get a good look at the child in the dim light of the stars. The girl raised her eyebrows at Sirix's questioning.

"Who I am doesn't matter. What does matter is that I know something that's about to happen in the Tolsan that can stop Aailaine from completing her quest." The mention of Aailaine's name bothered Sirix, but the girl didn't give her a chance to speak. "And that something revolves around a certain sorcerer we both have a score to settle with."

At this, Sirix changed into her human form, and walked closer to the girl. Now she noticed the girl had long white hair kept into a single neat ponytail and piercing yellow eyes. Her dark skin almost seemed black in the dim light and she stood with arrogance and importance. The slight wind of the plains blew at the opening of her cloak and revealed hints of the blue dress she wore underneath.

"What is your name, child?"

"It's Elmeye, and I am no child." She spat, looking Sirix straight in the eye, even as the dragon woman towered over her. "I am older than you and I am a powerful enchanter in my own right.

However, I didn't come to warn you to do you a favor; I'm coming with you."

Sirix was almost dumbfounded by the girl's brashness and lack of manners. She opened her mouth to reject the girl's offer, but Elmeye continued on as if she hadn't noticed.

"I'll tell you what he's planning to do there, and even help you stop him, but I have to go with you." Elmeye's eyes narrowed and her voice became very deep and serious. "I have my own wrong to right, and it begins with helping you and killing him. Besides, you can't refuse, unless you want Aailaine to fail."

Sirix mulled over Elmeye's words. If the child spoke true and something was about to happen in the Tolsan, then it was only natural that she should head there to stop it. However, she needed to know what was happening, and Elmeye had already made it apparent she had no intention of telling unless she was included. Sirix hated working with others, especially those who worked with magic, but the sorceress had effectively trapped Sirix and knew it. Her duty to Aailaine made it clear what her choice would be and Sirix growled with frustration. Elmeye simply smiled at her reaction.

"I guess that's all the answer I need, hmm?" She smiled coyly and looked in the direction of the faraway mountains. For a moment, Sirix thought she saw a twinge of regret in her eyes but the sorceress turned to her with the same arrogant look. "Well, shouldn't we get going, Sirix? The mountains aren't going to come to us."

"You are not riding me." Sirix retorted and the sorceress laughed, her pure child's laugh not matching her general demeanor. She gave Sirix a look of disbelief as she slowly began to levitate.

"Did I not just say I'm an old powerful enchanter? I don't *need* to ride you, neither do I *want* to." Elmeye shook her head as her laughter faded. "We need to get to Slalan, and I'll tell you more once we're there. Not going to risk you trying to leave me behind."

Sirix growled again in frustration as she shifted and began to fly through the night sky, Elmeye close behind her. She disliked the situation she found herself in, but in order to insure Aailaine's success, she would deal with the child sorceress. For now.

Chapter 10

"Say, Aia, you never said how long you wanted my help." Iasi spoke to her as they worked on organizing her belongings for the pack she planned to pick up the next day. The room they were in was simple, having two sleeping cots on the floor and a basic wash closet. There were two lamps placed on the floor, a small chair, and a desk in the corner; other than that, the small room was bare. Iasi knew of better accommodations in the city but didn't want to seem forceful and had allowed Aailaine to choose where she wanted to stay. She paused once he spoke and looked away before answering.

"Um, I've never actually travelled away from home before and I need to go to Hirie, so I...I was hoping you wouldn't mind traveling with me. You seem to know your way around fairly well. And I would gladly pay you for your help..." her voice faded, and Iasi sighed, standing and stretching. She looked up at him, waiting to hear his answer.

"I'm just stretching, I'm not used to sitting for so long." He gave her a comforting smile and she calmed down. "You don't know me that well, yet you want me to travel with you?"

"Well, um, it was suggested that I find someone to travel with and you seem trustworthy." Aailaine's voice faded as she fidgeted nervously. Iasi's ears perked up and his tail twitched as he tried to hold back his laughter.

"Hirie, is it? Well I guess you're in luck. I've been there a lot and I know that forest like the back of my hand." He finally answered, getting his laughter under control. "Wherever you need to go, I can get you there. And I don't need to be paid, getting to travel with a pretty woman like you is payment enough."

"Th-Thank you." Aailaine nodded toward him and quickly returned to organizing her things. She kept glancing at him, only to quickly look away. Iasi smiled as he sat on one of the cots to watch her. He started to wonder if he should go get his own room for the night when Aailaine spoke again. "Um, Iasi, can...can I ask you something?"

"Sure, go ahead." he looked over to her, as she pulled him from his thoughts. She visibly blushed, looking away from him again.

"Um, it's just, I've never seen anyone dressed like you before. It's so..."

"Revealing? Inappropriate?" Iasi offered, and Aailaine nodded. "It's kind of the point. I'm an exotic dancer."

"Exotic dancer?"

"Well, it's someone who dances in an erotic manner in order to sexually excite their audience." Iasi frowned at her puzzled expression and started to stroke his ear, his tail sliding across the floor behind him. "I suppose I could try showing you what I mean, but I have no music."

"Don't worry about it then. I don't want to make trouble for you." Aailaine started to fold the new outfit she had bought. Iasi sighed, dropping his hand away from his ear.

"It's no trouble, I know some of my dances by heart. Sit in that chair if you want me to show you."

Iasi waited patiently as Aailaine moved off the floor and into the chair he indicated. He stood and closed his eyes to calm himself.

Slowly, he could hear the music from the Chekari musicians rising through him, the sensual music filling him and moving him from within. He slowly dropped into a squat, earning himself a gasp from Aailaine, and he rolled upwards, running his hands over his body as he did so. He then slowly rolled down, dropping to all fours and his tail moved slowly back and forth as he crawled up to her.

Aailaine's eyes were locked on his as he put his hands on the sides of the chair and rolled his body up. Never breaking eye contact, he continued to dance in front of her, occasionally letting out erotic breaths and releasing the chair to run his hands down the side of his face to his collarbone.

He stood up completely and began to sway in front of her, running his hands over various part of his body. He avoided his pelvis, rubbing his hands along his inner thighs instead and moaning softly. He lifted off his shawl, tossing it to the floor as he fell to his knees again. He leaned back until his head touched the floor, slowly moving his hips. He slowly rose, glancing at Aailaine before looking down again. As the music in his head ended, he stood and strutted to where she sat, placing his hands on either side of her chair again.

"Understand now, love~?" He breathed into her ear lightly, and he felt her body shiver. As he pulled away, he saw that her face was a deep red and she had turned her silver eyes away from him.

"I-I think I understand now." She gulped, trying to fight down her wildly beating heart. He giggled again softly and stood, lying down on the cot and facing the ceiling.

"It's ok, I'm very aware of my sensuality. I took to dancing at a young age, and once I hit my teen cycles, I knew I wanted to be an exotic dancer. My sister didn't like it, but she supported me anyway."

"You have a sister?" Aailaine's eyes widened with interest at the mention of his family and she turned to face him. He smiled fondly as he twisted a ring he wore on his left hand.

"Yea, I have an older sister, Chadirra. We lost our parents when I was young, so I was pretty much raised by her and the Chekari." Iasi's smile faded as he began to remember the life he left behind. "Werecats usually travel in troupes. As a child, it's like being raised by a really big family, and as you grow up, it means you can't get away with anything."

"What does Chekari mean?" Aailaine queried and Iasi laid down on the cot, rolling over onto his stomach to look at her.

"It means desire. Some were dancers, although I was the only exotic dancer. My sister and a few other girls were singers and we had a number of talented musicians." Aailaine leaned closer, interested in his description of his family. "And what about you? What was your family like?"

At this, Aailaine drew back, and all of the enthusiasm drained from her. Iasi immediately regretted asking and opened his mouth to apologize when she spoke.

"I never really got to meet my mom, she died when I was too young to remember her." Aailaine looked away as tears welled up in her eyes. "I had a caretaker, but he died when...when the Shadows..."

"Stop," Iasi quickly rushed over to her and knelt in front of her. He gently hushed her, wiping away her tears. "I shouldn't have asked. It'll be ok, Aia."

Aailaine nodded and wiped her face. Iasi smiled softly, relieved that he had stopped her crying. She stood slowly and after checking the pack, sat down on one of the sleeping cots.

"I think we should get some sleep, so that we can be well rested for leaving tomorrow." Aailaine undid her hair as she waited for Iasi to lie on the other cot, but he shook his head. She looked at him, concerned, and motioned as if to stand again, but he quickly waved her down.

"I'll stay up for a bit longer. I don't really sleep, and besides, I shouldn't stay in here with you. You didn't pay for two people and you could get charged extra."

"Don't worry, I won't leave. I'll be right down the hall." He tried to give her a reassuring look as she watched him. Eventually, she lay down to sleep, passing out before her head even hit the pillow. Iasi smiled as he continued to look out the window into the night sky. The moon was a quarter full and glowed dimly over the dark city as he gazed out into the darkness. The soft light of the moon seemed to fill him with hope.

"Well, I guess I should get a room if I'm going to stay." He stepped away from the window and quietly left the room, making his way down to the front desk.

Chapter 11

Iasi stretched in the late afternoon sun as Aailaine paused for another rest. He humored her with all the breaks she took, taking it as a chance to enjoy the view. Although she seemed to have pretty good stamina, it was obvious from when they first set out that she wasn't used to walking long distances while carrying all of her belongings with her. Iasi never carried much while travelling, but to help Aailaine, he was carrying the big pack that they had picked up from the merchant, leaving her with just her bow, quiver and small leather pouch. Even so, she took several breaks and took swigs from a small bottle.

"What's in that?" His curiosity getting the better of him, he finally ventured to ask her about it. She looked down at it as if to contemplate if she wanted to share. He started to apologize when she offered it to him. He took it gingerly and took a small sip and instantly regretted it. "It's a wine, isn't it?"

"It's a rice wine my caretaker used to make." She took it back and smiled at the small container. "It's my favorite thing to drink."

"I don't like wines, they all taste too bitter to me, even the sweet ones." Iasi took a swig of his water to wash the taste out of his mouth. "I personally have a soft spot for honeymead, especially elven honeymead. Maybe once we get to Hirie, I'll treat you to some."

"Sure." Aailaine finished drinking her wine and stood, packing away the bottle in the pouch around her waist. Iasi settled the pack and took the lead again. As they walked, he noticed Aailaine staring strangely at the mechanical ruins they passed. She would stare at them as they walked by, sometimes jumping when a siraya caused one of the legs to move, or more of the structure to crumble. She would then quickly hurry to try and keep up with Iasi, only to repeat the process when they passed the next ruin.

"Do you know what that is?" Iasi pointed to the strange shape and Aailaine shook her head. "It's the remains of a Stroerire, a mechanical walker the gnomes make. They can only travel so far before they need to be recharged, but they can be recharged in any city in Dochel. Some people just forget and when their Stroerire dies, they abandon it."

"Why aren't we using one?"

"Because gnome items are expensive and for us, it'll just be easier to walk. At least most of the way." Iasi smiled and started walking again. "The only people who really pay for them are merchants, since it makes it easier for them to move their goods around the plains."

Aailaine nodded and Iasi smiled, walking off the path and sitting in the tall grass. Aailaine followed and sat next him, giving him a questioning look. He took the pack off and lay down on his back, gazing up at the clouds as they passed across the sky.

"Just wanted to give my back a break for a while. We have been walking all day." Iasi closed his eyes, enjoying the breeze over the plains. He heard Aailaine as she lay down next to him, and he opened his eyes ever so slightly to glance at her. She sighed deeply and closed her eyes as well.

"Hey, Iasi?"

"Yes, Aia?"

"Where'd the scar across your eyes come from?" At this Iasi frowned, and sat up, still looking up at the sky. She propped herself up on her elbow as she waited, and he eventually dropped his head to his knees, pulling at the grass in between his feet.

"It's…a complicated story. Maybe I'll tell you some other time." He continued to pull at the grass, avoiding her gaze. He wasn't proud of the scar and even less inclined to say how he got it. He eventually smiled down at her, hoping to ease the mood.

"Don't worry about it. It's nothing important and doesn't affect my eyesight. In fact, it's so faded I'm surprised you saw it at all." Iasi quipped, and pulled up more blades of grass. "Why did you ask, if you don't mind?"

"No reason, I suppose." Aailaine sat up as well, mimicking Iasi's pose. "It's just I haven't had anyone my age to talk to for a long time."

"Really? No one?" Iasi blinked in surprise when she shook her head. "Wow, that's…strange. Surprising really, considering how pretty you are."

At this, Aailaine turned away sharply and stared away from him. Iasi stared at her, puzzled by her reaction, and then returned his gaze to the sky, taking another drink of his water. He watched the clouds take shape and then break apart, like how the world was constantly changing. They were all just clouds, floating in the breeze; uncertain of what lay ahead of them.

"Well," Iasi stood and stretched, and bounced the pack back on his shoulders. "We should get going if we want to make it to Torora in a decent time. It's not so bad sleeping on the plains, but we really should try to limit how long we're out here."

"Why?" Aailaine asked, gathering herself as she stood to follow him. Iasi gave her a surprised and worried look, although he never stopped walking. "Um, I'm sorry, but what's wrong with sleeping in the plains?"

"I just find it strange that you wouldn't know, being from the farms. It tends to get really dark out here in the middle of the plains and on dark nights people can get infected with the Darkness and start to turn into Shadows." Iasi spoke as he walked, careful to move off the path when some merchants passed them. "It's fairly common knowledge, and most people know better than to stay outside for too long. The longer you're outside on a dark night, the higher chance you'll be infected."

"Oh," Aailaine said softly, staring at the ground as they walked. Iasi got the feeling that his words had disturbed her, and he reached back to touch her shoulder.

"Hey don't worry. As long as we make up for the number of breaks with how fast we walk, we'll make it to Torora by the end of the week. If we pass any farms, we can even ask the plainsfolk there to stay a night. Shouldn't be too hard if you ask for us." He smiled at her and she smiled back, easing his tension. "So, come on, let's get going."

Chapter 12

"Welcome to Torora!" Iasi spread his arms as if to show off the city. Compared to Lanol, Torora was tiny, but it's size reminded Aailaine of the dwarven caverns. It had a few gnome shops, which sold what Iasi told her were called Shi-Ratef, tiny guides that merchants bought to help them find their way around Dochel. Its buildings looked like small cylinders and the flat roofs were the same color as the red walls of the town. She noticed the school by its varied shape; it was the only square building and seemed tilted to the side a bit.

Aside from the school and gnome shops, the town mostly had inns and necessity shops, selling food and items needed for travel. Iasi had described it as a "pass city", saying it was more of a quick stop than an actual destination. The only people who stayed in the city constantly were the families who ran the shops and inns, depending on the merchants and travelers to keep their city going. He also mentioned there was another similar city to the north called Yarel.

Iasi didn't pay much attention to shops for the most part, until they reached a side stall in a large alley. Once they began to pass it, Iasi stopped suddenly and studied the sign for a moment before turning to Aailaine.

"Wait here a moment." Aailaine turned her attention to the rest of the traffic in the city as Iasi walked among the merchant's tables. Most of the foot traffic was merchants looking for a place to stop for the night, with a few plainsfolk whom she guessed ran the many inns. She saw some beings she thought were werecats, but she couldn't get a long enough look to see their tails. Some of the gnomes walked to and fro, mostly to get food and hurry back to their shops. She knew from her studies that gnomes preferred their workshops to outside interactions and heavily relied on the trolls and plainsfolk to help them function. She was surprised that she hadn't seen any of the little inventors in Lanol, but Iasi explained that very few lived in the city and that they preferred the quiet country towns.

"I'm ready now." Aailaine didn't recognized Iasi when he began walking toward her. His normal blue eyes were now a deep azure, so deeply blue that they almost didn't seem real. Despite the change, the new color seemed to fit his face perfectly. Iasi flashed her a smile as he fluttered his eyes. "Like it?"

"Ye-yes," Aailaine stuttered out, shaking her head to free herself from the allure of his eyes. "They fit you very well."

"Thank you. Blue is m-" Iasi paused, and seemed to consider his next phrase carefully. "My favorite color, so I often wear contacts to suit my mood. I prefer this color blue, but it can be hard to find sometimes."

"What's your true eye color?" Aailaine queried and Iasi visibly recoiled at the question. He shifted nervously, his tail wrapping around his leg.

"My...my eye color is taboo." He finally said, still refusing to meet Aailaine's gaze. "My family troupe doesn't really care but if I have to be among people for a long amount of time, I have get contacts to hide my eyes. Otherwise, people would be afraid and probably attack me."

"Oh." Aailaine didn't understand his explanation, but she didn't want to push him for an answer. She spoke quickly to change the subject. "Now what?"

"Well, let's find a place to spend the night. A lot of the inns here are kind of run down because it's just a pass city, but there is this really nice place I love. They have nice balconies facing out toward the plains." Iasi's tone perked up as they walked toward one of the larger inns and Aailaine walked silently behind him, watching as the streets began to thin out. The gnomes began to close up their shops, the merchants were filing into the inns like ants returning to an anthill, and the plainsfolk were returning to their businesses. It seemed almost unnatural to her; in Mathydar the city was never truly empty. The sun going down only meant the end of outside work while the work underneath the mountain continued far into the night.

"Aia, hey, you ok?" Iasi's voice snapped Aailaine back to reality and she turned to face him. They were almost alone on the deserted street as most of the beings had already disappeared into the other inns. "I assumed you were following me when I went inside, but when I turned around you weren't there. I know it's been a long week, so are you okay?"

"Yea, I'm fine. It's just..." Aailaine turned to the ghostly streets and felt a chill run up her spine. The sun was already far enough down in the sky that the buildings behind her blocked its light and the street seemed incredibly dark. She could almost feel the darkness trying to swallow her and she backed up instinctively, her step causing her to back up into Iasi. He placed his hands on her shoulders, gripping her tightly.

"It's imposing, isn't it?" She looked up at him as his usually happy tone had turned somber and dark. Even his face seemed darker in the shadows, and his eyes were narrow as he looked over the street. "It follows the light of the sun and threatens to swallow everything in its path. It's the Darkness of the Shadows, the Darkness we all try to avoid."

"Iasi?" Aailaine's voice quivered as she spoke, placing her hands gently on top of his. As if shaken, he quickly released her.

"Come on," his tone instantly changed, and he was the self of everyday again. "I already got our rooms."

"Rooms?" Aailaine queried, following him up the steps to the inn door. The interior of the inn was finely decorated with curtains and drapes hanging around the room. What she assumed was the main desk was right next to the door and another door was next to the desk. Past there were many set of tables, similar to large dining halls Aailaine had learned about in school. At the front of the dining area was a small stage, set a little higher than the tables.

"Yes, I assumed you'd want to keep sleeping in separate rooms. It's usually frowned upon for people our age to sleep together, and though I don't care, I figured you might." Iasi smiled at her as he picked up their room keys and held the second door open for her. "Don't worry, they're connected through a small doorway, so I won't be too far away."

"Ok." Aailaine sighed internally. While she had had her own bedroom with Rfkr, she was never in the house alone at night and it was comforting for her to be with others. In Lanol, once she woke up and found that she was alone, she was too scared to go back to sleep. She had tried to find Iasi's room, but since she didn't know his room number, she had no choice but to give up. This time, knowing that only a door separated her from him was a relief.

"Here's your room key." Iasi handed her a heavy metal key with the room number carved into it. "Dinner's in an hour downstairs so make yourself comfortable and freshen up a bit."

"Thank you." Aailaine managed to whisper, and she chanced a glance up at Iasi. "For paying for my room."

"Oh, that's no problem." He smiled at her and patted her shoulder before winking. "I know the owner *very well*."

Aailaine's eyes widened at his implied meaning and she quickly entered her room and closed the door. She heard Iasi chuckle in the hallway before she heard the door to his room close. Sighing a heavy sigh, she removed her quiver and bow, and setting them on the floor near the door, began to inspect the room.

The room was nicely designed, with a large bed as the main feature. The bed was easily twice the size of the bed she had slept on in Mathydar and could fit her plus five others easily. She fell on the bed and was nearly sucked in by the soft-pillowed mattress. Aailaine had never seen, much less slept on, such a soft bed, and she cuddled one of the pillows as she enjoyed the comfort surrounding her.

Along with the bed was a full washroom, with a toilet and a large wash closet. She touched the handle that jutted from the wall and nearly screamed with surprise when cold water rushed from the faucet above her.

"Aailaine?!" She heard Iasi open the door and rush into her room, only to find her wet on the washroom floor, staring in surprise at the wash closet. He released a long sigh, laughing at her slightly before helping her stand.

"Have you never been in a place with plumbing before?" He laughed again as Aailaine slowly shook her head. "A lot of inns nowadays have incorporated the gnome design that allows for running water. If you turn the dial, you can even control the temperature."

Aailaine watched in awe as he showed her how to use the wash closet and almost squealed when he let her touch the warm water. It felt delightful and soothing against her skin, and Iasi giggled again. She turned to see that he was watching her with a soft smile on his face, as if she was a young child who just started taking her first steps. She quickly turned away from him, embarrassed by her behavior.

"Thank you, for showing me how to use this." She murmured, and Iasi merely shrugged. He walked out of the wash closet and motioned to the large pack he had set on the floor of her room.

"You're welcome. If you want, clean up and change. When you're ready, meet me in my room and we can walk down to dinner together." With that, Iasi left Aailaine alone in her room again. Returning to the basin, she turned the handle again and adjusted the water to an appropriate temperature before stepping out of her garments and into the wash closet. She closed her eyes and lost herself in the warm embrace of the water as it washed away all her cares and made her forget about the world around her.

Chapter 13

Iasi waited patiently as Aailaine finished getting ready for dinner. As he was in the room alone, he stood on the balcony, watching as the last shred of light disappeared behind the faraway mountains. He watched as the sky became a deep blue and he could almost feel the Darkness that was riding on the edge of the vanishing light. He could feel the dark desires bubbling inside of him, but he ignored them, turning away from the sky. He walked into his wash room and studied himself in the mirror.

He was wearing a red crop top, trimmed with a sheer gold. He wore his usual chain around his waist, with the addition of two gold bracelets around each wrist. His pants were a similar red to his top and while they reached his ankle, the fabric opened up to show his inner thighs with small strips of cloth to cover his groin and buttocks. His makeup consisted of a dark red eye shadow with very thin gold eyeliner highlighting his bright blue eyes, and a very pale red lipstick to add a bit of color to his already plump lips. He could've tried to cover the scar with makeup, but he found that it only added to his allure. His black ears twitched ever so slightly, and his tail coyly wrapped around his left leg.

Examining himself in the mirror, Iasi felt a twinge of regret and slight pain in his chest. His once true-blue eyes only blue now thanks to the contacts he wore and his perfect tan skin hiding the changes within. He hated lying to Aailaine, but he knew he couldn't tell her the truth about the changes inside him; the dark thoughts that bubbled inside him and the desire to kill and maim that plagued his thoughts.

He shook his hips and stroked his chest, seducing himself with the mirror. He could feel the desire to kill lessen as he seduced his reflection, trying to push the dark thoughts from him mind.

Once he felt the desire had mostly left him, he walked out of the washroom to find Aailaine on his porch, looking out at the darkening sky. She was wearing a black skirt with a sheer overskirt that hung a little longer than the thicker material underneath and swayed in the evening breeze. Her shirt was a bright green with gold trim around the sleeves; at first, he almost took it to be the shirt she had been wearing earlier, until he realized that this shirt didn't have a collar. Around her neck was the amulet she always wore, its gem reflecting the dying sunlight, and instead of being braided, her long hair hung in a loose ponytail down her back. He looked around for her archery gloves but found that she had taken them off.

While there was nothing spectacular about her outfit, he felt that it suited her well. He stared at her awestruck for a few moments as she looked out over the dark plains before finally starting toward her.

"You look lovely," he silently came up beside her and leaned on the balcony next to her. She looked at him with surprise at first, and then a blush slowly spread across her face as she registered what he had said. Iasi laughed a little at her reaction.

"I'm...not dressed as well as you..." she murmured, looking away from him. He giggled softly as he stood, and he gently lifted his hand to her chin, turning her face toward him.

"You don't have to be." He smiled as he pulled away and released her, and he noticed how she swayed on her feet for a moment before regaining her balance. "C'mon or we'll be late to dinner."

He whisked her out of the room and locked the door behind them, before linking their arms and leading her down to the main hall. Most of the guests were already downstairs and enjoying their meal when they arrived. As they neared an empty table, a very voluptuous woman approached them and almost pushed her bouncing breasts in Iasi's face.

"Iasi! How nice of you to finally join us!" She placed a kiss on each of his cheeks and turned to see Aailaine, who was almost standing behind him. "And quite the catch you've brought with you! Who is this lovely lady, your escort?"

"This is Aailaine." He swung her forward and loosened his grip on her arm. "And I'm her escort actually. I'm helping her travel to Hirie, as she has been invited to visit with the elves."

"My, isn't she the lucky one, with beauty to match." The woman turned to Aailaine whose face was bright red as she avoided the woman's gaze. "A bit shy though."

"Weren't we all at some point?" Iasi waited until Aailaine was seated before sitting opposite of her and, after giving their drink orders to the waitress, started to study Aailaine. She sat still, her hands twitching in her lap and her knees shuffling. Despite her body language giving away her nervousness, her face was blank, no sign of her earlier blush visible. She made no effort to make talk or even look at Iasi, and he sighed heavily.

At this, she glanced up quickly and gave him a questioning look. He shrugged and said nothing, glancing around the room. Much of the room had been drinking for quite some time and was rowdy and loud. Groups of men and gnomes were sharing pints and screaming angry words at each other as Iasi waited for the waitress to bring them their food and drinks. Some of the human men were waving their hands around, throwing and catching the pitchers to entertain the other races until some of the waitresses came and stopped them.

"Here you go darlings, enjoy." The waitress slid their food in front of them and carefully placed their drinks before swinging by a nearby table to pick up the empty pitchers. Iasi turned his attention to the meal in front of him. It was mostly rice with a healthy amount of teyom meat, the savory smell of the boar meat filling his nostrils. Next to the meal was a small serving dish of gravy, which Iasi generously poured over his food. His drink was a thick honeymead, and he helped himself to a sip before beginning his meal.

"Enjoying the meal?" he asked, sneaking a look at Aailaine's food. She hadn't touched her food yet and was instead sipping on her drink. Iasi had ordered her a light ale, as she seemed to enjoy bitter drinks. He frowned as he watched her. "Do you not like it?"

"No, it's not that." Aailaine looked at his confused, before glancing at her drink and then his. "Oh, I apologize. I'm just used to drinking before I eat a meal. I actually can't wait to try it. I rarely had teyom meat at home."

Aailaine looked up and smiled, but it quickly faded as she finally began to pick at the food. "This is also something I'm still getting used too. Eating in a large group just isn't common where I'm from. I'm also not used to how luxurious this inn is either. I know you said it's run down, but this is more expensive than anywhere I've ever been."

"Oh, sorry." Iasi apologized and smiled reassuringly at her. "I'm kind of used to it. I get paid really well for what I do, so I tend to spend it on luxuries. I don't waste all of it, but I do enjoy doing things like this. I forgot that since you're from a troll farm this would seem strange to you. Outright wasteful, actually. Just try to enjoy it, and I'll try to tone it down in the future."

"Hmmm..." Aailaine hummed softly and started to earnestly eat her food as Iasi quickly finished his own plate. Downing the rest of his honeymead, he sat back in his chair and glanced around the room again. Many in the room were starting to calm down and were drunkenly trying to find their way back to their rooms. Some of the men were trying to entice the waitresses to join them, but the women were more than capable. The few who wouldn't take no for an answer were swiftly thrown out into the night, their money returned to them with a bump on their head.

The rest of the patrons were still calmly sipping their drinks but showing signs of being tipsy. The waitress who had served them and greeted them met eyes with Iasi and winked broadly at him. He smiled as he stood, startling Aailaine.

"Iasi?" She called his name out questioningly as he leaped and flipped his way to the front of the room, gathering the attention of everyone as he went. Once he got to the stage, he swept an elegant bow, receiving a quiet round of applause. He looked up to see Aailaine clapping slowly, her expression once again unreadable.

"Good evening everyone," he cooed as he stood up, almost springing to his feet. "As it was asked of me, I will be entertaining this lovely crowd of people on this wonderful evening. So, what will you have me do?"

"Shall I sing?" As he said this, he leapt to another table, landing on his knees and imitating a singer, sang a couple of sweet notes. The group cheered, and Iasi smiled as he leapt to another table and started to dance, pretending to dip another person. "Shall I dance? Or..."

With this, he slowly stalked his way over to Aailaine, whose stoic expression was slowly changing into a blush as he made his way toward her. He easily jumped up on the table and crawled on all fours toward her. He smiled slightly as her face grew redder and redder and the crowd began to hoot and holler at his actions. He leaned close to her face and released a breathy sigh before pulling back, his tail swaying slowly behind him and curling.

"...something a bit more sensual?" he offered, leaning backwards on the table. Aailaine quickly looked away from him, now aware that everyone was staring at her. Not wanting to push his little game too far, he quickly backed off and sashayed his way back to the stage, pausing every now and then to sensually interact with the crowd. A kiss here, a touch there; everyone in the crowd was longing for him and he loved it.

By the time he reached the stage, another werecat musician was already waiting and with a wink for Iasi, began to play. Iasi closed his eyes and lost himself to the allure of the music that threaten to overtake him.

Chapter 14

Aailaine's mind raced as she watched Iasi dance on the stage.
The dance he performed for the group was very different from the
private dance he had given her but was no less enchanting. The way
he moved his hips, the way his muscles shined in the light and the
way his hands would rub his skin; she could feel the blush her
thoughts brought to her face.

Aailaine quietly chastised herself for being flustered so easily.
Even Rfkr had mentioned that she would have a hard time finding a
mate if she hid away from every advance. In her defense, she would
remind him that she never had much interaction with other humans,
due to their cruelty and fear of her. She had never truly experienced
an advance that was not laced with a cruel scheme of getting a
reaction out of her. She didn't view Iasi's actions as genuine advances,
given his profession, but his honest flirtations and compliments were
enough to make her blush.

Aailaine turned her eyes back to Iasi, who continued to
seduce the crowd with his body movements and allure. He seemed to
truly enjoy the dancing and by his movements and smile, it was easy
to tell he was having fun. It was also obvious that the patrons enjoyed
the show as well, because both men and women were on the edge of
their seats. Aailaine watched the show in awe, surprised at his limber
movements; they had spent an entire week travelling since Lanol and
she never once saw him practice or even stretch. His natural
flexibility was truly to be admired and Aailaine felt a little jealous.

However, the music soon ended, and Iasi finished his dancing. Before leaving the stage, he leaned in and kissed the musician deeply. A lot of the audience cheered them on and soon the other werecat abandoned his restraint and drew Iasi close to him. Their tails intertwined as they pressed their bodies together and the crowd nearly screamed. Aailaine felt a strange twinge in her stomach and chest, similar to the one she felt when Iasi complimented her, and she watched with curious interest.

"Thanks honey." Iasi soon broke the kiss and stroked the cheek of the other werecat, who smiled and tightened his grip around Iasi's waist. Iasi gave him an inquisitive look and chanced a glance at Aailaine. She shrugged with her blank expression as the musician turned his face back to him.

"Just be careful, or I might have to take you to my room." At this Iasi laughed and broke free of the musician's grip, making his way back to Aailaine, who stood up when he got close to her. He offered his arm and for a moment she just stared at it, unsure of what she should do. She was aware of all the stares watching them, waiting to see if she would accept his gesture. Slowly, she locked her arm in his and they began to walk toward the hallway door that would lead them to their rooms. As they walked, Aailaine could almost feel her face turn red as she imagined the thoughts of all the patrons who watched them. She almost unlinked her arm from Iasi's when he released her first and walked in front of her instead.

When they reached the hall door as before, he held the door open for her as she passed through and then followed behind. As they got close to their rooms, Aailaine realized she didn't have her key and that she would have to go through Iasi's room again.

"Um...Iasi?" She spoke softly as she stopped in front of her room door. Iasi already had his key in the lock and was about to walk into his room when he paused at her soft words.

"Wha- oh. You forgot your key, didn't you?" Aailaine stared at the floor as she nodded. Iasi finished opening his door and held it open for her. "You are more than welcome to go through my room."

Aailaine stepped into Iasi's room and had every intention of going straight to her room when she noticed something odd on Iasi's porch. It almost seemed as if a person was kneeling on the exposed surface and her curiosity got the better of her. She cautiously walked toward the dark shape and Iasi walked in after her, puzzled. When he realized where she was walking, he looked over to the balcony and quickly grabbed her arm. Before she could protest, he pulled her close to him and pressed both of them into the furthest corner. Although the room was slightly lit, it wasn't very bright, and they easily blended into the dark corner. Aailaine opened her mouth as if to speak and Iasi quickly covered it. His musky scent filled her nose and she felt the familiar twinge in her stomach.

"Don't." He spoke softly and Aailaine's heartbeat quickened as the shape on the porch moved. It slowly stood, and she froze as Iasi pressed them further into the darkness. It was roughly the same height as Iasi, even mimicking his appearance. The biggest difference between the Shadow and Iasi was the jet-black liquid that hung closely to its skin, dripping off only to crawl back to it and its piercing red eyes. It looked inside of the room, stepping inside only to hiss and step back out.

That's when Aailaine noticed that the light in the room barred the Shadow from entering. The Elddess lamps in the Tolsan were very dull lights and the Shadows had run past them with no regard, but the bright light of the fire created a barrier that it could not pass.

Barred from checking the room, the Shadow's form shifted as it climbed over the balcony railing and slid along the wall toward Aailaine's room. After a few moments, Iasi released Aailaine and quickly closed the door to the porch and drew the curtains to keep the Shadow from looking in. Satisfied that it was safe, he looked to Aailaine and motioned for her to come out of the corner.

She slowly walked forward and looked over at the door between their two rooms. She thought she could hear soft sounds, as if someone was walking through her room and the sound made her heart leap in her throat. She glanced back over to Iasi, who shook his head as he sat on the bed.

"You should probably stay here for a moment." Iasi said quietly, his voice somber and dark, as it had been earlier when he spoke about the Shadows. Even though he was sitting right next to the light, he seemed to be enveloped by the darkness behind him.

"Are you alright?" Aailaine stepped a bit more in the light and the gem in her amulet reflected the small light all over the room, brightening the space with a bright flash. When she had recovered from the sudden brightness and looked over at Iasi again, he looked normal with a slight smile on his face.

"I'm fine." He laid down on the bed and stared up at the ceiling and Aailaine stood near him next to the bed. He shifted, and she noticed that he had rolled over with his back to her. Without his shawl to cover him, his back was exposed and covered in several old scars. Without thinking, she reached out to touch them; despite having a number herself, she found something fascinating about the number of scars Iasi seemed to have.

When her fingertips touched his skin, she felt as if something began to flow out of her and into him. Iasi purred with content and his tail wrapped around her arm as if to ask for more. She pressed the whole of her hand onto his back, and the amulet began to glow brightly. Slowly and softly, a trail of white light began at her shoulder and flowed like water over her arm before disappearing into Iasi. As Aailaine watched in wonder, Iasi's purring slowly changed to light snoring, as if the light had lulled him into a deep sleep.

Aailaine slowly removed her hand, and left Iasi to his sleep, passing through and closing the door between their rooms as quietly as she could. She took the amulet off to look at it, but it seemed the same as always. Then, as if struck, Aailaine felt all her energy drain from her and she collapsed onto her knees. She quickly replaced the amulet and felt some of her strength return.

"Did I...was that...my power?" Aailaine spoke softly as she stood. She carefully lit her lamp and felt her stomach churn as she watched the Darkness scurry out of her room, fleeing onto her porch and underneath her room door. She made her way to the balcony and closed it as Iasi had done, although she left the curtains open.

Content that she could sleep in peace, Aailaine slowly made her way to the bed. As she fell into the soft blanket of pillows and sheets, she held the amulet to her face, a slight twinge of fear and amazement rising in her. Rfkr had claimed to not know what the amulet was, or where Kleia had gotten it, as they had separated long before Aailaine was born.

Aailaine sighed as she rolled over to face the balcony. The endless darkness outside the glass caused her chest to tighten in fear for a moment, and she thought she saw movement. Aailaine carefully reached next to the bed and placed her bow and quiver on the bed, glancing out the window once more.

This time, she saw the eyes of the Shadow as it stood on the balcony, glaring at her as red met silver. It stood at the edge of the light, barred from coming near the window. Sirix's words about Irdrin hunting her drifted into her mind, and she began to regret asking Iasi to help her; she had not considered that she would be putting him in danger as well.

Aailaine glared at the Shadow in equal measure, removing an arrow and drawing back her bow. The Shadow's eyes widen, but it slowly slinked away, fading into the darkness behind it.

Relieved, Aailaine relaxed her draw, placing both items back on the bed. As the light protected her balcony, she decided to sleep facing the door, as the light from the lamp did not quite reach it. Even though her heart raced at the thought of the Shadow coming from her, exhaustion began to take its toll and her eyes drifted shut.

Chapter 15

Iasi was floating about in the mist above Exla, the vapor cool and wet against his skin. He softly drifted toward the bottom, like a feather falling in the breeze. He had started having this dream since he joined Aailaine and while it had troubled him at first, everything around him seemed calm and peaceful and he soon forgot about his worries.

As he drifted, he began to hear a voice calling through the clouds. It sounded so far away and unfamiliar, so he ignored it as he continued his slow and steady descent. However, as he drifted closer, he began to make out the words the voice was calling, and voice became more distinct.

"Iasi!! Scar, where are you?!" He turned to see the vague outline of a female werecat below him, searching for something. She seemed to run in small circles, clearly distressed and he recognized the shape as his older sister. He could hear the twinkling of the bells on her skirt as she ran around, searching for him. He reached out for her hand, hoping to touch her, but there was nothing he could do to speed up his fall. "Iasi!!"

"Chadirra!" Iasi cried, and he suddenly found himself in the desert, standing next to an oasis. He recognized that he was standing in the Redan Desert and he looked up to the sky to see a full moon hanging over him, just like that fateful night. Teasing him with its light and how it had failed to protect him in the darkness of the caves.

"Scar, are you out here?" Iasi heard his sister's soft voice behind him and in a panic quickly shifted into a siraya and leapt into the leaves of the frond next to him. He saw the edges of her skirt as she entered the oasis.

"Scar? Where are you?"

"Maybe he stepped out for some air." He recognized the voice of one of the male musicians and saw his feet appear next to Chadirra's. "You know he loves the oasis. Plus, we need to find those kids, it's dangerous for them to be roaming through the caves at night."

"Yea, I know..." Chadirra's voice quivered with her reluctance to leave and Iasi could feel his heart breaking. "It's just, I have a bad feeling about this."

"You know Iasi, he disappears sometimes, but he always comes back." The musician turned away and began walking toward the mouth of the cavern again. Chadirra turned to follow but paused before stepping inside.

"Iasi, please come back." His sister's final words to him caused Iasi's heart to ache as she re-entered the cavern and he shifted back into his original form. He dragged himself deeper into the oasis, his heart heavy with the fate that world had burdened him with. He made his way to one of the small lakes that littered the oasis and carmine eyes stared back at him as he gazed into the water. He closed his eyes and re-opened them, somehow hoping they would be blue again. That they would be any color but red.

Suddenly, he felt a presence behind him. Whipping around quickly, he turned to see that an elf stood near him, her pale pink skin standing out against bright moonlight. Her hair was a soft rose and when she turned to look at him, he noticed her narrow eyes were the same. She seemed so out of place in the desert and when she took a step toward him, he stepped away.

"Don't come near me! I'm...I'm not safe!" Iasi looked away as he spoke, and when he looked back up, she was considerably closer. She watched him with kind eyes and took a step closer to him.

"You were newly infected, weren't you?" She smiled at him softly and lightly touched her forearm. Iasi mimicked her motion, gripping his tightly. The blood felt cold as it ran down his skin, and Iasi already knew that soon it would close and heal, leaving no scar behind. He began to dig his fingers into his skin when the elf girl spoke again. "Concerning your change, there is hope for you, Iasi."

"How do you, how do you know my name?" Iasi glared at her, his tail twitching and his ears flattened. She looked at him kindly and opened her hands, holding some of the water from the pool. The water danced around her hands and floated over to Iasi, dancing around him before falling to the sand. This display of magic made Iasi even more wary, and he reached into his shrug, retrieving his daggers.

"My only intention is to help you." The elf girl looked deep into Iasi's red eyes with her own. "Go to the town of Lanol in Dochel and wait there. It is only there you can find your salvation."

"What? Why Lanol? Wait!" Iasi called after her, but the elf girl merely turned and disappeared into the dunes. He considered following her but decided against it. He stared down at his boots, flexing his toes inside. "Honestly, what is even happening here? I can either sit and wait to change or take this chance that I might be saved because some magically appearing elf girl told me to.

"This is all so absurd. None of this makes since. Why Lanol and what is even waiting for me there?" Iasi glanced at the water again and saw his own distorted face looking at him. He squatted next to the water's edge and stirred the water with his hand. He looked up and saw one of dune siraya drinking on the other side of the pool. The creature froze once it noticed him, its fur expanding with fear. His tail twitched behind him and it hopped away quickly, returning to its burrow in the sand. Iasi's thoughts drifted to his sister, whom begged for him to return and he stood, gripping his fists tightly.

"Alright, fine." he said to no one in particular. "I'll go to Lanol, as stupid as it sounds. What choice do I really have?"

He slowly shifted into an ozkok, his skin turning a sandy yellow. His arms and legs disappeared into his body, which lengthened and was almost three meters long. His face elongated, and his hair and ears disappeared as scales appeared to cover his body. His wings flew out from behind him and all that remained of his original form was his black tail. He slithered to the edge of the oasis, getting ready to take off when the same elf girl appeared in front of him. Her pink hair waved in some unknown wind and she seemed worried as she looked down at him.

"Iasi, I must warn you." She reached out to him, and Iasi slithered back. He wasn't sure how much he trusted this girl or her advice, despite her seemingly good intentions. "The Shadows, they will try to make you join them. To fuel the Darkness inside you. But you must be strong and wait in Lanol for your salvation."

"We'll sssssssee." Iasi managed to hiss from his dragon mouth and he glided past her, launching himself into the night sky. Toward the dark clouds, the endless horizon...

Slowly waking from his dream, Iasi rested his eyes on his ceiling. It was only because of the absurd events of that night that he had travelled to Lanol and met Aailaine. He had considered walking right by her when he saw her in the street, but something about her appearance was mesmerizing and drew him in. When she had asked for his help, both in the street and in her room, he felt as though he couldn't refuse her and that he had to accept. He didn't know if it was the Darkness in him or something else that drove him to help her, but it worried him nonetheless.

Iasi sat up on his bed, sighing heavily before feeling a strange sensation on his back. As he reached to touch it, he began to feel warmth spreading from his back all over his body. It seemed to flow through his entire being and calmed the rage and dark thoughts the Darkness within him created. He looked around but found himself alone.

Worried, he stood and opened the door that separated him from Aailaine. She was asleep in her bed, her hand resting on her bow that laid on the bed next to her. Iasi glanced toward her balcony and saw the numerous Shadows that stood on the edge of the light.

"Go away." He growled, lowering himself closer to Aailaine. She lightly shifted in her sleep but did not wake. The Shadows swayed in the balcony, ignoring his words. Instead he noticed one of them raise its hand and point toward him.

<One of us.> He heard the voice breeze through his mind, even as he tried to ignore it. He knew it was the voice of the

Darkness, the voice of Irdrin, trying to convince him to stop fighting. To stop fighting the dark desires and finally join in his rank of Shadows. His gaze slowly drifted back down to the sleeping Aailaine as the voice spoke again. <Soon enough.>

"No." he whispered, standing as he walked over to the lamp and made it brighter, forcing the Shadows to retreat further away. Some of the Shadows fell from the balcony as the rest tried to avoid the light. "I'll never become one of you."

At this the Shadows and the voice retreated, although Iasi remained in the room a long time afterwards. The clearness of the voice worried Iasi; while he usually heard whispers, he had never heard Irdrin's voice so clearly before. He was sure it signaled that his change was still progressing, although it seemed to be taking longer than he knew it should.

Iasi walked up to Aailaine's lamp and put his hand near the flame. Except for the usual heat, he felt no pain from the light of the lamp and he sighed as he dropped his hand. Carefully, he removed his contacts and looked at the light with his carmine eyes. The light seared his eyes and his head instantly began to ache as he quickly turned away. He turned the lamp back down to its original brightness, and replaced his contacts, blinking as they reseated.

When he finally returned to his room, he left the door between him and Aailaine open a crack, in case the Shadows tried to return. Reluctant as he was, he laid back down on his bed, staring at the ceiling above him. With a heavy sigh, he closed his eyes again, and whispered an answer to his sister's plea.

"I'll come home, Chadirra. I promise."

Chapter 16

"Aailaine, time to get up." Aailaine moaned into the soft bed as Iasi called for her through the door. The sun had barely risen in the sky and she finished watching the sunrise through half-closed eyes before she stirred from her comfort. Living in the mountains kept her from being able to watch sunrises and sunsets and it astounded her that no two seemed the same. The way the colors were arranged and even what colors one could see were always different and she loved how the warm sun felt on her face on the morning or watching the moon rise behind the array of orange, pinks and purples.

Aailaine worked her way to the wash closet and turning on the warm water, stripped out of her skirt and top before cleaning herself and waking up. She had washed her other set of clothing before heading down to dinner with Iasi and hung them in the wash room to dry. She quickly dressed in her travelling outfit and slipped on her boots. Upon leaving the washroom, she found Iasi waiting on her bed in his typical blue outfit with the large pack next to his feet. He still only had the small pouch he wore around his waist, so she started to question where he carried the outfit he had worn the night before. Iasi noticed her looking at him questioningly and he tilted his head sideways, his ears perking up.

"What is it?" he asked, waiting for her to pack away her skirt and extra shirt before he picked up the larger pack to carry.

"Where's the outfit you wore last night?" Aailaine's ears grew hot, as she remembered his show from the night before. "You only ever seem to have that small pouch, so I was curious."

"Oh, that wasn't mine." Iasi smiled, adjusting the pack on his back. "It was an outfit I was borrowing from the owner for the show. It was part of the deal for giving us rooms here."

"Then what do you keep in there?"

"My money." Iasi shrugged. "I don't have much else beyond the clothes I'm wearing and the jewelry I wear."

"Oh. And I suppose I have these." Iasi reached into his shrug and pulled out two small daggers from the fold of the fabric. They were very short blades that would only be useful for slashing or throwing and he showed them off for a moment before hiding them back in his shrug. "But those are just for my protection. What about you?"

"Well, I have the pack and my bow." Aailaine shrugged as she fastened the quiver around her waist and slid the bow inside. She handed Iasi the room key as he looked at her expectantly. When she said no more, his brow furrowed.

"You don't carry any close-range?" He queried as he stood and locked her room behind them. Aailaine shook her head, confused.

"Why would I need them? I'm just fine with the bow."

"Because you won't always have time or the range to use your bow. What if you run out of arrows? You should have a close range back up just in case." Iasi explained, handing their keys to the same voluptuous woman who served them the night before. "It's always better to be safe. We'll see if we can find you something when we arrive in Pasyl. They'll be more farms along the way this time, so we won't have to sleep outside as much. Besides, it would take at least a week and a half no matter how fast we walked."

"In the meantime, I'll teach you how to use my daggers." Iasi promised, stepping out into the waking town. It seemed as if most of Torora hadn't roused from its sleep, save a few vendors who were offering food to those preparing to leave. Iasi bought some fruit from one of them and handed Aailaine a roundish red fruit with a smooth texture and a short stem coming out the top.

"It's an eri. Enjoy it, they can be very filling even though they're not that big." Iasi bit into the juicy fruit and hummed with delight as they began to leave the small pass town. Aailaine looked at the fruit and took a small bite. The skin was a bit tough but the minute her teeth broke through, the fruit's juice jetted into her mouth and the meat of the fruit was soft and easy to chew. As she kept biting into the fruit and chewing the red meat, more and more juice would jet into her mouth. The eri was both a meal and a drink, and the skin itself reminded her of eating paper. Regardless, it was delicious, and she quickly finished off the fruit and tossed the core into the grass alongside the path. She was almost sad when it was gone and looked over to Iasi.

"Um, Iasi?" He glanced down at her, halfway through his own eri. She knotted her hands and look around nervously before continuing. "Um, do you have any more? Eri, I mean."

"Of course." Aailaine's face lit up as he tossed her two more eri from the pack he carried on his back. "I picked up enough for us to have three each."

"Thank you." Aailaine quickly bit into the fruit and hummed with delight as Iasi had done prior. He smiled and finished off his first eri before starting his second.

"No problem Aia. I'm just glad you like it." Iasi laughed as he ate the delicious fruit. "It would've been a bit of a problem if I had to eat them all by myself."

"You'd still look handsome." Aailaine giggled softly and Iasi paused to stare at her. For the first time, she saw a slight hint of red spread across his face as his ears flattened and he quickly looked away, polishing off his second Eri and starting his third.

Confused by his reaction to her compliment, Aailaine slowly turned back to eating her fruit and enjoying the crisp morning air.

Tolsan
Where Old Friends Meet

Chapter 17

Sirix tapped her foot impatiently as she waited for Elmeye to finish talking with the dwarven merchant. It had been almost two weeks since their arrival in Slalan and not only had the child still not told her what was happening, the sorceress spent most of her time talking to the Viwl clan merchants, buying various jewelry. She had said they were waiting for someone to come join them in Slalan but Sirix's patience was running thin. She hated being within the tight spaces of the Tolsan, which confined her to her human form. She preferred to be in her dragon form, but even from her days with Kleia, the dwarves were never accommodating to dragons, even ones that were Vuiej. Viregda, the Viwl SkiRyldes, had made a bit of an exception for Sirix, but still requested that the dragon stay in her human form to avoid causing commotion.

Finally, Elmeye finished her transaction, and skipped her way back over to the dragon woman, clearly pleased with the proceedings. The girl's yellow eyes twinkled as she beamed a smile at Sirix.

"Well, I'm all done for the day, so let's go back to the dwelling." she sang, cheerfully walking past Sirix and heading in the direction of their temporary home. As the dwarves rarely welcomed visitors, the cities in the Tolsan had no dedicated inns, but rather dwellings that visiting merchants could rent from the local SkiRyldes, something Sirix always considered bothersome. Kleia had more patience with the mountain dwellers than Sirix did, and Sirix would often be forced to wait outside the dwarven cities before Rfkr joined them on their travels.

Thinking of Rfkr brought a slight pain to her chest, which Sirix strongly tried to ignore. She knew his cycles were numbered and that Rfkr had longed for death but the reason he died haunted her and fueled her frustration with Elmeye. Pushing down her sadness and giving way to her anger, Sirix reached out with her scaled hand and caught the back of Elmeye's cloak, stopping the girl in her tracks. She could feel the energy around the sorceress change as her emotions went from happiness to annoyance.

"How much longer must I play your games, girl?" Sirix growled deep in her throat as Elmeye turned around and quickly yanked her cloak away from the dragon woman. Her deep, animalistic voice caught the attention of some of the dwarves and humans passing by and a few stopped to stare. However, one quick glance from her burning eyes and they hurried on their way. "I do not have forever to wait."

"No one is holding you here." Elmeye retorted, crossing her arms defiantly. More onlookers were taking notice of their exchange and slowed their walk, although none dared to stop due to Sirix's menacing appearance. "You came of your own free will and you have stayed for the same reason."

"I have a duty-"

"A cage you have created yourself, Sirix." Elmeye deflected, using Sirix's name. This gave the dragon pause, as the child had never actually spoken her name beyond their first meeting. "So, again, only you have kept yourself here. I will not rush on your behalf and I will not needlessly endanger lives that have nothing to do with our affair. I will not create a bloodbath to satisfy your impatience."

Elmeye turned to walk away again and Sirix begrudgingly followed. As usual during their daily trips to the market, many dwarves eyed Sirix strangely. Due to her short stature, Elmeye was more easily ignored but Sirix easily towered over the tiny mountain dwellers. Even the few deep-dwellers and plainsfolk that were buying and selling with the dwarves were tiny compared to her giant frame and she began to feel uncomfortable under their stares. She heard Elmeye snort in front of her and Sirix quickly began to walk normally again. The sorceress had offered an enchanted necklace that would make her appear normal sized, but she had refused, not trusting the girl or her magic.

"Home sweet home," Elmeye sang as they stepped into their temporary home and Sirix followed her in, immediately walking to her corner and sitting. The home was uncomfortable for her to move around and she preferred to sit in the largest corner that accommodated her tail, which now revealed itself from inside her dress. Elmeye moved around the home freely, removing her cloak's hood and shaking her white hair free from its ponytail. Just as she recovered some fruit from the stores in the kitchen, a timid knock came on their door and a familiar voice called through the frame.

"Elmeye? *Ritye*, I hope this is the right one..." Sirix's eyes widen in surprise as Elmeye opened the door to Hvidr. The she-dwarf stepped in and upon eyeing Sirix, bowed her head with respect. Sirix returned the gesture as the sorceress embraced Hvidr tightly. Hvidr was wearing her typical sleeveless tunic and shorts, although Sirix could see the outline of the breastplate with the Nivim clan symbol hidden underneath her tunic.

"It's been too long, friend. Also, I heard about Rfkr, my condolences for your lost." Hvidr said nothing to this as she sat with the girl at the table and accepted the food that was offered to her.

"He has the rest he longed for and the peace he desired. It won't be too long before I join him." Hvidr sighed, undoing her ponytail and allowing her red hair to tumble across her shoulders. Elmeye patted her shoulder as the dwarf ate. "What brings you and Sirix back to the Tolsan? Your messenger was frustratingly vague in delivering the message. Also, meeting in Mathydar would've been better. The Viwl may be our merchants, but they still don't truly trust my clan like most."

"I know but we couldn't afford to be in Mathydar; we can't have too many people knowing either of us are here. Especially me. Viregda's clan has tighter lips." Elmeye smiled, leaning back in her seat as she helped herself to some of the raspbessires. She offered some to Sirix, who refused and continued to watch the pair and listen from her corner. It seemed strange to her that Hvidr knew Elmeye, although she didn't know the dwarf very well. All she knew came from Rfkr, and he had become very bitter after Kleia turned Aailaine over to him, refusing to talk about almost anything. "Anyway, with autumn almost over, shouldn't the second Covern be happening soon?"

"Yes, in the next few weeks or so. Why?"

"Well," Elmeye's expression became very coy and she leaned forward on the table, lacing her fingers together in front of her. Her change in demeanor peaked Sirix's interest and the dragon woman leaned closer out of her corner. If Elmeye noticed, she made no notion, keeping her eyes locked on Hvidr. "What if someone was planning to destroy the Covern and the Threrayrt?"

"I'd say you'd better have some damn good proof, because Nivim is still stretched thin at the moment." Hvidr huffed, eating more food and drinking more water. "We lost quite a few numbers beating the Shadows out of Mathydar a few weeks ago and no one besides me even knows why we got attacked. A lot of people are jumpy about Shadow activity in the Tolsan and Dhonir is already ready to start a war over it."

"Well, I wouldn't worry about your clan. The Shadows shouldn't be returning anytime soon, as long as we succeed. Rather a very obnoxious wizard that we have a score to settle with. Right, Dragon?" At this Elmeye shot a glance at the dragon woman, and Sirix nearly felt herself burst with rage at the implication. Unable to stand, she slammed her tail into the ground, fighting her urge to shift. Elmeye had already mentioned his involvement with events in the Tolsan, but Sirix hated the very thought of him.

Hvidr seemed shocked by Sirix's reaction at first, but then her eyes widened in surprise before she turned to look at Elmeye again.

"You don't mean...?"

"You mean the only person Rfkr was worried would find him and Aailaine here? My one mistake." Elmeye nodded, her face calm and devoid of emotion. "Soseh is here and he is planning to throw Tolsan into chaos. If the Tolsan falls, the Shadows will tear through the mountains and onto the rest of A'sthy."

"But daylight... they can't survive sunlight." Hvidr stammered. It was obvious that this news disturbed her, and she was having a hard time accepting it. She played with the cup in her hands, gripping it tightly. "Taking Tolsan won't help that."

"Aye, but it does bring them out of the Void and closer to the rest of A'sthy," Elmeye pointed out. "Sunlight is still a problem at the moment, but how often do you get sunlight down here, Hvidr? Does the sun ever illuminate your caverns?"

Hvidr slumped in defeat, the fear plain on her face and Sirix felt a twinge of empathy for the dwarf. Elmeye however, kept her stoic expression as she continued. "I thought so. Soseh will make the Tolsan tear itself apart by destroying the Covern, allowing the Shadows to overrun in the confusion."

"Sounds like him." Sirix growled and Hvidr looked between the pair, clearly worried. "And he would be the best to do it. Throw Tolsan into chaos without involving the Shadows. That way the dwarves will see it as an internal problem and start infighting with the deep-dwellers again rather than uniting to act against the Shadows."

"Agreed. He prefers to keep his hands clean and the situation she mentioned is perfect." Elmeye returned her attention to Hvidr, who fidgeted. "If Tolsan falls, the rest of A'sthy will shortly follow."

"Why are you telling me this? I don't know anything about this Soseh person." Hvidr glanced at Sirix. "Rfkr never told me much, other than if Soseh found him and attacked Mathydar, I should take Aailaine to the trolls in place of him. Ironically enough, rather than Soseh, the Shadows came themselves."

"Soseh was here." Elmeye casually mentioned and Sirix stood quickly, despite her large form not fitting. Hvidr looked at the dragon woman with surprise and alarm.

"There was no mention of anyone being here but the Shadows by my clansmen." Hvidr argued, still looking at Sirix. Elmeye finally broke her stoic expression and sighed.

"Soseh is a werecat, Hvidr; he can change his form and he loves turning into other races. Always a flaw when I knew him. He's the one who followed Sirix and after confirming Aailaine's presence, he led the Shadows here. If he had known Rfkr was in Slalan, then he probably would've just killed Aailaine before anyone found out. A coward as always, he sent the Shadows to avoid facing him." At this point, Sirix's emotions threatened to burst. She had led Soseh to the Tolsan. She had led him to Aailaine and Rfkr was dead because of her.

Sirix could feel her control slipping and quickly left the dwelling. She was a blur as she ran through the streets, unconcerned for anyone she bumped into. She hurried out of the mountain and once she stood in the evening air, she lost her control over her human form. Her body began to elongate as her legs and arms shortened. Bones snapped and cracked as they reformed to accommodate her larger frame as her backbone extended to its original length. Her face contorted and pushed out as she finished her transformation. Full of rage, she launched herself into the air and flew high into the sky.

<*SOSEH!!!!*> Sirix screamed, her thoughts reaching no one. She hadn't known that he was the one who had tracked her to Mathydar. She *should* have known; the Shadows had never managed to find her before but now, to know that it was *him*. The coward, that snake who sent the Shadows to kill Aailaine and cost Rfkr his life.

<*Soseh kodad ritye!*> She growled helplessly and landed fiercely on the ledge she had taken off from. By time the other women found her, she was in her human form kneeling on the ledge, her head touching ground as she balled her fists. Neither Hvidr nor Elmeye said a word as they stared at her, waiting to see what she would do.

"I must apologize, Hvidr." Sirix's voice was soft and empty of emotion. "I have allowed Soseh to take Rfkr away from you."

"Don't apologize to me, Sirix. If anything, Soseh had taken two people from you. First Kleia and now Rfkr." Sirix felt a stab in her chest at the mention of her former Teieimoko. "Besides, if anything, I lost him a long time ago. When Kleia turned Aailaine over to him, that's when he was never the same."

"Few people could come home the same after seeing what those three saw. Rfkr did his best, all things considered." Elmeye commented and Sirix finally looked up, the two women staring at her as they sat on the stony ground. Elmeye merely shrugged and said nothing else. Sighing heavily, Sirix dragged herself up from the stone and walked over to the two. Hvidr stood as well, although Elmeye remained seated.

"Let us return into the mountain. There is much to do if we are to stop Soseh." Sirix spoke calmly, pushing down the raging sea of her emotions. Hvidr nodded solemnly and turned her gaze to the sorceress. Elmeye watched her a little longer before chuckling and standing.

"Agreed, although we don't have much time or much help. Soseh is too tricky for the average dwarf and we have no solid proof other than my word. Luckily, I know him extremely well." Elmeye grinned and for a moment, Sirix thought she saw something move underneath her cloak, but quickly dismissed it as the wind. "I can't go to Mathydar, however, until we know exactly where he is and what's he's planning to do. If he sees me there, he'll run or worse, try and do something unexpected to throw me off."

"So, I'll have to be your eyes in Mathydar, like usual." Hvidr sighed, running her hand through her loose hair. Sirix stared at the two tiny women, confused by their relationship. Elmeye had already mentioned she was older than she appeared, and it seemed she had known Hvidr for a long time. Hvidr was younger than Rfkr but was still old by dwarf standards, meaning it was impossible for this to be more than their second or third meeting.

"Don't sound so glum about it. It's simpler than last time; just do your job. You manage the city's workforce, including the workers who fix the Threrayrt and the guards who will be on standby during the Covern." Elmeye smiled and patted Hvidr's back. "Soseh will try to be one of those, so that he has an excuse to be there without raising conflict. If one of your workers seem strange, like he doesn't know what's he's doing, or a guard asks too many questions about the Covern, tell me. I'll be able to determine whether it's him or not."

"How am I supposed to tell you? It took me a week myself to get here, and the Covern will be in the next few weeks. By the time I return and could send a messenger, the Covern will be taking place." Hvidr crossed her arms, fully turning to face Elmeye. Sirix felt alienated by their conversation but understood that she didn't have much to add and silently listened to their planning. "And what are you planning to do once you find him? I can't raise my clan or even the brigade until he's dragged into the open and his plans revealed."

"The communication part is easy. I'll merely cast an enchantment that will allow you to speak with me whenever you please." Hvidr looked uncomfortable at the mention of the enchantment, which Elmeye ignored. "As for once we know who he is, that's where Sirix comes in."

"What is my part in all of this?" Sirix finally spoke and Elmeye sighed heavily before turning to speak with her.

"You're the only one who can confront Soseh. Hvidr can't do much against him and can't raise her clan until after he has been revealed. I can't go to Mathydar for several reasons, but the most important is that Soseh thinks I'm dead." Hvidr scoffed before uncrossing her arms and placing them on her hips.

"Everyone thinks you're dead, Elmeye. That's the point, isn't it?" Hvidr offered and Sirix glanced between the two of them. Hvidr seemed smug about something and Elmeye was clearly annoyed by her response. "If you're seen in Mathydar, it'll take two days before all of Tolsan knows you're alive."

"I am aware of this Hvidr, thank you for reminding me. However, it is not a problem if Tolsan knows; only if Soseh does." Elmeye asserted and then continued to speak to Sirix. "Once we know who he is masquerading as, you have to go to Mathydar and confront him. You've never been there in human form, right?"

"No." Sirix answered. "After Kleia passed, I did go to visit Rfkr and Aailaine, but I did so in my true form. Rfkr has never seen this form, so I thought it better to see him as he knew me. Only the Viwl recognize this form and only because you have brought me here."

"Good. No one there will recognize you in human form then, not even Soseh. He'll probably masquerade as a deep-dweller if he's smart, since Hvidr would recognize right away if it was a dwarf she didn't know." Elmeye seemed pleased. "I'm fairly sure he's aware of her connection to Rfkr, so he should be careful around her."

"I'll be confronting him as a human?" Sirix frowned. If their goal was to stop Soseh, she felt that she should confront him in her true form, which was much better for fighting.

"Yes, I just said that. Your true form is too large and would draw too much attention." Elmeye's annoyed tone didn't match her savage grin and her eyes continued to light up as she went on. "You'll convince him to go with you to a more deserted part of the city. I'll tell you where once we know who he is. There we can confront him openly and stop him from destroying the Covern."

<And end his life.> Sirix could almost feel the unsaid words in Elmeye's plan and from Hvidr's expression, so could she. The very air around them seemed to vibrate with Elmeye's anger and passion to destroy Soseh. Hvidr chanced a glance at the dragon woman, and it seemed Hvidr didn't quite understand Elmeye's passion against the wizard either. Sirix's curiosity made her want to question, but she doubted that the sorceress would answer her anyway.

"Well," Hvidr interrupted the silence between them. "I guess I should get back to Mathydar quickly, preferably tonight."

"Indeed." In a moment, the air around them returned to normal and Elmeye was her calm self again. "I'll send you back, along with the enchantment. And don't worry; this time it is an enchantment on an item, so you won't have to deal with it."

"Wonderful." With that, Hvidr turned to walk back into the mountain and Elmeye turned to follow. Sirix paused for a moment, turning to look at the night sky. They had such little time to do anything and were depending on Hvidr's help. It seemed that Elmeye was hoping Hvidr's love and care for Rfkr and her clan would spur her to help and give it her all, which Sirix didn't doubt. It was Elmeye's motives and knowledge that troubled the dragon. It seemed she had a wealth of knowledge regarding Soseh at her disposal and from her anger, it sounded like she might have been the one who trained him in magic. On top of that, she seemed to know quite a bit about Kleia and Aailaine, which worried Sirix greatly. She was always vague and cryptic in her statements, however, never truly revealing if she knew the truth or was merely guessing.

"Are you coming, Sirix?" Hvidr called back to her from the opening and Sirix tore her gaze away from the night sky and began to walk back into the cold embrace of the stone.

Dochel
Where the Darkness hides

Chapter 18

Aailaine quietly poked the fire as Iasi walked back toward the main path. In the last week since they left Torora, he had insisted they camp away from the main path in case the Shadows were checking it for them. After the incident in Torora, Iasi had gotten more paranoid about sleeping at night in the plains and would only sleep if Aailaine woke up. It bothered her that he wasn't sleeping, and she made every effort to get them space on a farm if possible. On nights like tonight however, when they were far from the closest farm, they had no choice but to sleep under the sky.

"Well, it seems ok for now," Iasi conceded as he stepped into their little camp and sat near the fire. Aailaine took this chance to open the large pack and pull out some of their food. The trolls had packed her some salted teyom meat that she finally pulled out and Iasi's eyes widened in surprise.

"Where did you get that?"

"The trolls that my family lived with packed it for me when I left." Aailaine shrugged, laying out the meat to cook. "We're almost out of the fruits and vegetables, so I figured we could eat it now. You said we should reach Pasyl soon, right?"

"If all goes well, we should be there within six to eight days." Iasi nodded as he spoke, helping Aailaine to spear the meat with the wooden rods that were also in the pack. Once speared, they held the meat over the fire to wait for it to cook. "So hopefully before the weekend. Wish we had a pot though."

"Why?" Aailaine asked, packing away the rest of the meat and checking her own dinner. It wasn't quite as done as she wanted it, so she thrust the other end of the rod into the ground, angling the meat over the fire.

"We could've made a stew. Although I suppose a pot would only make the bag heavier." Iasi sniffed the meat and bit into it. There wasn't any blood, but Aailaine knew it wasn't cooked all the way through from the color and that made her stomach churn. She stifled her disgust and turned away, looking up into the night sky. The moon was starting to disappear again, a slice at a time, and the sight made Aailaine a little sad. Aailaine recalled from her studies that unlike the sun, which was always the same, the moon went through a cycle. It would start with a dark night, where the moon wasn't visible and then a little at a time, the moon would appear until it was a full circle, also known as a full moon. Then after being full, the moon would begin to disappear again. Every once in a while, when the moon started to disappear, another moon would start appearing and would follow the same cycle, then disappear again for a long while.

"It doesn't seem like we'll see the second moon this time around." Iasi remarked, and Aailaine glanced over at him. He was watching the night sky, still eating his nearly rare meat. Aailaine remember her own meal and rescued her meat from the fire. It was burnt slightly, but still mostly edible and she began to nibble on her food, still turned away from Iasi.

Eventually she heard him stand and watched as he wiped his face with his shrug before taking it off and setting it on the ground next to him. A small part of Aailaine hoped he wouldn't put the shrug back on until it was washed and the thought of him wearing it almost made Aailaine's food come back from her stomach. She coughed to mask her disgust, and Iasi looked at her confused and then glanced back down at his shrug before sighing.

"Oh. Yea, I know it's gross. Sorry." He apologized, rubbing his hand through his hair. He looked away shyly and then looked back up at her, his ears flattened and his tail swinging slightly. "I'm glad you saved the meat till the last minute. To be honest, I would've eaten it raw, but I didn't want to disgust you."

"It's ok." Aailaine gingerly ate her own meat and she felt bad that she had made Iasi feel like he was wrong. "Feel free to eat the way you want to."

"I'll go wash this. You'll be alright on your own for a moment, right?" Aailaine nodded as Iasi stood, picking up his shrug and removing the daggers, setting them down next to the fire. "Good. Now let's see..."

"Wait, are you going to shift?" Aailaine asked excitedly, and Iasi gave her a strange look before laughing.

"Oh, right. You've never seen me shift. Yea, I was going to." Iasi winked at her as he spread his arms wide. "For you, beautiful."

Before her eyes, Aailaine watched as Iasi's arms became thinner and feathers started to spout from his skin. His legs grew shorter, becoming covered in hard, ribbed skin and his mouth jutted out into a beak. His cat-like ears and hair disappeared into his scalp and black feathers took their place. His eyes grew smaller and the contacts began to fall out. Aailaine moved quickly and caught them before they hit the ground. She watched in awe as Iasi completely shifted into a giant black eagle, his black feline tail the only feature marking him as a werecat.

Iasi flapped his wings once, as if to test whether they worked before picking up his scarf in his beak. He seemed to stare at Aailaine for a moment and she nodded, never taking her eyes off his beady black ones. With that, he took off and Aailaine watched him fly off into the distance.

Once he disappeared from view, Aailaine promptly finished eating and threw some dirt over the fire. She stood to remove her quiver from around her waist and she laid back down on her back so she could watch the sky. The deep-dwellers had ridiculed her for loving the stars and studying them, but now Aailaine grinned with delight as she identified the various patterns in the sky. Just as Aailaine rolled on her side to follow the path of the stars, she heard a rustle in the grass behind her. She quickly jumped up to her knees, pulling the bow out of the quiver and notching an arrow. She waited with baited breath and almost laughed when a small black siraya hopped out of the grass into their camp. She sighed nervously, standing and putting down the arrow.

"Found." Aailaine's blood ran cold when she heard the creature speak and watched with horror as the siraya morphed into a werecat Shadow, its tail twitching like a cat ready to pounce. In the grass behind it, more Shadows appeared, some standing up out of the grass and others appearing as if they had teleported from the Void itself. She glanced up to the sky to notice that the moon was temporarily covered by clouds and chastised herself mentally for putting out the fire.

She notched the arrow and aimed it at the closest Shadow. She relaxed and released the arrow, and it flew straight through its target and through the Shadows behind it. At first, Aailaine was worried that her arrow had no effect, but the Shadows slowly melted away, turning into puddles of darkness before evaporating. However, her victory was short-lived because as the first row passed away, the others behind it took its place and Aailaine quickly realized she was surrounded.

She began to fire off her arrows as quickly as she could, but it seemed for every one that disappeared, more took its place. Aailaine began to panic as her arrow supply was steadily depleted and there seemed to be more and more Shadows encroaching in on her. Soon she reached into the quiver and discovered she had no more.

She quickly used her bow to knock away some of the Shadows that tried to grab her, and she managed to knock away a blade from a human Shadow. The sword clanged the ground, revealing its silver blade as the Darkness left it. She heard a strange hum coming the handle as it lay on the ground and she swore it was vibrating.

Aailaine dropped her bow as some of the Shadows lunged at her. She picked up the blade and stood to face the onslaught, silently hoping she had inherited some of her mother's natural ability. Now in her hands, she could feel the hum of sero that ran through the hilt and she jerked the sword, causing the electricity to shoot out over the blade. The Shadows stepped back at this, and Aailaine smiled savagely.

"Alright." She smiled as she swung the blade and killed some of the Shadows that stood near her. She continued to slice and dodge them as best she could, being especially aware of the shifting werecats. However, she found that she was still being overwhelmed by their sheer numbers and her strength was failing her. Even though she managed to wield sword with a level of proficiency, her swings were clumsy, and very few of them connected. She glanced at the never-ending hoard and prayed for the moon to come out from behind the clouds.

< Please come back, Iasi. I need you. > Aailaine mentally called out for her companion and suddenly, she noticed a lot of the Shadows disappeared at once in front of her. She didn't have much time to think about it, however, as one of the human Shadows managed to sneak around her and grab her from behind. Aailaine dropped the blade in surprise and struggled to get away from it. It suddenly dropped her and as she fell to the ground, she watched the Shadow melt into a puddle before evaporating.

She looked up to see Iasi moving around her, jumping and leaping around, taking care of the Shadows. He moved like a black blur, and she could barely keep up with his movements. She looked to where he had left his daggers and saw that they were no longer there. She grabbed her blade quickly as one of the elven Shadows leapt at her and she quickly turned and slashed it, having the Darkness cover her as its host died. She coughed as some of the liquid went into her nose and mouth.

"Aailaine!" she heard Iasi call her name as she felt the liquid evaporate off her skin and she coughed out what had gone up her nose. She didn't have much time to recover, as another Shadow lunged at her and she found herself back to back with Iasi. He glanced back at her and she saw his red eyes glowing in the dark, similar to the rest of the Shadows. The sight caused her heart to jump a bit; now she understood why he wore the contacts and was reluctant to reveal his eye color.

"Stay close, the moon should reappear soon." As if summoned, a sliver of moonlight appeared through the clouds and the Shadows around them quickly backed up, disappearing in clouds of black smoke as the sliver of the moon came out from behind the clouds, giving off just enough moonlight to drive the Shadows away.

At the sight of the moon, Aailaine dropped her blade again and fell to her knees coughing. Iasi knelt beside her, rubbing her back as she coughed.

"Aailaine, what's wrong?" Aailaine couldn't answer as more of the black liquid came out of her mouth, splashing on the ground in front of her along with her meal. She vomited up enough of the liquid to fill a bucket and it almost seemed to stick to the ground before evaporating in the moonlight. Once the substance was out of her, she sat up on her knees, and deeply breathed in the night air to sooth her aching throat and mouth. Iasi quickly grabbed her face and searched her eyes with his.

"Wha-?" Aailaine started to question him, when he sighed deeply and released her. His uncanny red eyes were filled with relief and he worked on restarting the fire. Once it blazed again, he sat down and took his daggers from where it lay in front of Aailaine. He slid both back into his shrug and gazed into the fire, the light dancing in his eyes. She sat closer to the blaze and worried about his expression. "Iasi?"

"I don't suppose my contacts survived that." Iasi sighed as Aailaine shook her head and he gazed up into the sky. The clouds were mostly scattered with a few large groups and he poked the fire with one of the wooden eating sticks. "I suppose I'll see if I can find new ones in Pasyl."

"Iasi, I'm sorry. Your eyes...I understand now." Aailaine placed her hand on his shoulder, but the werecat showed no sign that he noticed. Worried, she grabbed the blade and sat next to him, laying it across her lap. Iasi finally sighed, looking away from the fire and closing his eyes.

"Where did you get that?"

"One of the Shadows dropped it. I picked it up when I ran out of arrows." She jerked the hilt and Iasi's eyes lit up as the electricity ran over the blade again. "I've never seen anything like it."

"It's a Sassrane blade." Iasi held his hand out and Aailaine gave it to him. Iasi twisted the guard and Aailaine watched in awe as the blade became permanently covered in sero. He twisted it again and it became a normal blade before he handed it back.

"Hold on to it; it's a good blade. I can teach you how to use it." Aailaine quietly accepted the sword and continued to wait. It was obvious that there was more on his mind, and Aailaine gently placed her hand on his shoulder again.

"I should've been here." Iasi whispered angrily, and Aailaine released him. "I should've known better than to leave you by yourself."

"I took care of myself just fine." Aailaine argued, standing and moving in front of him. His carmine eyes looked up at her surprised and it caused her heart to jump again. She swallowed her fear as she continued. "Yes, I ran out of arrows and I had to use a weapon I'm not really familiar with yet, but I was not helpless.

"I did fairly well by myself and it is in no way your fault, nor do I need you here to protect me. You are my guide," Aailaine glanced away and stared at the dirt, her voice shaking with frustration. "And my friend, but I am no little girl that needs protecting."

"Then why did you put out the fire?!" Iasi finally yelled, standing to look down on her. Iasi just stared at her for a moment and Aailaine felt her ears grow hot as she refused to meet his gaze. She could feel his eyes burning into her and she chanced a glance at his face. His heart-shaped face and shaggy hair glowed in the firelight and her eyes ran around his flawless skin. She felt ashamed for her actions as she tore her gaze away from him again; she couldn't deny that putting out the fire was what had allowed the Shadows to attack in the first place.

After what seemed like eternity, Iasi began to move near the edge of the camp. His movements portrayed his anger as he stomped around the fire, his tail twitching quickly. Just as he started to sit down, Aailaine called after him.

"Iasi?"

"Yes?" Iasi paused, turning around to face her. His voice was still full of anger and she glanced away again, clasping her hands in front of her.

"I'm sorry. You're right, it's just...I'm sorry." Aailaine chanced a glance at him and he was watching her cautiously. "It was stupid of me to put out the fire without fully considering the consequences. I...I won't do it again."

Iasi looked at her a moment longer before looking away from her again. He picked up the quiver and bow where they lay abandoned and handed them to her. He stood in front of her and a slight twinge of red began across his cheeks. At first Aailaine thought the fire was casting its light on him, until she noticed that the color began to fade as he spoke.

"I...also didn't mean to make it sound like I was belittling you." He sighed and ran his hand through his hair. His tail was wrapped around his leg and his ears were flat as he spoke. "I'm just...frustrated with myself for not being here. I knew the Shadows were tracking us, but I didn't think they would come directly after you. And I know this is all new to you, so I should've warned you about the fire."

"But I don't doubt your abilities at all. The best fighters I know are all women and you held up well against them before I came back." Iasi let out a little chuckle before glancing at her again, any hint of his blush gone. "So, I'm sorry, for leading you to believe that I doubted you. I'm just angry at myself for my lack of foresight and I took that out on you."

"It's alright. Just, let's work together okay? I just don't want you to think I need you to protect me." Aailaine spoke softly and Iasi smiled.

"I don't; you showed tonight that you don't need protection. Any idea as to why they're after you though?" Iasi gave her a worried look and Aailaine was forced to avoid his gaze. "I thought they were tracking me, but then it wouldn't make since for them to come after you."

"I...I don't know. Right before I left on my journey, the Shadows also attacked my home, killing my caretaker." Aailaine closed her eyes to stop the tears as she tried to think of a reasonable excuse. "The letter we received didn't seem to indicate anything more than a friendly visit to Hirie, but maybe..."

"There's a reason they don't want you to reach Hirie." Iasi finished and she nodded, chancing to meet his gaze. He was looking away from her with contemplative look on his face. "Or maybe..."

"What is it?" Aailaine watched him carefully, but Iasi smiled his usual smile at her and stroked her arm.

"Don't worry about it. We'll get to Hirie, no matter what." He released her and took his seat on the edge of their camp. "Try to get some sleep, I'll make sure the fire stays lit to keep them from coming back. We may have to take a different route to Pasyl now, but we can talk about that tomorrow."

"Alright." As she undid her braid and laid down to sleep, Aailaine started to wonder if Rfkr would have been proud of her. While he never attended her training, he always pushed her to train with the Nivim trainees, and that training was now beginning to pay off. She never expected in her life that she would have to fight other beings, but if she hadn't trained, the Shadows would have easily overwhelmed her.

<Thank you, Rfkr.> Aailaine thought as she drifted to sleep. <I'll become the person you want me to be.>

Chapter 19

"So, what's Pasyl like? Is it anything like Lanol or Torora?" Aailaine queried, walking briskly behind Iasi. The fall sun was high in the sky, but a cool breeze danced through the empty plains. It was clear that winter was on its way, and Aailaine wondered if snow had already begun to fall in the Tolsan. The thought excited her, and she felt a slight ache as she missed the mountains.

"Not really." Iasi paused, waiting for Aailaine to catch up. Since they had no sheath for the blade, Iasi had made a simple sling that allowed Aailaine to carry it across her back. He mentioned that Sassrane blades had special sheathes that prevented the electricity from flowing, so Aailaine had to pause every now and then to reseat the blade. "I mean, it's not quite as big as Lanol, but Pasyl is mostly the home to gnomes who make boats. There aren't many plainsfolk around, save those who run the inns and shops. Other than that, any plainsfolk you'll see will be merchants or apprentices. Oh, and there might be some elves."

"Apprentices?" Aailaine fixed her empty quiver around her waist before walking after Iasi again. The many charms around his waist clinked against each other and Aailaine caught herself watching before quickly looking away.

"Yea, apprentices. See, Lanol is special; all of the plainsfolk making gnome items there were once apprentices at different cities. That's why there aren't many gnomes in Lanol, but a lot of plainsfolk." Iasi explained, pausing as they neared a farm. He glanced up at the sun, as if to consider stopping, but instead began to walk around it. Aailaine waved at the trolls and plainsfolk working the fields and waited until they were past them to speak.

"Hey Iasi?"

"Yes?" He paused to look at her as they passed the last building on the farm and Aailaine shifted the sword on her back.

"Um...why..." Aailaine swallowed her reluctance and adjusted the quiver around her waist again. "Why aren't we stopping at farms anymore? If we did, you wouldn't have to stay awake so much."

Iasi watched her for a moment and without answering her question, started walking again. Aailaine chastised herself for asking and followed silently behind him, watching the clouds roll by in the sky. Occasionally, she would spy a farm off in the distance, its crop rising high above the short plain grass. The farms in the Tolsan were tiny compared to the long stretches of land the trolls farmed. She felt a slight ache thinking about the faraway mountains and to clear her mind, Aailaine decided to try and make conversation again.

"So, are there skyboxes in Pasyl?"

"Skyboxes?" Iasi called over his shoulder and almost immediately started laughing. Aailaine felt a blush spread across her face and she was glad he didn't turn to look at her. As his laughter subsided, Iasi paused in his walking, bending over as he took a deep breath and waited until she was beside him to start again.

"They're called gondolas and yes, there are some in Pasyl. Almost every city, besides the pass cities, have them. They make it easier to travel across the city in a day. It would be impossible to accomplish otherwise." Aailaine nodded as she remembered how they had used the gondolas to get to the Guild and to the inn they had stayed in. Being so high hadn't bothered her as much as the slight swinging had, which made her feel like the gondola would fall at any moment.

"Aia, look." Iasi's voice yanked her from her thoughts and Aailaine looked out in the direction Iasi pointed. Down from the hill and across the long stretch of grass was another large city and beyond that was a large body of water, shining a beautiful blue and reflecting the sun's light. The pointed pink roofs of the city seemed like fish scales shimmering in the sunlight and Aailaine was glad to see that this city appeared to have no wall. However, she could still make out the tiny shape of the Guild and its flying akhby, which resembled large birds at this distance.

"It's that Pasyl at the bottom?" She smiled as he nodded, and he pointed to the body of water.

"Yup and that's the Risck Imyd. We're going to commission an Orare in Pasyl so we can cross it." Iasi's face seemed a little pale and he visibly grimaced before sitting down in the grass. "But first we can take a break."

"What's an Orare?"

"It's what the gnome boats are called that we use to cross water. It's the fastest way to Hirie." Iasi looked up at her and motioned for Aailaine to sit next to him.

"Oh. Wait, Iasi, I thought you said gnome-made things were expensive," Aailaine wondered, sitting next to Iasi and plucking at the grass. He took off the pack and set it down between them, lying down in the tall grass. "Why are we taking an Orare?"

"Because it'll be quicker than going to the land bridge, and I'd rather take the shortest route across the water. Don't worry, I don't expect you to pay for it." Iasi crossed his legs and tapped his foot in the air. Aailaine waited for him to elaborate, but when he said nothing else, she gave up and continued plucking at the grass.

Quickly becoming bored of the grass, Aailaine turned her attention to the sky. The clouds were scarce and flowed by slowly, despite the wind that was blowing across the plains. Aailaine was about to lay down to watch them when Iasi moved, stretching his long figure.

"Well, Aia, you ready to go?" He quickly stood and stretched again, picking up the pack and swinging it on his back. He glanced down at her and offered her his hand, which she gingerly took. He pulled and lifted her up in one fluid motion, and she sprung up, faster than she could catch herself. She continued forward and, afraid of falling, clung to Iasi. Soon she found herself rolling down the hill, Iasi with her. She felt a sharp pain in her back as the rocks and other various objects they rolled over activate the sword. Aailaine closed her eyes, trying to ignore the pain, when she felt the ground fall out beneath her.

"Iasi?" Aailaine opened her eyes to see the ground of the plains far beneath her and became aware of the sharp claws in her shoulders. She looked up to see a large black akhby carrying her, circling above the hill they had been standing on. His long body waved behind them as he dove toward land and Aailaine let out a little yelp. Before her feet touched, Iasi slowed down, gently placing her next to the pack that had fallen from his back. She gingerly picked it up, looking it over to make sure it was fine and that none of its contents had spilled. One of the straps had snapped, and Aailaine frowned, looking back up into the sky. Iasi continued to dance around in his dragon form, his large wings blocking out the sun every time he flew underneath it and his long body wriggling behind him.

Eventually he flew back down, shifting as he grew closer to Aailaine. It seemed almost unbelievable to Aailaine as she watched his long black body shrink and split into his legs and his front claws lengthen and became thinner. The black scales disappeared up his legs until they reached his shorts and then the scales flattened and became cloth. By the time he landed, only his wings were left, and those quickly shrunk and folded across his chest, becoming his shrug as he stood up next to her.

"Is the pack and your bow okay?" he asked. Aailaine moved to show him the broken strap when Iasi mentioned her bow. She quickly reached into the quiver and her heartbeat quickened when she failed to find it. Aailaine panicked as she ran back up the hill, finding her bow among the grass there. She felt her heart break as she expected the worse.

The bow was in perfect shape, with no evidence of the roll at all; there were no scratches on its upper limb or lower limb and no indications of damage were visible on the notches. Aailaine carefully picked up the bow and used her half skirt to clean away the dirt. Iasi stood behind her as she stood up, cradling the bow in her arms.

"Is it alright?" Iasi asked tentatively and Aailaine nodded, tucking it back in the empty quiver.

"It was enchanted by elves; it's not surprising that it didn't take damage." Aailaine smiled, turning back to Iasi. "It was a gift from my mother, who passed away when I was young. I guess...she hoped I'd take to archery."

"She probably knew," Iasi offered, shouldering the one strap of the larger pack. "Mothers are like that. Anyway, we'll see if we can find a way to fix or replace this thing once we reach Pasyl. And get you a proper sheath."

"Yea," Aailaine could still feel the pain in her back from the jolts the blade had given her, and she took it off her back to readjust it's sling. "How far away are we?"

"At the most, three days, more likely less." Iasi glanced down at the rest of the hill. "I'm pretty sure our little tumble probably saved us an hour or two."

"Sorry." Aailaine rubbed her thumb against her forefinger as she stared at the ground. She felt a warm touch against her cheeks and looked up to see Iasi smiling at her. He wasn't standing close enough to touch her and Aailaine reached to her cheeks. As soon as she touched them, however, the warm feeling faded.

"It's fine, we'll just have to be careful so we don't take another one." Iasi stuck out his hand, still smiling at her. Aailaine carefully took it and he smoothly wrapped his hand around hers and began to carefully guide her down the hill. A slight warmth seemed to travel from his hand to hers and she found herself smiling.

<What is wrong with me?> Aailaine wondered silently as they walked, but she made no effort to remove her hand from his, content to enjoy the feeling as long as it lasted.

Chapter 20

Aailaine stood outside as Iasi conversed with the gnome in his workshop. Apparently, Iasi had commissioned Orares from this particular gnome before, so he insisted that Aailaine let him do all the work. He had explained to her that gnomes were very picky, and they only worked on commission basis.

Iasi had also insisted on buying more contacts the moment they reached the city. It took quite a bit of searching, but they managed to find a merchant who sold them and she also happened to carry bladed weapons. Aailaine was able to find a sheath for her Sassrane blade that had a quiver attached as well. The woman was also very eager to buy Aailaine's extra quiver; apparently dwarven made quivers were a rarity and the woman offered a hefty amount for it, making the sheath Aailaine was buying a nominal price. Aailaine was sad to part with her belonging, but after some reassurance from Iasi, she sold it to the merchant, who showered her with thanks.

They also bought some needle and thread so Iasi could fix the strap of the backpack. Although he seemed embarrassed about it, he admitted that he had some knowledge of sewing and could repair clothing and cloth bags, as long as the repairs were simple.

She drew her blade from the sheath on her back as she waited for Iasi to finish. The woman who sold her the sheath had described it as a Sassrane Bastard. The pommel was small and rounded and the grip constantly vibrated in her hand. Iasi had shown her how to lock the guard to stop the sero from flowing, so she jerked the blade without worry. She looked up to see some merchants staring at her with worried looks, and she quickly moved to put the sword away.

Bored with waiting for Iasi to finish his negotiations, Aailaine decided to sneak off to refill her quiver and after walking a while, she found an elven merchant sitting on the side of one of the busy streets. He motioned for her to come over and she did, mesmerized by his dark green skin and bright blue hair. His narrow eyes looked over at her bow and he motioned for her to show him. Still entranced, she slowly took it out and held it out for the merchant to inspect. The elf ran his delicate fingers over runes, and gently plucked the string. Satisfied, he turned to his numerous bundles of arrows, mumbling to himself in Eroir before selecting two very distinct sets and laying them on the table in front of her.

The first set had black shafts, and the point was narrow, not much thicker than the shaft. The fletching was made with red feathers and felt stiff under her fingers when she touched them. The notches were painted red as well and she liked the sleek design of the points.

The second set had green shafts and the black points were a strange shape. Both the points and the shafts were covered by what seemed to be black vines and when Aailaine reached to touch it, it moved to blunt the point, surprising her. The fletching was as black and soft as Iasi's fur, and the nocks were the same deep green as the shafts.

"Which will you choose, *Earibuoko*?" the elf's voice was smooth like honey and offered the same sweet taste. Aailaine ignored his use of Eroir and carefully looked between the two sets. For a moment, she considered buying both sets, as she liked the both designs. However, the vine-like design on the second set seemed to reach out to her hand, and when she touched it, she immediately felt that she needed those arrows.

"This one." Aailaine chose the second set and the elf handed her the bundle of arrows, untying the string that bound them together. He slid the arrows into her quiver and motioned her away, refusing to take her money. Surprised, but thankful, Aailaine slowly made her way back to the gnome workshop, and she reached back to blissfully brush the soft fletching as she walked.

"We're all set now. Let's go get you arrows." Iasi's voice drew Aailaine from her thoughts as he stepped out of the workshop and stood next to her. Aailaine smiled as she showed him her quiver.

"I already got some." She announced, and Iasi looked at her with surprise before glancing at her full quiver.

"Well, I guess you did." Iasi affirmed and put his hand on her shoulder. He was looking at her softly and he slowly smiled, looking away. "It'll be about two or three days before our Orare is ready, so we should find an inn and book a few rooms for a while."

"Ok." Aailaine followed closely behind Iasi, who seemed to be considering their best choice of an inn. As he had stated, there were only four inns in Pasyl, and to Aailaine they all had seemed decent. However, she barely knew anything about inns, and so she left the decision to Iasi, whom definitely seemed better versed in the matter.

Soon, Iasi chose the smallest of the inns and quickly walked inside. Determined not to be left behind this time, Aailaine followed him and stood next to him at the counter.

No one waited at the counter, so Iasi picked up a small bell on the counter and rang it. After a moment, Aailaine saw a small door on the other side of the counter slide open and soon the torso of a short woman stepped up behind the counter. Her long white hair was pulled back into a braid, although her bangs cleverly covered most of her face. She didn't seem to wear much clothing to cover her black skin, just a strip of cloth around her small breasts and Aailaine wondered if she was an exotic dancer like Iasi.

"Iasi! It's been too long. How is your sister, Chadirra?" The woman greeted Iasi warmly and he smiled, his tail swinging happily.

"Chadirra is good, Yraly." Iasi beamed, flashing her a seductive smile and kissing her hand. The woman didn't blush and instead, to Aailaine's surprise, leaned forward to steal a kiss from Iasi's lips. Iasi returned her kiss in kind, although a small blush did spread across his face as he glanced down at Aailaine. Yraly followed his gaze and once becoming aware of Aailaine, leaned back from him.

"And who is this lovely lady you're with today?" Yraly smiled at Aailaine kindly and extended her hand. Aailaine carefully accepted the offer and was taken aback when Yraly softly kissed the back of her hand as well. "She is quite the catch if I do say so myself."

Aailaine's ears grew hot and she slowly withdrew her hand and started to wish that she had remained outside. Iasi noticed her embarrassment and quickly responded to Yraly.

"This is Aailaine. I am helping her to reach Hirie." Iasi smiled again, lightly draping his arm around her shoulders. Aailaine felt her blush subside at his gentle touch, but she continued to keep her gaze on the floor. Yraly whistled, which drew Aailaine's attention, causing her to chance a glance up. Yraly was nodding at her with approval and opened the large book in front of her. She seemed to be looking over it, as if searching for something.

As they waited, Iasi's grip on Aailaine loosened, and he soon let go of her altogether. She chanced a look up at him and he winked down at her, mouthing something silently. Aailaine failed to catch what he said and frowned at him. Iasi sighed and leaned down toward her, not taking his eyes off Yraly.

"Sorry," he whispered, quickly standing up straight as Yraly exclaimed softly, marking a section of the page with her finger and reaching over for her quill and ink well.

"I'm guessing you two will need rooms for a few nights, but unfortunately, the only rooms I have left are double bedded rooms." Yraly turned the book to face them, never moving her finger off the page. Aailaine noticed that her finger marked two empty lines on the page, which she assumed was for an empty room. "I assume that won't be a problem?"

"Yraly, you know tha-"

"Not at all." Aailaine managed to find her courage and, taking the quill from Yraly's hand, quickly signed the page and placed the coins on the counter. Iasi gave her a strange look as he slowly took the quill from her and signed his name as well. As Yraly took the book and money before disappearing behind the desk again, Aailaine thought over what she had noticed about the tiny woman. She was easily small enough to be taken for either a dwarf or a gnome, but her face was baby-ish and she seemed too slender to be a dwarf. She could've been a gnome, but even female gnomes preferred inventing to anything else.

"Here you go." Yraly appeared above the counter again and smiling, handed the pair their key. "Dinner is right after sunset, so feel free to rest in your room until then. You must be tired after all that walking. Where did you come from this time?"

"All the way from Lanol. My thanks, Yraly." Iasi answered as he accepted the key and the woman winked at them, stepping off her stool and disappearing through her door again. Aailaine waited for Iasi to show her where their room was, but he stood in place, waiting expectantly. Aailaine opened her mouth to ask him what he was waiting for, when Yraly appeared out of a door behind Aailaine.

Behind Yraly was a spider-like abdomen and four extra limbs, which she had kept tucked behind her back out of sight. Aailaine watched her in surprise as Yraly walked over to Iasi and pulled on his shrug using one of her extra legs, whispering something to him. Iasi's eyes widened, and he quickly whispered something back. After that, Yraly giggled and continued off, walking toward the main dining area. Iasi watched after her before turning to face Aailaine, who was still looking after Yraly in surprise.

"Never seen a spindly before?" Iasi waved his hand in front of her face to break her from her stupor, but Aailaine couldn't help but stare. She continued to watch as another spindly, this one male, joined Yraly and seemed to be helping her clean the dining area.

"Not in person." Aailaine admitted, slowly tearing her gaze away from the spindly pair. Following behind Iasi as he finally took the lead, he held open the hall door for her. Aailaine had been curious about the door at the previous inn and finally her curiosity got the better of her. "Why are the hallways for the rooms separated from the main hall by a door?"

"To keep people from sneaking into the rooms and getting a free night." Iasi made sure the door closed behind him before walking in front of Aailaine. "That's also why the door is on the other side of the desk. So not only do you have to walk past the desk first, but this door is locked until the owner opens it for you."

"But the rooms have keys." Aailaine frowned and Iasi glance at her, his eyebrows raised. "How could someone sneak into a room?"

"Not everyone is as honest as you, Aia." Iasi spoke quietly as he found their room and opened the door, allowing Aailaine in first. This room was not as nicely decorated as her room in Torora but was better than her room in Lanol. Rather than full of decorations, the room was simply painted teal and the two beds were large enough for two people each. She gingerly stepped into the wash room and noticed that the wash closet was like the one in Torora, with a small handle to turn and a faucet above it. The main difference between that closet and this one was that this one had a basin.

"Mind if I use that?" Iasi came in behind her, his shirt and shrug already removed. Aailaine found herself staring at him before moving out of the wash room. Iasi smiled at her and leaned his head out the door after starting the water. "Before I forget, Yraly or another spindly should be coming up here with a change of clothes for me and a set for you."

"You don't have to wear it tonight or anything, but they're a gift from Yraly." Iasi said offhandedly, disappearing back in the washroom before peeking out again. "Just knock on the wall and slide my clothes in here."

"Alright." Aailaine nodded and slid off her half skirt as Iasi disappeared back into the washroom. After removing her sheath and leaning it against the bed, Aailaine sat down and was overjoyed to find out it was just as soft as the bed she had in Torora. Unlike that bed, however, this bed only had a handful of pillows and Aailaine grabbed one and fluffed it.

A soft knock eventually came at the door and Aailaine stood to answer it. The spindly at the door was the male one she had seen earlier and he carefully handed her the two soft packages wrapped in paper. His legs twitched behind him and he grinned brightly before walking back down the hall. Aailaine took both bundles over to the bed and, unable to tell which one belonged to Iasi, opened the first one examine the contents.

The first bundle consisted of a dark blue top that had short sleeves and opened about mid stomach. The bottoms were poufy dark blue pants and the outer material was sheer, revealing the black fabric beneath. The shoes where black slippers obviously made for dancing and Aailaine was even more confused. The outfit didn't seem revealing enough for Iasi's tastes, but she didn't understand why she would be given dancing shoes.

The other outfit seemed to be a dark grey and similar to the first outfit she unpacked. However, this outfit's top was shorter, barely reaching past mid stomach and had no split. The pants also weren't poufy, with the sheer overlay closer to the base material. The dark grey boots had a sliver heel and the heel seemed to be made of a different material than the rest of the sole. Aailaine looked between the two set of clothing for a moment before sighing heavily.

"Um, Iasi?" Aailaine walked over to the washroom and gingerly knocked on the wooden door. She heard some bumps and then Iasi's head appeared in the doorway, his shaggy hair dripping with water. "The outfits came, but I can't tell which one is yours."

"Well that's no good." Iasi frowned, and looked down at the floor, thinking. "What colors are they?"

"Dark blue and a dark grey, almost black." Iasi's frown deepened as he continued to stare at the floor. Aailaine began to hum as she rubbed her thumbs with her index fingers, waiting for Iasi's response. Eventually Iasi sighed and looked up at her, smiling shyly.

"To be honest, I have no idea which it is. I don't think I've ever seen these outfits before. Yraly must have just made them." Iasi shrugged, shaking some of the water off his skin. Aailaine turned her face away from him as she realized that he was probably still undressed in the doorway. "I guess you can slide both sets in here, and I'll try to tell. Actually, let me see your feet first."

"Why?" Aailaine turned back and pointed her boots for Iasi to see. He glanced down at her feet and nodded, apparently pleased.

"You could try on the shoes and if those shoes are close to fitting you, I guess that one is yours." He smiled coyly. "My feet are way bigger than yours."

"Ok." Aailaine nodded and Iasi waited a moment before disappearing back into the washroom. Confused, she moved back over to bed where the outfits lay and she carefully removed the shoes from the second set.

Just as she sat down to remove her boots, she heard a humming sound come from the washroom. Curious, she moved to the doorway and placed her ear against the wall to hear Iasi singing. Despite hearing him sing a few notes before, Aailaine was surprised by the hypnotic nature of his voice. It was strong and deep, and reverberated through the wall as he sang a song that Aailaine had not heard in a long time:

"There's a storm rattling beneath my bones.
A caged *earmom* condemned to sing off-key notes.
I would leave if I only had the chance to follow,
To live in a happy place that held no sorrow.
Orassul cries me to sleep,
as the stars trace the tears from my cheek,
and I become lost in the embrace of *Yelaneri*.

Fa ided fohto ashe gibdeod bia ...
Fohto, I can't stand to be without you.
Fa ided fohto ashe gibdeod bia ...
Fohto, Fohto, I need you to love me too..."

Aailaine stepped away from the wall as Iasi started the song over again, obviously lost in his own world. She wondered how he knew the song, as it was an old dwarven and elven lullaby. Rfkr had sometimes sang it to her when she was young, but his voice was no where as sweet as Iasi's.

Filled with curious interest, she returned to the bed and slipped on one of the short grey boots. The boots swallowed her feet and she sighed heavily, glancing over at the black slippers. She slipped one of them on her other foot and the slipper fit fairly well, although it was still a bit loose. She wiggled her foot in the shoe, enjoying the soft plush material.

"Figure it out yet?" Iasi called out from the doorway and Aailaine looked up to see his face peeking out again. His hair was drier and was starting to curl, resembling his normal shaggy look.

The rest of his arm and chest still gleamed with moisture, although it no longer dripped and she couldn't hear the water running in the background anymore.

"Greyish-black one is yours." She slipped off the shoe and placing it back on the second bundle, carried the clothes over to Iasi. He reached out of the washroom to accept the clothing and nodded his thanks, before disappearing again. Aailaine turned to walk away when Iasi's head popped out of the washroom again.

"Thanks sweetheart." Iasi winked at Aailaine, who smiled warmly to hide her blush and turned back toward the bed. She heard him giggle softly as he began to dress in the washroom and she held her hand over her pounding heart. She wasn't sure why the compliment had caused her heart to race; he had called her sweetheart on numerous occasions before.

Once she had calmed down and she was sure that he wouldn't return for a while, Aailaine took the opportunity to undress from her traveling outfit and change into the outfit provided. The opening around her stomach bothered her slightly, but for the most part, the cloth fell over itself. The only time the opening was even visible was when Aailaine pulled it open herself or if she spun.

She sat on the bed to slide on the other slipper just as Iasi stepped out of the washroom, dressed in the dark grey outfit. Aailaine noticed that there was a split in his shirt, and it ran from the collar to a little below his chest, making most of his chest visible. It was now that Aailaine noticed that Iasi's chest was covered in various scars and marks similar to the ones she had seen on his back, although none were as pronounced as the scar than ran across his eyelids.

The boots seemed to fit his feet perfectly, and Iasi clicked the sliver heels against the floor. She assumed that he had taken his contacts out in the washroom, because his eyes shined like rubies, the red frightening and enchanting her. His feline tail wrapped around his leg coyly, as if it were a separate entity and trying to grab his attention. She swallowed hard and forced herself to meet his gaze.

"You look lovely, Aia." Aailaine felt as if her heart would burst as Iasi walked toward her, but she forced herself not to look away. Iasi gave her a strange look as he sat on the bed next to her. Aailaine took this chance to examine the marks and scars on his chest more closely, and Iasi followed her glance, and laughed once he realized where she was looking.

"I was rowdy in my teen cycles," Iasi admitted, shaking his shaggy hair and sliding his hand across his chest, tracing the scars absently. "I got into quite a bit of trouble sleeping with people's children. Although some of these scars are from such endeavors."

"Sleeping with people's children? Men and women?" Aailaine croaked, raising her eyebrows as she chanced a glance up at Iasi. He wasn't looking at her anymore and was instead looking up at the ceiling as he leaned back on the bed.

"Yea. I am very aware that I'm attractive, and I used to use it to sleep with whoever I wanted. Being a werecat also helps." A slight blush spread on Iasi's face as he brought his gaze down to the floor and he flattened his ears. "I grew tired of it as I got older though."

"Do you still…" Aailaine felt her ears grow red as she tried to think of a polite way to word her question. She felt Iasi's warm hand on hers and she looked up to see his face.

"No, Aia, I don't sleep around anymore. Nowadays I only do it if it's related to my job. Sometimes I do sleep with customers who pay extra for it," Iasi admitted, still blushing, but he maintained eye contact with Aailaine as he pulled his hand away. "And even that is rare nowadays. Most are satisfied with just my dances. My job is all about the illusion that I belong to you, not that I actually do."

"Oh." Aailaine looked away from Iasi, staring into her hands as she stroked her thumb with her middle finger. "Um, Iasi?"

"Yes, Aia?"

"Why," Aailaine paused, taking in a deep breath. "Why did you take out your contacts?"

Iasi looked away from her at this, and Aailaine began to regret asking. He moved his hand to his face, covering one of his eyes as he looked at the floor.

"Do...do they scare you?" he asked softly, and Aailaine felt her heart leap into her throat. She couldn't deny that they always initially frightened her, especially after that night. When she woke up in the morning, she often had to squash her fear as she tried to remind herself it was only Iasi. Her fear also made her feel terrible; since red eyes were always associated with the Shadows, she couldn't imagine how horrible Iasi's life must have been. Being born with such a taboo eye color would certainly have made people treat him horribly, just as the deep-dwellers had treated her because of her appearance.

"They did at first, when we were fighting the Shadows." She admitted, and she saw his shoulders fall. She moved quickly to finish her thought. "But not now. I trust you and if you were turning into a Shadow, you would've already turned completely."

"Most wouldn't agree with you." Iasi whispered, and he covered his face with both of his hands. "I took them out to give my eyes a break. I'll put them back in before we go downstairs."

"I'm sorry." Aailaine wanted to admit that she understood some of his pain, but kept silent. She remembered what the plainsfolk head had told her at the beginning of her journey and knew that admitting her past would contradict her story. Instead, she gently placed her hand on his shoulder and saw a slight glimmer as some light flowed from her hand into him. She felt the tension from his body fade and Iasi dropped his hands from his face, a slight smile on his lips.

"It's not your fault, Aia." She felt the bed move as Iasi stood and looked up as he moved in front of her, offering his hand. She was surprised to find that he was looking away from her, his ears still flat as he held his hand out for her.

"Anyway, would you...would you mind dancing with me? Yraly usually has large dances with her dinners, and I usually lead the group if I'm here, although I usually dance with my sister." Iasi's blush deepened and Aailaine watched in surprise as he continued to look away from her. She had never seen him so flustered, especially when talking about dancing. "You...you don't have to if it makes you uncomfortable. Yraly already mentioned that she would love the chance to dance with me."

"It's fine, I'd rather watch. You should dance with her." Aailaine took his hand and enjoyed the cool breeze that brushed against her skin as Iasi pulled her effortlessly to her feet. She was careful this time to catch herself and although she swayed, managed to stay on her feet. He drew her close, his arm around her waist and the other holding her hand. His tail moved to stroke her leg, and his warm breath tickled her neck. Aailaine was surprised to suddenly be so close to him and had to swallow her wildly beating heart before she could continue speaking. "Although if you teach me, I wouldn't mind dancing another night."

"Fine by me."

Tolsan

Where Trouble is Brewing

Chapter 21

Elmeye truly hated to admit it; Sirix was a relatively good person to get to know. Elmeye wanted to hate the dragon woman on principle; she had a general dislike of people who bound themselves to their so-called "duty". However, Sirix seemed to be fine with her self-built cage and even seemed proud of it. She almost never complained about her responsibility to Aailaine, only occasionally bring up her impatience with Elmeye herself. She never seemed to feel bitter about Kleia's daughter or her part in Aailaine's success and instead seemed pleased that she had a part to play.

Elmeye sighed as she leaned across the table, watching the writing that appeared in the notebook next to her. Hvidr was constantly sending her information about new and unusual workers and guards, even if they weren't related to the Covern. Hvidr mentioned that she was never told who the list for the Covern would be until two days before, so it would be best to try to catch Soseh before he was put on that list. The only trouble was that apparently a large group new deep-dwellers had just come of age and had moved into Mathydar. Much to the deep-dweller Commune's pleasure, the new arrivals were all too willing to help the city.

Also, following the attack on the city, most of the inhabitants were still mourning the death of Rfkr and Aailaine, who they assumed also perished in the battle. This meant a large number of dwarves from all three clans were also currently in the city, many of them being dwarves Hvidr didn't know. They were trying to find a single tree in a large forest and Soseh held the advantage, even with Elmeye's existence being unknown.

Elmeye absently traced the small scar on her cheek, reminiscing about her days with the werecat sorcerer. He had been such a good student; studious, careful, polite and eager to learn magic. He had seemed so pure and full of good intent and now Elmeye wondered how much of that was false. How much of his good heart was just an act to get her to teach him? Or was it her teachings, her values that changed him?

A short knock came at the door and Elmeye sighed as she stood to answer it. She flipped the notebook to an empty page and carefully opened the door, her cloak dragging on the stone. Sirix calmly walked in and headed straight for her corner, arranging herself so that she sat comfortably. She offered no words and Elmeye stayed silent as well.

There wasn't much for Sirix to do until they discovered Soseh's assumed identity and she still had the Shadows that constantly tried to find her. She left during the day to wander around Dochel, to keep them thinking she was still there. If she was discovered to be waiting in the Tolsan, the Shadows might try to warn Soseh, which would ruin their chance to catch him.

Elmeye was skeptical of Sirix's daily trips but considering that the Shadows had never caught her before, kept silent. It was only Soseh who had been smart enough to follow her to the Tolsan discreetly, so she allowed Sirix to do as she pleased. The small enchanter returned to her table and began screening through the names and descriptions Hvidr was sending her.

"No...too dopey.... too high minded...no..." She spoke to herself as she read through the beautiful handwriting. The writing was slowing down and Elmeye imagined it was because outside work was coming to an end. The harvest was in full swing, so Hvidr was busy with mostly gardeners helping to bring in the harvest before the first freeze. Winter in the mountains usually started earlier than anywhere else in A'sthy and since there were only a few weeks left of autumn, it was important to bring in the harvest quickly.

Deep, soft snores rose from Sirix's corner and Elmeye turned to see the dragon woman asleep on the floor. She was lying on her side with her tail curled underneath her and it seemed that even with a human form, Sirix still tried to sleep as she would in dragon form. Elmeye chuckled to herself as she looked on, leaning against the table.

"A dragon that can turn into a human and a dwarf that lived long past his time." Elmeye grinned to herself, leaning back in the chair. She stared at the stone ceiling above her as she considered Soseh's previous travelling partners. "Aailaine couldn't be normal if she wanted to, regardless of how hard she tries. It burns within her too brightly."

"She is allowed to try, if that is what she wants." Elmeye looked over to Sirix, who hadn't moved but had opened her eyes and was looking at the small enchanter. The dragon's silver eyes were slightly red at the corners from sleep, but she stared at Elmeye calmly. "It is her choice to make. It would not be preferable and could be disastrous, but if she chooses to refuse her destiny, then she does."

"You won't let her. Rfkr won't let her. Kleia won't even let her." Elmeye scoffed. "You've already brainwashed the girl into doing

- 161 -

what you want her to do. You have even managed to brainwash help for her."

"She is on her own now, free to discover the world and form her opinions as she pleases, just as...Kleia, requested," Sirix responded, closing her eyes again. "Kleia knew that Rfkr and I would push Aailaine down the right path initially, but we are forbidden from interfering directly with her now that she has begun her journey. We are too tied to her past and future and Kleia didn't want us to push her. She must learn and grow, accepting the world on her own."

"Then I guess it's good that Rfkr died when he did. He wouldn't have been able to resist trying to coerce her. He, almost more than Kleia, wanted the Shadows gone." Elmeye casually mentioned, trying to raise a reaction from Sirix, but the dragon simply shrugged.

"It's true, but he was ready, I think. He always cursed the extra time he was granted and longed for eternal slumber. Although I think he did enjoy raising Aailaine, as much as it cost him and he assured everyone he didn't." Sirix shrugged, rolling over so that she faced away from Elmeye, adjusting her tail beneath her. "I wish his death could have been peaceful, but Rfkr was never the type to go down without a fight. I think dying while facing the Shadows was the way he preferred."

"As for me, Aailaine is stronger than she realizes. She will find her own reason for doing this and she doesn't need me to give her one." With this, Sirix closed her eyes, attempting to go back to sleep.

<For someone who has bound herself to a silly promise, it's strange to hear you talk about choice. Although, I suppose you've

made yours, even if it is ridiculous.> Elmeye thought to herself and once she heard Sirix's snores renew, she returned to the tedious task of filing through Hvidr's writing. Hvidr hadn't written anything new, so Elmeye guessed that she was done for the day. Sighing heavily, she flipped through the pages filled with the dwarf's handwriting. Almost two weeks had passed, and they still had no sign of Soseh's assumed identity. The Covern would meet at the end of autumn, leaving the trio only fifteen days to find him.

Elmeye stood and made her way to the food stores again. Much to her disappointment, they were close to being empty. Glancing at Sirix from the kitchen, Elmeye carefully pulled her hood over her face and left the temporary home. The other dwellings in their crevice seemed dark, meaning the occupants were asleep or nighttime workers.

The enchanter quickly climbed out of the narrow hole, sliding down onto the ledge beneath her. She hated the side crevices; she preferred to stay in ground ones. Side crevices made her feel trapped, as she had stone surrounding her on all sides as she tried to leave. Ground crevices required a ladder to get in and out, but she would prefer a ladder if it meant avoiding feeling as if the stone could trap her in the passageway.

Shaking herself free of her discomfort, Elmeye quickly continued down the side of the cavern toward the marketplace. Since it was night, much of the marketplace was quiet, but a few vendors that sold food remained open for the night workers. Elmeye quickly made her way to one of these and bought a simple meal of potatoes, carrots and totiriel meat. She sat close to the stall as she ate, her mind still wandering to Soseh and the Covern.

<I have to find him. I won't, can't, let him slip away from me again.> Elmeye promised herself, carefully eating her food. Once she finished, she tossed away the disposable container and gathered herself to return to home when she heard someone call for her.

"Elmeye? Is that really you?" She looked up sharply to see an old male dwarf with yellow hair looking at her and trying to examine her. The dwarf's blue eyes lit up with recognition and he smiled at her broadly. "It is you! What a surprise. I thought you would be de-"

Elmeye moved quickly and grabbed the dwarf, dragging him away from the marketplace. She soon spotted a dark alley and tossed the dwarf down the alley roughly. She looked around to make sure no one had followed them before turning to the face the man. He was rubbing his hips, clearly aching from having been thrown. Elmeye felt her heart sink as she recognized him; he had been a good friend to both her and Hvidr, and had helped them out of more than one predicament. It seemed that his age had finally caught up with him and he was slow to stand.

"Yeesh, is that any way to greet me? After all I did for you." The old man groaned and Elmeye felt her chest become heavy as she considered what she had to do. She carefully removed her hood as the dwarf continued to nurse his sore body. "Anyway, aren't you supposed to be dead? I thought you died cycles ago."

"I've been alive far longer than that, long before you knew me." The man looked up to see Elmeye's yellow eyes change to a piercing black, almost melting into her dark skin. He tried to back away from her as she came toward him but soon discovered he had nowhere to run. Elmeye eyed him softly as she slowly came toward him. "I'm sorry it came to this, old friend."

"No! I-I-I could still help! Just tell me what to do! What you need!" His eyes grew large with fear as she stood over him. Elmeye slowly embraced him tightly, and she felt his body relax for just a moment. Before he could try and pull away, her cloak enlarged and engulfed them, hiding them both completely from sight. There was a flash of red light, and she could feel the jolt as the magic ran through his body and the sag as it drained the life from him.

Slowly, she allowed his body to drop to the stone, the magic eating away at his bones and flesh until no evidence remained. As her cloak fell to rest on her shoulders, she sat on the ground to watch as her spell finished eating away at her former acquaintance. Drawing her knees to her chest, she sighed heavily.

"I am truly sorry. I wish it hadn't come to this. You were a good friend, and I'm sure Hvidr won't be happy when she finds out." Elmeye whispered, offering her deepest condolence to the smelly pile of meat and bone. Her heart weighed heavy with the dwarf's death, but she tried to shake the feeling off, thinking of Soseh. "But, I can't risk him finding out. I can't let him continue to be my blight on the world."

Satisfied that the magic would erase all evidence, Elmeye dragged herself back to her shared dwelling. Much to her pleasure, Sirix was still sound asleep, her soft snores filling the empty space. The girl glanced at the notebook where it still lay open, debating whether to keep up her search or to rest for the night. Her thoughts returned to the old dwarf she had killed and her brow furrowed as she tightened her fists.

With renewed purpose and determination, Elmeye sat down at the table and began to flip through the pages again, looking for anything that could give her a clue.

Chapter 22

Sirix soared over the Dochel plains, looking for easy prey. She quickly spied a pack of wild teyom, drinking the irrigation water on the edge of a troll farm. The boars were hardly a threat, as they had no horns and rather short snouts. Their stubby little legs only allowed them to move so fast and they would be no match for her majestic wings. She was in the mood for some yineru, but didn't want to steal from any of the farms and shops in any town would already be closed.

Having settled on them, she began to circle them, slowly dropping to get closer. The boars, sensing danger, became skittish as she circled above them. Before the pack could scatter, Sirix dove quickly and caught two of them with her hind claws. They squealed wildly in her grip and she squeezed them with her powerful legs, breaking their necks and stopping their movements.

Tossing them into an empty area of the plains, she quietly landed next to them and began to tear into one of them as the rest of the pack fled. She lifted her head up to let the meat slide down her gullet and hummed with delight as she tore away more of the meat, the blood dripping down her scales. She had barely begun eating when she heard a small 'Tsk, Tsk.'

"That's not very ladylike of you, Sirix. What would Kleia think?" Sirix stopped eating to see a werecat standing in front of her. His medium-length blond hair swayed in the autumn wind and his slitted green eyes stared at her. His pale skin glowed in the twilight and many layers of clothing served to hide his true stature. Sirix raised her body, her clubbed tail in the air much like a cat ready to pounce.

< Soseh. > Sirix growled, readying herself to launch at him. The werecat stood proud, his tail twitching behind him. His many bangles clinked together in the strong wind of the plains. <How dare you show your traitorous face around me.>

"To be a traitor, I would have needed to have been aligned with you, no?" His voice was deep and enchanting, filled with vacant promises. He folded his arms with a look of disdain on his face. "Since I never was, I think that hardly makes me a traitor. Just a travelling companion who you naïvely assumed had the same purpose."

With a roar, Sirix lunged at him, only to have him duck underneath her. She quickly shifted as she landed, producing a long white staff and rushing at him. He produced a black staff of his own and sweeping his staff downwards, stopped her attack before it reached him. She slid past him and used her staff to stop herself. She carefully stood and placed the long stick behind her back, standing ready.

"That's a pretty nice form you got there, Sirix." Soseh seemed genuinely impressed, leaning against his staff. "I'd have to say though, I prefer you as a dragon. Those curves just don't suit you."

"You killed Kleia," she hissed, her clubbed tail whipping out from behind her dress. It danced behind her like an enchanting snake. Soseh's interest faded as he yawned, leaning back on his blond tail as if it were a chair. "And you killed Rfkr."

"That boring woman killed herself, thinking she could hide the chosen one from my master. My master's Darkness is everywhere and sees everything. Although hiding her in the mountains was clever, I'll give her that. The dwarves hardly let strangers in and I suppose Rfkr was counting on that. But his death, too, is his own fault." Soseh threw away his staff and jumped up, morphing into a dairn before aiming for Sirix's head. She hit him away with her clubbed tail, and he rolled across the plains, slowly changing back into his original form. He was able to roll away quickly as she brought her staff down on him, picking up his staff from where he had thrown it.

The pair danced up and down the hillsides, the sounds of their staffs hitting causing a 'clack!' to echo across the plains. The occasional troll came to see what was happening, but quickly scrambled away to avoid being injured.

Finally, Soseh thrusted at the dragon woman, but she easily dodged and grabbed his wrist. Sliding her staff under his extended arm, she used his momentum to flip him, claiming his staff as well. She threw his staff a great distance away and raised hers high above her head.

"Your bones aren't worth picking from my teeth." She brought the staff down on him, but the crafty man morphed into a snake and slithered away at the last moment.

"*Rizid Kea, ashe muireod i fear i Washck.*" As Soseh finished his spell, Sirix found herself surrounded by Shadows. Soseh himself appeared outside the circle with his back to her and waved his hand. "I'd love to stay and chat, but I have a chosen one to find and a world to condemn."

"SOSEH!!!" Sirix bellowed, leaping at him with her staff, but several of the Shadows blocked her way and threw her back into their circle. The magician chuckled and glanced at her over his shoulder.

His slitted eyes watched her coldly and his smile conveyed all his evil intent.

"Sorry, but I don't have any more time to play with the likes of you." With that, the werecat vanished from sight and the Shadows began to slowly encroach on her. Sirix took in a deep breath, and pulling the fire from deep within her belly, let out a torrent of white flames. The Shadows around her screamed as she burned them all to cinders, scorching the ground around her. She glanced around for Soseh, but the werecat was nowhere to be seen.

Sirix rubbed her sore mouth as her stomach rumbled, reminding her of her immense hunger. She growled as she shifted back into her dragon form and returned to her dinner.

< I must go to Aailaine. I must find her. > Sirix's thoughts raced as she quickly dug into the Teyom meat once again. <I have to find her to make sure...>

<No,> she thought sorrowfully. <I already know that I cannot. I cannot risk Soseh tracking me again, and I must ensure that Soseh fails with his plan to throw the Tolsan into chaos. Elmeye is my only chance to help Aailaine, as infuriating as she is. And now there's a hitch in her plan. >

<I need to practice meditation again. >Sirix growled in frustration and thought back to her Teieimoko's teachings. <I still need to learn to control my temper. Kleia, I need you now more than ever. For your future and your daughter.>

Sirix quickly finished her meal and waited until the sun had set completely and the moon was high in the sky before heading back to the Tolsan. On bright nights like these, she would merely fly high above the clouds, higher than any creature could follow and the

Shadows would be forced to lose her. It was never a perfect plan, for they would always track her again once she landed, but it usually gave her a day or two of reprise.

Once she arrived in the Tolsan, she quickly shifted and disappeared into the darkness of the stone. Hurrying back to their shared dwelling, Sirix arrived to find Elmeye still slaving over her book, her finger dragging across the pages as Hvidr wrote. Sirix didn't quite understand the charm, but she knew it allowed the enchantress to read everything Hvidr wrote in a matching book.

"Gi-" Sirix started to speak, and then paused, clearing her throat. She was at fault, and understood that she needed to be calm. "Elmeye."

At this the girl looked up, clearly surprised by Sirix's use of her name. She turned to face where Sirix crouched in front of the door and watched the dragon woman with careful eyes.

"What is it? The Shadows catch wind of you?"

"No," Sirix paused, closing her eyes as she tried to keep her raging emotions in control. When she opened them again, Elmeye was now eyeing her suspiciously, her arms crossed in front of her tiny chest. "It's Soseh."

At this, a flash of concern flashed across her face, but was quickly replaced with suspicion. "Did *he* follow you here?"

"No," Sirix growled, and adjusted her position, moving from the door to her corner where she could stretch out, albeit still cramped. "He confronted me while I was eating in Dochel and now recognizes my human form. According to your plan, I can no longer confront him."

Just then, the tiny woman jumped to her feet and began to rant in a language Sirix didn't recognize, though it sounded strangely familiar. It wasn't Eroir, but it still had a melodic and magical air about it. Rather than ranting, the girl seemed to be singing as she paced the floor.

"-Kogå kogå shooke. Foånonneg hun tun." Elmeye finally finished her rant, slamming her hands on the stone table. Sirix became concerned when she noticed blood running down the grey stone. Before she could say anything, however, the enchantress spoke again.

"I didn't want to put Hvidr in danger..." Elmeye sighed, picking up her bloodied hands from the table to stare at them. It was then that Sirix noticed that many of the girl's fingers were sliced open, as if she had slammed them on glass. There was no glass on the table however, and Sirix's eyes widen as she realized they were magically inflicted.

Looking from her bloodied hands to Sirix, Elmeye's usual yellow eyes were now an empty black. Sirix readied herself for an attack, but the girl merely healed her cuts instead. For what felt like an eternity the pair stared at one another, Elmeye's hands slowly healing as Sirix kept her defensive stance.

"There can be no hitch." Elmeye finally spoke, her voice as empty as her eyes. Sirix held her gaze, refusing to be intimidated as the sorceress continued. "No faults, no errors. You-We have to be perfect. I cannot lose Hvidr. I will not."

Sirix relaxed and sat down in her corner as Elmeye's eyes faded back to their normal yellow. This was a terrible situation and

Sirix owed it to Rfkr's memory to keep Hvidr alive. Once again, she found herself completely agreeing with the enchantress' emotions.

"We won't."

Dochel

Where days pass in peace

.

Chapter 23

Their few short days in Pasyl seemed to fly by for Iasi. Both nights Yraly provided Iasi and Aailaine with a new outfit, and although at the dinners he danced with Yraly, he would practice with Aailaine far into the night. She seemed to enjoy dancing with him, although she was easily worn out after each session and often fell asleep immediately.

Iasi giggled to himself as he thought about their practicing. The gnome looked at him strangely for a moment and then returned to his work. Iasi watched in awe as the gnome finished making the Orare, attaching the fins that allowed for forward movement. Iasi spent his days watching the gnome, enjoying the simple rhythm of the gnome's tools and the constant hum of the energy that ran through the coils. The gnomes were the first to discover sero and harness its power to run their machines. It would only be much later than humans would adapt to this and create items like Aailaine's sword.

Aailaine would sometimes visit him in the shop, usually to ask him various questions about different topics. She would never stay for long and would eventually leave, although Iasi was never sure where she went. It had occurred to Iasi that Aailaine wasn't truly from the plains; she asked too many questions that she should've known the answers to. He sometimes considered asking her about her true origins, but always withdrew his questions. With the

Shadows having an interest in her, she was probably lying to protect herself and Iasi didn't want to endanger her by asking.

After making sure Aailaine wasn't walking toward the shop, Iasi stood and made his way to the gnome's crafting table. A thin charcoal stick and a few sheets of paper were laid out and Iasi carefully removed a single sheet. He sat at the desk facing the gnome and using the stick, he lightly sketched the outline of the gnome at work, trying to capture the gnome's studious nature in the drawing. He almost never glanced at the paper, keeping his eyes on his subject.

Iasi had started sketching in the dirt in his younger cycles, and Chadirra, noticing that he had a talent for it, bought him a book with blank paper and a few charcoal sticks for his sixth birthday. Iasi spent much of his free time sketching in the book, sketching everything from the environments they passed to the people scurrying to and fro in the cities. Whenever he filled the book up or when one of his sticks became too small to use, Chadirra would buy him a new set.

However, when he left the Chekari, he had left his book and sticks behind, and he occasionally found himself longing for them. They often helped him pass his free time during the day, and the long hours he didn't sleep at night. It still seemed all too surreal for him, to believe that he had not seen his sister for almost a season.

"She must be worried sick about me." He sighed over his sketch, glancing down to see his progress. He had unknowingly started sketching the Orare, his fingers following his eyes as he traced each line of the metal scales, mimicking the nymphs that lived below the surface.

"You're really good." Caught up in his own thoughts, Iasi had failed to notice Aailaine as she entered the shop and he jumped as she spoke over his shoulder. His knee bumped the table, knocking it over and shocking the gnome as well, who dropped the fin he was holding. Aailaine stood away from him as he examined his knee. The area had already turned a light red and he was sure it would bruise. He sighed as he stood, and he let out a hiss as the pain hit him again. Aailaine reached out to touch him but changed her mind and slowly withdrew her hand. "I'm sorry, I didn't mean to startle you."

"It's fine, really." Iasi forced a smile as he picked up the table and the scattered papers and tools that had been on it. Aailaine helped him and organized everything on the table again. He smiled at her as they finished and put his hand on her shoulder. "My knee is just going to hurt for a little while."

Aailaine frowned and looked away from him. He sighed and turned to face the gnome, who had recovered the fin and was watching the pair fix his work station.

"Tomorrow, then?" he asked and the gnome huffed, attaching the fin to the body of the boat. The gnome ran his hand over his handiwork, and a small smile graced his face.

"Most likely." The gnome grunted as he stood, his hand still on the metal. Iasi walked over to the gnome to stand next to him and to admire the Orare up close. "I just have a few more details to add, then it's just to make sure she runs."

"Will you paint her this time?" Iasi whispered, touching a scale with his fingertips. The gnome laughed softly.

"Do you want to wait two more days? Thought you were in a hurry."

"I guess we are. Shame though, I love your painting." Iasi assured the gnome, who merely grunted before disappearing outside of a door on the other side of the workshop. Iasi then turned to face Aailaine, who still stared at the floor, refusing to meet his gaze. He walked over to her carefully and placed his hand on her shoulder.

"It's not that big of deal, Aia." He laid a light kiss on her forehead and smiled at her slight blush. Although he initially enjoyed teasing her, he now found he also enjoyed the little displays of affection he gave her. "Let's head back to the inn, alright?"

"Ok. But I want to buy bandages first." Her voice was soft and quiet, and Iasi frowned, releasing her. He held out his hand and she took it gingerly. Squeezing hers lightly, he led her out of the shop.

They walked to a small stall not far from the shop and he held the door open for her to go in first. She looked at him surprisingly and he nodded, smiling gently at her. He followed in after her and sat down in a chair near the door as Aailaine wandered around the shop.

The merchant sold various cosmetic items, ranging from jewelry to the contacts Iasi wore outside of their room. The shop also sold bandages and basic medical supplies and Iasi watched with a slight smile as Aailaine roamed through them. She seemed uncertain as to which bandages to buy and Iasi smiled a little.

"Um, Iasi?" He looked up at her as she held two very distinct bandages in front of him. He carefully felt each one with his hand and chose the one in her left hand. She carefully hurried to put away the other one and walked up to the merchant to buy the bandages. Iasi watched her with a smile on his face, and sighed deeply, closing his eyes.

"I think we're ready." Aailaine stood in front of him, holding the bundle to her chest and looking away from Iasi. He winced as he stood and walked beside Aailaine back to the room. Yraly wasn't at the main desk, so Iasi was able to slip back into the hall without any questions. Once back in their room, he collapsed on the bed, sighing from the slight pain. Although he had endured worse pains, he had a very low tolerance for it, something he was often teased for.

"Um..." He sat up to see Aailaine still standing at the door, her head down and still clutching the bandages close to her chest. Iasi sighed and motioned for her to move to the bed. However, she didn't react to his motion and he stood, a quiet groan escaping him as he did so. Aailaine looked up quickly at the sound and rushed over to him, placing her hand on his shoulder. "Are you alright?"

"I'm fine, I just don't deal with pain very well. I really don't need bandages; the pain will fade on its own in a little bit." Iasi sat back down on the bed, sighing with relief.

"But..." Aailaine's voice faded as she glanced down. With a heavy sigh, Iasi took the bandages from her and motioned for her to sit next to him. She watched as he wrapped his knee, careful not to wrap the bandage too tightly. Using one of his daggers, he cut the bandage and tucked the end into the rest. He handed the leftover roll to Aailaine, who placed it into the backpack.

His injury dealt with, the pair sat in silence and Iasi tapped his foot nervously. He glanced over to Aailaine and she stroked her thumbs with her other fingers, something Iasi noticed she did instead of fidgeting. He looked up to see her raise her gaze as well. He looked deep into her silver eyes and could see his blue irises reflecting in her pupils.

Carefully Iasi removed his contacts, and looked back up to Aailaine, whose eyes widen a little. In the nearly white canvas of her eyes, Iasi could see the red glow reflected at him and he feared the sight a bit. He closed his eyes and folded his hands in his lap.

"Sorry," he mumbled, a weight coming to his chest as he leaned back on the bed. A warm sensation touched his hand, and he looked down to see Aailaine's hand on top of his. From her shoulder flowed a glowing white light that disappeared where both their hands met and the amulet she wore glowed, creating a bright light. Iasi felt a calm, warm feeling spread from where their hands touched, and he began to feel peaceful. Just as he began to close his eyes, Aailaine removed her hand from his and took in a deep breath before speaking.

"Iasi?" Whatever she had done with the amulet seemed to wear her out and Iasi carefully touched her forehead. Feeling no fever, he relaxed and leaned away from her.

"Yes, Aia?"

"Are you going to be able to dance tonight?" Aailaine queried softly. Iasi giggled a bit, and she looked up at him confused.

"Like I said, I'm not hurt that badly. Actually, whatever you did seems to have erased my pain." He smiled at her kindly. "More importantly, tonight is our last night. Do you think *you're* up to the dance?"

"Um...I really don't want to dance in front of the group..."

"I'll talk to Yraly. I'm sure she can lead with Sillyph," Iasi offered, mentioning the male spindly who ran the inn with Yraly. "I mean, that's if you want to."

"I...I think I wouldn't mind. But only if Yraly is ok with you not leading." Aailaine smiled up at him, and Iasi felt uplifted and glowed with warmth. He immediately stood and made for the door.

"I'll go talk to her right now. Take the chance to wash if you want to." Iasi beamed a large smile at her as he walked down the hall to find the spindly owner.

Chapter 24

Iasi started to feel nervous as he sat on the bed, waiting for Aailaine to get ready. Yraly had readily agreed to lead the dance with Sillyph, confessing that she would like to see how well Aailaine had learned the dance. Although he had told her of her approval, he had left out that detail, worried that it might make her change her mind.

He began to pluck at the pink-holed material that clung to his body. It was more like strings twisted together to give the impression of a shirt, but with its numerous small holes and occasional large ones, Iasi felt as if he was wearing nothing. The darker pink bands around his biceps shifted a bit as he crossed his arms, tapping his foot. The dark pink pants he wore hugged his body tightly and he appreciated the dancing boots Yraly always gave him, although he would've preferred slippers.

"I'm ready." Aailaine looked down as she stepped out of the wash room, and Iasi took the chance to take in her appearance. The color of her outfit was a sea green, which looked lovely with her shell-like hair. The top was longer in the front than in the back and came to a single point near her knees. Her pants clung to her body as well and her dark green slippers curled near the toes. Instead of her usual braid, she had her hair up in a high ponytail.

"Beautiful as always," Iasi remarked as he stood, making his way to her. She allowed him to take her hand and lead her to the banquet hall, but she stayed quiet. Iasi began to worry about her when she didn't talk or look at him, only speaking to say her drink choice. He opened his mouth to say something when she looked up at him. Her eyes were blank and she tried to smile, but it soon faded.

"It's alright, Aia. We really don't have to." Even as Iasi said the words, he felt a heavy weight in his heart. During all their practices, he had desperately looked forward to dancing with her. Aailaine looked away from him again and said nothing, not even when their food was placed in front of them.

Tonight's dinner was a stew, filled with yineru meat, peas, corn and cabbage. Iasi was disappointed to find no rice in the stew but enjoyed the flavor and aroma. He ate slowly and carefully, his desire to dance weighing heavy on him. When Aailaine finally spoke, it surprised him.

"I still want to." She looked down at her bowl, smiling softly. "After all, that's why we practiced so much. I'm just nervous, even though I know the attention won't be on me. I'm afraid I'll mess up."

"It's not about being perfect, Aia." Iasi reached across the table to touch her hand. She slid it into his and he squeezed gently "It's about having fun and enjoying yourself."

"Yea." she smiled at him, but he still felt her worry. He opened his mouth to speak when he heard a soft 'tsk...tsk...tsk' coming from the stage. He watched as the form of the musicians appeared and soft music quieted the crowd. Although many were still eating, Yraly preferred to start the music early, as the soft sounds often helped to relieve stress and calm down the more nervous individuals. He glanced to see Aailaine looking at the musicians with interest, as she did every night.

Rocking her head slowly to the beat, she closed her eyes and a smile softly spread across her lips. Iasi quickly finished his stew, not taking his eyes off her. The lights had dimmed once the music started, but she still seemed to glow, even in the soft light. The many colors seemed to ripple through her hair as she rocked, like the waves of the sea and Iasi found himself lost in them. Slowly Aailaine stopped to look over at him and found him staring. Embarrassed, Iasi coughed and looked away, staring at his empty bowl. He could feel Aailaine looking at him and he felt his face become hot.

"Ia-" She was interrupted as the music stopped and everyone began clapping. They both turned their attention to the stage as Yraly and Sillyph walked on from opposite sides, meeting in the middle.

"Thank you everyone for joining us tonight. We hope you have enjoyed the food we prepared for you." Despite his childlike stature, Sillyph's voice was deep and mesmerizing, capturing the attention of all who were present. Iasi had never gotten to know Yraly's partner very well, although he knew through talk that Sillyph was a perfect match for the inn owner. "Now, for those who would like to, we ask that you join us in a dance."

Sillyph took Yraly's hand and led her down to the floor as several people stood and moved their tables to clear the dance space. Iasi stood as well and extended his hand to Aailaine. She carefully took it and he slowly led her to the cleared area, standing among the many other dancers.

"For those of you who have never danced with us before, follow our lead. Most of all, enjoy yourselves." Although they could not see her, Iasi heard Yraly's voice easily and pulled Aailaine close, placing one hand around her waist and gently holding her other hand. She placed her free hand on his shoulder and looked down at her feet as they waited for the music to start.

A quick build and then once the drums came in, Iasi stuck out his left foot and Aailaine her right, and they began a slow spin around each other. After switching places, they changed directions, returning to their original spots. The sweet mellow tune of the saxophone and keyboard began, and they swayed gently with the group, moving in a slow, but obvious circle. Iasi loved the mellow music as well as the harmonious nature of the instruments.

The build began, and Iasi reached their hands up, spinning Aailaine quickly. She stumbled a moment, but quickly caught herself as they gripped each other's hands tightly. Extending one arm out and bending the other across her chest, she quickly stepped to one side of Iasi and then the other. When she moved to step on his other side again, he released his opposite hand and she swung out, reaching for the female dancer closest to her.

Their fingers almost touched before Iasi spun her back to him and grabbing her hand again, they both stepped to the side and dropped down. Quickly standing, they switched sides and dropped again, this time spinning. They both rolled their bodies up, although Aailaine's was a bit more forceful than Iasi's. They swayed slowly as the music slowed down again, moving to the opposite side of the group.

The build began once more and this time, Aailaine spun Iasi, who kept his arm bent. Once he faced her, he quickly placed both hands on her waist and lifted her up. She swung her legs to one side of him and then to the other before he slid her in between his legs. She twisted on the floor, so when he swung her back up to her feet, she was facing away from him. Her arms were crossed in front of her body and as she slowly raised them, Iasi caught of glimpse of Yraly.

She was smiling with pure glee as Sillyph gently kissed her neck and he cleanly spun her.

Iasi, feeling a bit brave, did the same to Aailaine's neck before spinning her. He delighted in the smoothness of her skin and loved the feel of her silky hair touching his face. He was delighted at the smile she had on her face and he quickly smiled at her, before swinging her out again. She spun cleanly this time, reaching her hand out to grab the hand of the female dancer. Releasing him, she grabbed hands with the woman, and they rocked side to side while Iasi and the other girl's partner came toward them.

Wrapping his hands around her from the back and touching the back of the other male's hands, Iasi rocked behind Aailaine for a moment, breathing in her scent deeply. It was a scent he had grown used to from his time with her; the smell of fresh vanilla and soft clean snow. He rocked behind her, loving the feel of her back pressing against his body and he tightened his grip on her, careful to keep his hands on her top to avoid touching her skin.

In a quick movement, both he and the other male lifted the girls away from each other, spinning in a tight circle. Swinging her legs to his right, Aailaine leaned over his shoulder and threw her arms open, careful to avoid hitting the other girl's arms. He slowly let her down as the music began to fade and they ended with her standing on his right, their hands linked behind them.

At this, the remaining audience began to clap and cheer, and Iasi released Aailaine. He smiled at her and she beamed back at him. She was clearly exhausted from both the dancing and her worry about doing it right, but she had also clearly enjoyed it. He had never seen such joy on her face and it touched him deeply. He leaned close to her face and laid a soft kiss on her cheek. Aailaine's hand immediately moved to her face and a light blush graced her cheek. Still holding her cheek, she stood on her tiptoes as if to do the same and Iasi found himself holding his breath in anticipation.

"Thank you everyone for joining us and those who watched." Once Yraly began speaking, she stopped and they all turned to face the spindly couple. "I hope you enjoyed it as much as we did, and I wish you all a good night and safe travels. May Orassul watch over all of you."

"May Orassul watch you." The whole host repeated the blessing and with that began to disperse. Iasi allowed Aailaine to lead the way, following closely behind her. When they reached their shared room, he fell backwards onto his bed, releasing a large breath. Bringing his legs onto the bed, he folded them as he sat up. He watched as Aailaine sat on his bed next to him, gazing toward to the ceiling with a slight smile on her face.

"So, did you enjoy it?" Although he had seen the happiness and enjoyment on her face while she was dancing, he strongly wanted to hear her opinion as well.

"Yea, it was...it was really fun. I felt so free." Aailaine smiled, turning her gaze down to her lap. "Although I was really nervous when I had to dance with the other girl. I was so nervous, I thought I was going to fall over."

"But while we were rocking, she told me she was really nervous too and somehow, that made me feel better." She finally looked up at him. "It also made me feel better knowing you were my partner. I don't think I could've done it with anyone else."

"I'm glad I could help." Iasi felt his heart swell with pride and emotion as he returned her smile. She leaned back on the bed as if to stand, but instead stayed like that, returning her gaze up toward the ceiling. Iasi watched her and burned the image of her sitting next to him into his mind. She seemed so happy and carefree in her sea-green outfit, practically radiating light and comfort. The light shimmered through her beautiful hair and Iasi found himself wanting to embrace her.

She glanced down at him, and having been caught, Iasi's ears flattened as he quickly looked away. Coughing to mask his desire, he carefully pulled off his boots and placed them on the floor next to the bed. "Well, we should probably go to sleep soon. We still need to get up at a decent time tomorrow to leave."

"Mhmm." Aailaine agreed as she nodded but she made no effort to move. Iasi tilted his head slightly at her odd behavior when she quickly leaned over and kissed his cheek. Her lips were pursed too much and her kiss was rough and hard, but it sent a shock through him nonetheless. After kissing him, Aailaine quickly stood and after slipping her feet out of her shoes, slid into her bed, refusing to look at him.

"Good night," she called over her shoulder as she pulled out her ponytail, allowing her hair to flow freely. Iasi sat dumbfounded on his bed for a moment, trying to register what had happened. He slowly reached his hand up to his cheek and gingerly touched the place where she had kissed him. He fell over on his side, his hand still up to his cheek, a small warmth enveloping him. Slowly, he started a soft chuckle that grew into full laughter, his tail wrapping around him as he curled up to keep the warmth from escaping. Even as

Aailaine rolled over to look at him, Iasi closed his eyes as his laughter died away. He sighed, rolling onto his back and half opened his eyes to look at the ceiling. He wasn't sure what this was, but he never wanted to lose the feeling.

Chapter 25

Aailaine began to notice that Iasi was uncomfortable as they drifted gently in the Orare. He sat on the floor in the center of the boat, and refused to move, even when Aailaine tried to point out the beautiful sights in the water. He sat with his knees to his chest, humming softly as he rocked back and forth.

"Um, Iasi?" Aailaine softly called out to him and he barely moved his head to look at her. He seemed sick and ready to throw up. "Are you ok? You've been like that for the past few hours. You haven't even eaten."

"I...I don't deal well with being surrounded by large bodies of water," he whispered, returning his face to his knees. "I can swim just fine, and I don't mind looking at them from the shore. I just don't like being surrounded, like this."

"Oh." Aailaine seemed thoughtful. "Then why did you suggest we take an Orare?"

"Because this is better than taking the land bridge." Iasi mumbled. "The land bridge takes a day and a half and this only takes a couple of hours."

"Hmmm," Aailaine frowned as she watched the werecat continued to comfort himself on the floor of the Orare. "Well don't you think you should see how-"

"No."

"But it's really beautiful when-"

"No."

Aailaine frowned at his rejections. "If you would-"

"No. Aia." Iasi turned his whole face to look at her, his red eyes narrowed. His ears were pulled back and his tail had doubled in size. Seeing his eyes gave Aailaine pause; she wasn't aware that he had taken out the contacts again. "Stop. You're not the first and you certainly won't be the last. Just leave me alone until we get to Hirie. I'll be fine once we get there."

Aailaine sighed with defeat as Iasi returned to his rocking and humming. She gazed over the blue waters and marveled at how clear the water was. Due to the different minerals and occasional mud, the water that flowed through the mountains was often cloudy and usually had to be strained to be considered drinkable. She reached her hands into the water and brought the sweet liquid to her mouth. Although she wasn't fond of plain water, the water of the Risck Imyd seemed to have a sweet taste to it.

Just as Aailaine reached down to drink more of the sweet water, she thought she saw a face looking back at her. Its eyes were large and round, and its skin seemed to have a pink tint to it. Aailaine tilted her head and the face beneath the water did as well. When she reached her hand to touch the surface, a pink hand rose to meet hers, almost like a reflection.

Once their fingers touched, there was a just rise of water as the male creature rose from the depths. He had pink webbing between his feet and hands and stood completely naked on the Orare, which continued moving undeterred. He towered over both passengers and Aailaine was surprised that he had not tipped the boat over. Iasi, who had not moved from the center of the boat since they began, was now pressed up against the side opposite of Aailaine. She looked up at the creature with awe as he carefully walked toward her. He seemed to walk awkwardly, like a child taking its first steps and she focused her eyes on his feet, trying to ignore his scaled naked form. Once near her, he leaned his face into hers and Aailaine turned away. He smelled strongly of fish and the smell was nauseating.

"*Ura. Hez. Earibuoko.*" Aailaine's eyes widened as he used the same name for her that the elf in Pasyl had. She hadn't given it much thought then, but now this creature had called her the same.

<The one who shines...> Aailaine pondered as behind the nymph, Iasi slowly stood, keeping his eyes on the pink creature. It was obvious he was still nervous by the way his tail wrapped around the seat of the boat.

"*Fa nuif, anggerad kei feahtum or?*" Iasi called out to the nymph, his voice steady despite his nervousness. The man turned to face him and after glancing at him for a moment, moved closer to Iasi. The werecat stood still as the nymph looked him over completely and Aailaine opened her mouth to speak. Before the words could leave her tongue, the nymph stood up from Iasi, looking down at him.

"*Yoltri. Or gibdeod ngea.*" With that, the nymph leaped out of the moving Orare and slid back into the water. Aailaine watched as he swam deeper and deeper until she could no longer see him. When she looked back on the Orare, Iasi had already slid back into the middle and resumed his humming. It was now that Aailaine noticed that the boat was now filled with soft pink scales and only the space Iasi sat in was devoid of them.

"I didn't know you spoke Eroir," Aailaine offered, trying to get Iasi's attention. His humming stopped, but he didn't move to look at her.

"I've spent a lot of time in Hirie, so I speak it fluently." Iasi immediately resumed his humming, not waiting for a response. Aailaine considered offering that she spoke it as well but paused. She wasn't sure how many plainsfolk could speak the ancient language fluently. In the mountains, it had been mandatory to learn Eroir and Common, as the dwarves spoke both interchangeably. However, she knew outside of Hirie and Tolsan, fluent Eroir speakers were rare.

Not sure what else to say, Aailaine stayed quiet and gazed over the water again. Soon trees began to appear in front of her and she squealed excitedly. She had never seen trees before, much less so many together. Their strong thick trunks reminded her of the pillars of stone in the mountains and the leaves were a beautiful shade of green. Some of the trees had lost their leaves, and the ground surrounding their roots was colored with shades of brown and orange.

"Iasi, is that Hirie?" Aailaine excitedly pointed to the trees and the werecat looked up, stretching to see over the side of the boat.

"Yea, that's it." He slowly pulled himself into one of the seats as more and more trees began to appear. Aailaine watched his hair slowly sway in the breeze as his tail tightly wrapped around the seat. She didn't quite understand his fear of being surrounded by water, but she was glad that soon they would be on land again and Iasi would be his normal self.

Hirie
Where Magic Blooms

Chapter 26

"So where is it you need to go?" Iasi queried as they finished removing all of their luggage from the storage unit. It was too big for the amount that they had, but he had explained to Aailaine that mostly merchants used gnome inventions. Therefore, it made sense to have a large storage area away from the seating so merchants could stow away their many goods and calmly enjoy the scenery of the water as they sailed.

"Um, I actually don't know," Aailaine admitted, sliding her bow into her quiver. It had never occurred to her to ask Sirix where she needed to go once she got to Hirie and she hadn't seen the dragon woman since their parting near Lanol. "The letter didn't mention where and if it did, I don't remember."

"You don't have it still?"

"No," Aailaine admitted quietly. "It was lost when my caretaker died. I'm sorry."

Iasi sighed as he stood, closing the storage compartment. He started the Orare and pushed it back into the water. It slowly turned itself around and to Aailaine's amazement, began drifting back the way they had come, slightly heading toward the setting sun.

"Well, then I guess we can head for Yoltri. It's the closest city anyway." Iasi stretched, not picking up the pack from where it sat. "We'll stay here for tonight. It's already late and Yoltri is more than week away, if not more because of the undergrowth."

"Undergrowth?" Aailaine began to unfasten her quiver and sheath as Iasi tapped his foot. He tilted his head for a moment, and then motioned for her to follow him. They walked a little way into the forest and Aailaine marveled at the sight. The trees seemed to be leaning close and the winds blowing through their branches sounded like whispers. Their footsteps echoed on the crunchy leaves that littered the forest floor and Aailaine couldn't help but giggle. After a while, Iasi stopped and pointed out the low bushes and vines.

"That's the undergrowth. See how light is barely coming through? The trees get the most sunlight, so the other plants tend to gather toward the rest. Although I suppose now is a bad example with the sun setting." Iasi walked among the plants and fallen leaves and showed Aailaine his foot. The innocent-looking vines had entangled his leg and were squeezing his boot. "Also, since this forest is teeming with magic, the plants more or less have a will of their own."

Iasi rapped on the vines three times and they released him, sliding back to the ground. He quickly stepped out of the undergrowth and stood next to Aailaine. As they walked back to their makeshift camp, she carefully watched the ground, quickly stepping away from any vines that reached out to her. It seemed as if the whole forest was alive, reaching out to them and trying to understand who they were.

"Ahh!" She let out a cry when a tree branch caught the back of her shirt and lifted her up, holding her well above the ground. Iasi quickly turned and leapt for her, only for the branch to move her out of the way at the last second. The sudden move made Aailaine nauseous, and she groaned as the tree held her aloft. The werecat quickly pulled out his daggers and leaped again and for a moment, she thought he might cut her shirt.

Just as she opened her mouth to stop him, she felt herself falling and landed safely in Iasi's arms. He landed hard, falling backwards with her in his lap. Aailaine quickly reached around to her back and found the branch still clinging to her. Frantically, she pulled it off and threw it away, clinging to Iasi. They both watched as the branch flopped on the ground like the tail cut off a wevran before finally becoming still.

Sighing with relief, Aailaine looked at Iasi, who still sat on the ground with his arms around her. A blush spreading, Aailaine quickly stood up from his lap and brushed herself off. He stood as well and slid his daggers back into his shrug.

"Let's hurry back before any more trees find you delicious," he commented, getting behind Aailaine as they returned to the river bank.

"Delicious?" she gasped, turning to look back at him. He pointed in front of her and she looked just in time to dodge another branch trying to grab her.

"Well, I suppose 'delicious' isn't the best way to put it." Iasi pushed the last few branches out of her way as they returned to their belongings. The sun had already passed on to the south and it seemed that the moon would soon appear. Iasi sat down and stretched as Aailaine moved as far away from the forest as she dared, sitting very close to the water.

"The trees especially take interest in the people who walk through the forest. If they find you particularly interesting, whether it be how you dress, how you smell, or even how you feel, they'll carry you off." Iasi reached into the large pack and pulled out an eri for himself, tossing one to Aailaine. She caught it with ease and began to nibble on the sweet fruit. "Where they take you, only Orassul knows. But most people probably just go mad."

"Go mad?" Aailaine inquired as she finished off her fruit and moved over to the pack to grab another one. Just as she reached in to grab one, she saw a vine quickly moving toward her hand. As Iasi sat up to grab it, Aailaine quickly grabbed the fruit and glided back over to her seating area. The vine tried to follow but found it could not reach her and receded back into the forest. Iasi raised an eyebrow at her before laying down again.

"Hirie is full of magic, so much so that most people besides elves and spindly who live here go mad if they stay too long. Plainsfolk and goldsman have the least amount resistance, probably because neither visit the forests often." Iasi tapped his foot in the air. "You can build up a resistance to it if you come often enough, but the best way is to have an elf give you an amulet that will absorb the excess magic."

"Do you think this will work?" Aailaine held up her amulet, gazing into its white gem. It seemed dull, as if some of its brightness had faded away. Puzzled, she reached for her quiver and pulled out her pouch with the gems. Iasi rolled over and watched her curiously as she pulled out one of the white emeralds to compare it to her amulet. They both watched in amazement as a thin light flowed from the gem into her amulet, which pulsed lightly. The mo'qire seemed to wriggle in the stream of light, as if pleased. Some of its color returned as the emerald became transparent, dissolving into thin air once it was completely drained of color. The mo'qire's red eyes began to pulse, as if asking for more.

Aailaine glanced up at Iasi, who nodded and came closer as she pulled out another gem. Again, light from the gem flowed into her amulet and she stared in blank wonder. Ever since the first time the light had flowed from her into Iasi, Aailaine had tried to figure out how the amulet worked. However, no matter how hard she tried, she seemed to have no effect on when the amulet activated or not.

"Where did you get that?" Iasi marveled, never taking his eyes off the pure light that flowed from gem to gem. Aailaine shook her head to clear her mind, his voice bringing her back from her own thoughts.

"I've had it ever since I can remember. I have no idea where it came from," she confessed, taking out a white agate. "Even R-... my caretaker, said that he has no idea where it comes from. It was never something he saw Kleia have, and the sapphire resembles nothing mined from the mountains."

"Kleia?" Iasi wondered, looking up at her. Aailaine lifted her hands as the last gem evaporated and the amulet finished absorbing its color and shined brightly once again. She looked down at the ground, refusing to meet his gaze.

"It's what he called my mother. From what I'm told, it's not her real name, but rather the name she gave out to strangers." Aailaine smiled softly at the amulet. "I'm told she was a Teieimoko and a fierce woman, proud and strong. She was an extremely skilled fighter, and nothing could stop her once she started."

"Huh, that's interesting." Iasi seemed lost in thought as Aailaine spoke and Aailaine's eyes widen with realization. It was very possible that Kleia was a well-known name throughout A'sthy, just as Rfkr's had been. However, since Rfkr had always insisted Kleia was not her real name, she hadn't thought twice about mentioning it. She jumped when Iasi continued speaking. "What was her Vuiej?"

"A-an akhby."

"Interesting." Iasi uttered, looking away for a moment. Aailaine slipped her pouch back into her quiver and let the amulet fall back against her chest. "Well, that amulet will probably work, considering how magical it is. Although that trick with the gems is a new one."

"Then what about you?" Aailaine queried, and Iasi giggled, laying on his back again. His tail wrapped around his bare mid-section and his ears twitched happily. "Iasi?"

"I have a natural tolerance. I seem to remind you a lot, but I've been here plenty of times." Iasi hummed sweetly. "I used to have an amulet when I was younger, but I haven't needed it in cycles."

"Oh." Aailaine sighed, a wave of sleepiness washing over her. Yawning, she reached into the pack and pulled out the sleeping mat that she had bought in Pasyl. Wary of any encroaching plants, she laid out her mat, still staying close to the seabed. Iasi sat up as she laid down, her head feeling heavy.

"I'll watch out for any plants. We don't want you waking up every few moments to deal with them," Iasi assured her, turning his back to her and facing the forest. "Sleep well, Aia."

"Thank you." Feeling safe and protected, Aailaine allowed herself to fall into a deep, comforting sleep.

Chapter 27

Iasi kept his back to Aailaine until he heard her breathing slow down and her soft snores came from behind him. Certain that she was asleep, he stood and stretched under the waning moon. It seemed truly surreal that he had only been infected for a couple of weeks. The quick cycles of the moon had never bothered him; in fact, he hardly noticed how quickly the moon appeared or vanished. The week cycle now seemed so short, another new moon just a couple nights away.

"Sometimes, light can be so cruel." He sighed, glancing back down at Aailaine. She seemed so radiant even in her sleep, as if light just poured out of her. It even seemed that she couldn't be infected by the Shadows either; she had vomited up all the Darkness that had gotten inside of her body. Even now, he saw no traces of the change beginning in her eyes, which remained as clear as ever. He reached down to touch her shoulder, causing her to shift in her sleep. "But at the same time, so beautiful."

Reaching into his wrap, he pulled out one of his daggers, admiring the clean blade. He tried to cut his own skin, but the Darkness spilled from the wound and closed his skin. Sighing deeply, he struck the blade into the ground and waved his hand over the pommel.

"*Or gazud bo.*" He quickly stepped back as a wall shot out of the ground around the sleeping girl, stopping once it towered over three meters. The vines from the forest quickly rushed to claim the wall, but the streams of magic shot from the stone, destroying the vines completely.

Satisfied, Iasi removed his contacts and stepped into the forest. Magic was an art he preferred to avoid, as usually he couldn't concentrate well enough to push his intentions through. His father had been an enchanter but after his passing, there had been no one in the troupe to teach him properly and so Chadirra discouraged him from the practice. The elves however, had secretly encouraged his slight talent, and in Hirie, where magic was thick, Iasi enjoyed casting simple enchantments.

Shifting into a wonir, Iasi quickly ran through the trees, dodging and snapping at the vines that tried to grab him. The trees also tried to stop his advance, but he swiftly evaded them as well. He made his way to the lake in the forest and morphed back into his werecat form. He walked close to the water's edge, hoping that the elf would appear.

"I don't know what I'm expecting. It's not like she told me to come here." He squatted down to look at himself in the water. On that night, the red in his eyes had seemed so pronounced and the Darkness that clung to his skin seemed more intimidating. Now, the red appeared dull and lacking luster, and thanks to the moon's soft light, the Darkness was nowhere to be seen.

"I see you have found what you were seeking." He looked up to see the pink elf standing along the water's edge near him, holding a small bundle against her chest. She turned to him as he stood, although this time she kept her distance from him.

"So, she is what I was going to Lanol for." Iasi reasoned, folding his arms across his chest. The elf stayed where she was, holding her small bundle. Her pink skin seemed darker, and her red hair stayed still around her shoulders. "Why didn't you just tell me? Who is she? Why are the Shadows after her?"

"Stay with her." Ignoring his questions, the elf swung her arms out, releasing her bundle. The leather package shattered, spilling out hundreds of pieces of glass. The glass seemed to hang suspended in the air as Iasi gasped in horror and then looked at the elf. She regarded the mess with sadness, pushing the pieces of glass and causing them to collide with one another slowly. "She is much like this glass right now; she is suspended in her destiny, unsure of the correct path to take. Unsure who is friend and who is foe. It is up to you to protect and guide her. You, the one who is becoming a Shadow."

"I...I know..." Iasi stammered, looking into the lake's water. He couldn't deny the dark rage that continued to grow within him, the strong need to kill. Try as he might to hide his red eyes, he could always see them behind the contacts, reflecting the Darkness he couldn't escape. The Darkness around them pulsated, as if waiting for the last sliver of the moon to disappear as it hid in the shadow of the trees. The elf looked deep into that Darkness before turning her gaze to him.

"Stay with her, Iasi. Continue to be her guide." He looked up to see the elf walking away into the forest.

"Wait! You haven't answered any of my questions!" He started after her, only to be stopped as the wall of glass fell to the ground. He quickly leapt back, helpless, and watched as she disappeared. Her voice echoed back from the dense vegetation.

"Keep Nerissa's dream alive..." Iasi's mouth dropped in awe. Nerissa had been a famous Teieimoko nearly 500 cycles ago; the only Teieimoko to have a dairn as her Vuiej. She was the first to venture into the mists of Exla and not return. Most who attempted merely reappeared outside the mist, but Nerissa and her dairn simply disappeared.

"If she is Nerissa's dream, then maybe, Aailaine is somehow *Fogeako*?" Iasi's soul swelled with hope as he finally understood. "She is the one to awaken Orassul and banish the Darkness again. But, will that truly save me?"

Thinking deeply, Iasi slowly made his way back to their camp. Unlike before, the trees and vines moved from his path, the Darkness quickly wrapping him in its cold embrace. However, his deep thoughts overruled the dark compulsions and he walked on silently, never straying from the path.

As he returned to Aailaine, he found the vines still trying to get at the sleeping girl, but as the Darkness rolling of his skin touched them, they soon turned black as coal, and blew away like dust. Iasi sighed deeply, stepping out into the dim moonlight. The Darkness fell from him like a coat and he rubbed his tan arms, relieved to see color.

Kneeling carefully, he pulled the dagger from the ground to remove to wall from around Aailaine. She had rolled over several times in her sleep and her once-perfect braid was now twisted and rumpled. He stared at her awhile, thinking over what the elf had said about her.

"Nerissa's dream, the hope to banish the Darkness." he murmured, carefully removing her hair tie and unraveling her braid.

She barely reacted in her sleep, only rolling over farther away from him. He giggled softly as her beautiful hair spread out on the ground around her, like rays of sunlight. His voice came out quiet, full of longing and hope.

"I guess I can believe that."

Chapter 28

Iasi helped Aailaine over a root that jutted out of the ground on the forest path. The plants had been less active during the past few days, so the pair only had to fend off the occasional vine or tree that came after Aailaine. Iasi noticed that, just like the Shadows, they seemed far more interested in her than in him. The trees would reach out to grab her amulet and the vines kept wrapping themselves around her braid. Iasi had suggested she wear it in a bun, but the girl had quietly refused.

"Iasi!" The werecat turned around to see that several trees had a branch in Aailaine's hair and were each pulling it toward themselves, leading to a tug of war with the poor girl's head. She had tried to pull out her blade, but a vine held her hand still. Iasi carefully walked over to her, stepping on the vine to release her hand, and hitting each of the branches three times to force them to release her.

"How does that work?" Aailaine grimaced, un-doing her braid once again as she began to walk in front of him. "The hitting them, I mean."

"It's a trick the elves use. It's no good if they get your hands, but you hit them three times as a warning." Iasi quickly knocked away a tree branch that reached for her and Aailaine continued walking, none the wiser. "If you must hit them a fourth time, it'll be with a weapon."

"Oh, so it's basically a 'Stop before I have to hurt you' situation?" Aailaine glanced over her shoulder, done with her fishtail braid. Iasi nodded quickly and continued behind her. His eyes began to wander as he looked out for any curious vegetation and he noticed that her half skirt was slipping. The band now crossed over her buttocks rather than sitting around her hips and the cloth was dangerously close to dragging on the ground. The vines were already very aware of her presence and the skirt dragging would just alert them more.

"Aia, your-" Iasi stopped as he realized what telling her would mean. Aailaine stopped and turned to face him, tilting her head slightly. Iasi quickly glanced back down at her skirt and his ears flattened as a very light blush started on his face. Aailaine's confused expression quickly turned to worry as his tail wrapped around his leg.

"What is it?"

"Oh, um, it's just, your, uh, skirt is falling," Iasi stumbled, managing to get the words out before quickly glancing away. He chanced a peek as Aailaine lifted the band and adjusted the skirt around her waist again. "I didn't want it to drag on the ground."

"Thanks. I don't really need anymore I guess, but I like it." Aailaine merely smiled and continued walking and Iasi stared after her surprised that she didn't seem to notice the implication of his observation. Confused but relieved, Iasi started after her when he heard something moving quickly through the trees. He paused to listen carefully; it was moving much to quickly to be a plant. An animal should've been able to move quieter and Iasi's eyes widen as he realized what the sound was. He began to run up to Aailaine as the sound started to get closer.

"Aia!" Iasi quickly threw the pack and jumped at Aailaine as a dark blur flew over them, cutting the back of his top. The rocks and the tree roots dug into his back as he landed, Aailaine on top of him. He hissed with pain as they both quickly stood, and she quickly drew her bow, notching an arrow. Iasi tore off what remained of his shirt and drew out his daggers from his shrug, looking at the shape that had cut him.

"That's-" Aailaine voice faltered as she stared and she lowered her bow slightly in surprise. The small dwarf stood in front of them, licking the blade of his large axe. Iasi mentally sighed with relief that only his shirt had been cut, considering the size of the weapon. Readying his blades, he stood between Aailaine and the little being.

"Some people side with the Shadows and Darkness, serving as daytime fighters to its will," Iasi spat, the words leaving a bad taste in his mouth. "Truly they are worse than the Shadows, who at least have no choice."

"I'm not here to listen to you preach at me, boy." the dwarf spat back, pointing the axe at Aailaine over the werecat's shoulder. "I'm here for her."

Aailaine gasped and drew back her bow, pointing the arrow over Iasi's shoulder. He glanced as the plant-like tip wriggled around the shaft, ready to be buried in the dwarf's flesh. His ears perked up as he heard leaves crunching and he quickly glanced around to find the source. He saw no one, and the sound stopped suddenly once he started glancing around for it.

"Be careful, there's another here somewhere." Iasi leaned back to whisper to her and she nodded curtly, never taking her eyes of the dwarf. Satisfied, Iasi rushed at his opponent and the dwarf prepared to stop his frontal assault. At the last moment, Iasi changed direction, dropping to the ground and slashing up at the dwarf. However, his blade connected with the axe's handle and the dwarf hit Iasi in the stomach with the flat edge of his axe.

Iasi twisted as he flew through the air and landing on one of the trees, launched himself back at the dwarf, whom was heading for Aailaine. It seemed that the dwarf was only interested in her, and Iasi used this to his advantage. He landed between them and thrusted at the dwarf. However, the dwarf reacted quickly and blocked with the handle. Iasi consistently found his blades connecting with the metal as he tried to throw the dwarf off balance, but the little man was versatile with his weapon, and blocked Iasi at every turn.

"Iasi!" Both the dwarf and Iasi pushed away from each other as Aailaine's arrow flew between them, killing the dwarf that had been notching an arrow to shoot at the werecat. Aailaine's shot caught the archer in one of his eyes, and the shaft buried itself deep in his skull. The dwarf with the axe let out a terrible cry as he watched his companion fall and launched himself at Aailaine.

"*Guofi ei!*" Aailaine notched another arrow and hit the dwarf in his midsection, but he still came at her, yelling in pain. Iasi quickly threw himself into the little man's body, using his superior size to knock him away. The dwarf landed with the dexterity of a cat, using the axe's pommel to keep him from running into any trees. Iasi also landed on his feet in front of Aailaine, who had put away her bow in favor of the sword. The energy crackled from the blade like lightening and Iasi glanced back to see Aailaine looking at the dwarf with a blank expression.

The dwarf, blinded by rage and pain, came at them again, and this time, his blade caught Iasi's arm, slashing his deeply. Iasi was forced to quickly leap away to avoid being injured more seriously.

Aailaine managed to block the swing the dwarf aimed at her and used her strength to push the dwarf back. Their difference in stature didn't seem to bother Aailaine, and as Iasi watched, it became obvious that she had experience fighting dwarves.

The dwarf swung his heavy axe at Aailaine's leg and she quickly leapt up, neatly landing on the blade. Unable to hold her weight, the dwarf was forced to lean down and didn't see Aailaine as she swung her blade down at him. The sero that shot crackled from the blade pushed the dwarf back, slamming him to a nearby tree. The sounds of his bones cracking were clearly audible and the black burns marks that ran across the dwarf's skin caused Iasi to grimace.

"You think my master can be stopped but there is nowhere you can run." The dwarf laughed as blood mixed in with the spit that poured from his mouth. He tried to stand but found he could not. Instead, he stared at Aailaine with ice cold eyes meeting Aailaine surprised gaze. "Where there is Light, there will always be Darkness."

Iasi spat at the dwarf's words as he stood and made his way to where he had thrown the pack. He pulled Aailaine away from the being, even as the dwarf began to gurgle laughter as he lay dying. After the laughter faded from hearing, Iasi stopped, sitting on a large root near the path. Aailaine joined him silently, sheathing the blade as she sat. Pulling the bandages from the pack, Iasi began to address the cut on his arm.

Neither of them spoke a word as Iasi dressed his wound. Iasi glanced over at Aailaine as he finished, who was staring at her hands. It seemed that she was trying to grasp the situation that had just played out and from her expression, Iasi could tell that this was the first time she had killed someone other than a Shadow with her own hands.

"I didn't know there were people who joined the Shadows by choice." she whispered, her voice sounding strained and filled with tears. Iasi leaned back on his hands, looking up at some birds in the trees. They landed for only a moment and quickly took off again, heading for some unknown destination. He sighed deeply, trying to think of what to say.

"It's unfortunate, but not completely unexpected. Daywalkers are rare, since most people are too afraid, but there are always those who are willing." Iasi remarked, rubbing his hand across his now-bare chest. Aailaine looked at him with a horrified look and his mood dropped even further as she stood angrily, disbelief across her face.

"How can you say that?" Aailaine shouted, and several birds launched themselves from the nearby trees. Although this was not the first time Aailaine had shouted at him, Iasi's chest began to ache as she raved at him. "Two, *alive* beings attacked us, not Shadows and all you can say is it's not unexpected?!"

"When you travel around a lot," Iasi began, refusing to meet her gaze and gazing instead into the gaps of sky that were visible through the canopy. Her implication that Shadows were not alive sat poorly in his stomach as he tried to answer her demand. "You see a darker side of people. Most people are indifferent, willing to leave well enough alone if you don't bother them."

"A few people, like you, are good to the core, always willing to lend a helping hand, and wanting to improve things for the benefit of everyone. And that's when nothing bad is happening." Iasi dropped his gaze down to his feet, flexing his toes inside the boots as he kicked up some of the dead leaves. Aailaine remained silent, but he could still feel her burning gaze. "When bad things start to happen, you see that third group of people; the ones who would sell you out to save their own skin, or for the right amount of gold."

"But, why?! How can anyone be like that?" Aailaine begged him, and Iasi glanced at her with pity. Her childish innocence struck a chord in him, and he hated being the one who would have to take that innocence away. His thought drifted to the words the pink elf had said to him. "How many deaths have those two caused with their selfishness?"

"I...don't know, Aia. Maybe it's because they're afraid and they think the Shadows will win. Maybe they think 'I should join the winning side before it's too late.'" Iasi sighed. "People really don't have hope anymore. It's been over thousand cycles and no chosen one has appeared while Orassul remains sleeping. After Nerissa never reappeared, most think one never will, and well, that makes some people desperate. Desperate enough the turn against their own."

"But that's-" Aailaine started to speak, but stopped herself, looking down in despair. Iasi noticed the tears rolling down her cheeks silently and he quickly jumped up, pulling her into an embrace. She let him and buried her face into bare chest, and he gently stroked her.

"Don't the Shadows kill enough?" she cried into his chest and he gripped her tighter, kissing her hair gently. "Why do we have to kill each other?"

"Don't worry Aia. Regardless of who comes chasing after you, I'll make sure you make it to Yoltri. So how about we get going before it gets dark?" He pulled back from her to meet her gaze. Her eyes were red and poufy, but no more tears flowed as he smiled at her softly. Taking a step back, he offered her his hand, which she took gingerly. "Tonight's a new moon and we need to find enough space to get a fire going before sunset comes."

"Th-Thank you, Iasi." It was clear that she was still upset, but Aailaine managed to smile back to him. He gently kissed her hand. "Is your arm going to be okay?"

Iasi released Aailaine as he gripped his wrapped arm tightly. He had only wrapped it to keep Aailaine from noticing the Darkness that was leaking out to heal it. Even now, he knew by nightfall the cut would be completely healed, despite its size.

"It'll be fine." He managed to smile, taking her hand with his other arm. "I heal fast, so by time we reach Yoltri, it'll be completely healed."

Aailaine merely nodded and Iasi led her deeper into the living forest, praying for Aailaine to never learn his secret.

Chapter 29

She was floating, high above the sea of Darkness, drifting through the air. The Darkness below her rumbled and spoke, the sound echoing throughout the clear skies above her. She couldn't make out what it was trying to say, and she instead kept her eyes on the sky. Sometimes she thought it's rumbling sounded like words, but despite her best efforts, she could not understand what the Darkness was trying to communicate.

She shivered. She didn't want to return to the Darkness. The thought of returning scared her, but she knew she couldn't float above it forever. After all, it was within the Darkness that she had awaken and to the Darkness she must return. The Darkness wanted to keep her all to itself, but she hated being trapped within. She loved the light the sun and stars provided. If only she could tell it how she felt. If only they could understand one another...

Aailaine slowly opened her eyes, watching as a wall of stone slowly sank back into the ground. Once the wall had completely disappeared, she sat up, noticing one of Iasi's daggers in the ground next to her. She glanced over to where he lay asleep, curled up on the soft ground on the other side of the fire. She slowly touched the dagger and she felt a slight jolt run through her, and Iasi twitched in his sleep as if hit. Aailaine carefully withdrew her hand as the werecat rolled over onto his other side.

She slowly raised her gaze to the empty night sky; Iasi had insisted that they start a fire as soon as they had found the small clearing, even though the sun was still up. He insisted on doing so every new moon, saying that the new moon was the most dangerous night of the week. He mentioned that most people considered the first day of week taboo because it was the night of the new moon and she had to admit it was a new idea to her. No one thought much of a new week starting in Mathydar; under the layer of stone and rock, they had no fear of the moon's cycles, and life continued as if it were any other day.

Aailaine's thoughts returned to dream she had woken up from. She knew from Rfkr's telling of the story that she was dreaming of Orassul; something that had started happening since they entered Hirie. She wondered if the forest had something to do with the dreams, as it was well known that the forest was one of Orassul's favorite places.

Aailaine felt a deep twinge in her stomach. Rfkr had been right; although she had wanted to leave the mountains badly, she often found herself longing for the life she had with the old dwarf. The past season seemed like a bad dream and she still felt that she would wake up to Rfkr calling her name. Seeing the dwarven Daywalkers had only caused her to miss him more and her heart dropped even further in her chest.

Sighing and trying to ignore the ache, she drew her head to her chest, letting her long hair shield her face. As she stared into the light of the fire, she began to hum and slowly she started to sing.

"Sometimes I look at them and I look into their eyes,
I notice the way they think about the stone with a smile,
Curved lips,

they just can't disguise,

With stones and jewels,

reflected in their eyes.

But they think it's adventure that makes their life worthwhile.

Why is it so hard for them to decide,

which they love more?"

"Is that a song about dwarves?" Aailaine stopped as Iasi spoke, opening his eyes to look at her. She smiled softly, returning her gaze to the ground.

"Yea, it's the only one I know. It was taught to me by an old dwarf." she replied, rocking her head to the rhythm of the song. "It's about the two thing they love the most as a race: the stone that surrounds them and adventuring outside it."

"Huh, that sounds about right." Iasi chuckled, rolling onto his back. "Most dwarves I've met can't shut up about one or the other."

"That's not to say that's all there is to them." Aailaine laid her head on her knees, moving her hair so she could see him. "It depends on the clan."

"Clan?"

"Yea, there are three main dwarven clans; the Nivim, the Stryn and the Viwl." Aailaine's face grew brighter as she began to talk about the clans. "The Nivim are the warlike ones. They are always looking for a fight, regardless of with whom. They almost started a war before the Shadows appeared, but since then they have served as the protectors of the mountains. They're also the ones who like to go adventuring to win glory and fame.

"The Stryn are the miners and farmers. They mine for materials and gems throughout the mountain and farm the land in Mathydar." Iasi frowned, but Aailaine hardly noticed. "The Viwl take the goods mined by the Stryn clan and refine them. Most merchants are from the Viwl clan. Most Hongekako also come from the Viwl clan, although some come from the Stryn. There are also smaller clans, but they are mostly religious sects of the main three."

"I've never heard of Mathydar," Iasi remarked, frowning as he glanced away. "Is it a newer city?"

"I-I don't know." Aailaine mentally chastised herself; she had forgotten that the rest of the world didn't know about deep-dwellers or any deep-dweller cities. Although Mathydar was a shared city, it still wasn't on any map outside of the Tolsan. "I suppose so. He just said that's where the good farmland was."

"Huh, I do remember being told that there wasn't much good farmland inside the Tolsan." Iasi shrugged. "I suppose if they found a sizeable amount in one area, they would've immediately built a city there."

"Hm," Aailaine nodded as if she agreed. She reached into the large pack and pulled out the last bottle of Smibi she had. She uncorked the bottle and breathed in the sweet scent of the wine. She took a small sip and let the liquid roll down her throat. The slight bite of the alcohol was soothing, and she purred with content as she drank more.

She glanced up to see Iasi looking at her curiously and she turned away from him. She started tapping her fingers on the ceramic container while she spoke.

"What is it?"

"You really like that stuff." he remarked, still watching. Aailaine nodded as she looked into the milky white substance.

"My caretaker used to make it. It...reminds me of home."

"Isn't that the last bottle? You only had six or seven."

"It's fine." Aailaine pulled out her letter from Rfkr and showed Iasi the back. "I have the recipe on how to make it. I actually bought all I needed from Pasyl."

"So that's what you were doing in Pasyl. And I wondered why the pack felt heavier," Iasi joked as Aailaine nodded.

"I'll have to wait till we get to Yoltri, but that's fine. It doesn't take long to ferment."

"At least you can make more." Iasi's tail twitched. "Personally, I can't wait to have some honeymead. It feels like it's been forever since I've been to Hirie."

"Iasi, if you don't mind me asking, why are you travelling without the Chekari?" Aailaine put away her smibi and watched the werecat. His happy expression turned sorrowful and he rolled away from her.

"I- I lost track of them in near Lanol. I sometimes end up getting left behind because of my profession and my tendency to get sidetracked. I suppose my sister figured I'd eventually catch up and didn't worry about me. And she'd be right to think that." His voice came muffled over his shoulder and Aailaine had to lean closer to hear him. "But I...ran into you and taking you to Hirie seemed like a good sidetrack while I look for them."

"But don't think I'm not taking this seriously." Iasi rolled over to look at her again and his usual smile was back. "It won't be that hard to find them, so I'm not worried. My sister knows that I can take care of myself."

"But don't you miss them?" Aailaine glanced at the letter still in her hand and fought back the wave of sadness that threatened to wash over her. "Isn't it hard being so far from them for so long? I mean fall is almost over and it'll be winter soon."

"I miss them," Iasi admitted, drawing little circles into the dirt. "I haven't seen my sister for almost a season. But I know that I can find them when I'm ready, so it's not so bad."

"But-"

"On top of that, I have such a beautiful woman to keep me company." Iasi winked at her and Aailaine lost her train of thought. She knew he was just trying to change the subject, but his words still caught her off guard. She turned away from Iasi and her voice came out quietly.

"Well, you're not so bad yourself. I'm sure you know a good time when you find one." Aailaine refused to look at Iasi as her entire face turned red. Yraly had spent some of Aailaine's free time giving her books to read to help her deal with Iasi's flirtations. According to what she read, he shouldn't be as suave as he let on, and could easily be embarrassed when called out.

As she chanced a glance at him, she was surprised to see him staring at her wide-eyed and slack-jawed and his face had a light blush spreading across his cheeks. She felt a sense of pride and power and she couldn't help but giggle. Iasi quickly shook his head and standing, made his way over to her. He dropped his body down in front of her, squatting almost on top of her. Shocked, she tried to back away from him, but he crawled after her and grabbed her wrists, pulling her up onto her feet.

He ran one of his hands through her hair, loosening her tangles as he wrapped his other arm around her waist. He leaned close and whispered into her ear, his voice sultry and raspy. Aailaine kept her gaze away from his as she fought to swallow her pounding heart.

"I could show you so much more than that, Aia~" Pulling back, he released her and Aailaine swayed on her feet, her knees feeling suddenly weak. The book had warned her that he might take her comebacks as challenges, but Aailaine found that she wasn't ready to be the center of Iasi's sensual attention. As she began to fall, Iasi quickly reached out to catch her and held her steady. His expression changed from coy to worry as he held her up. "Are you okay?"

"Yea...I'm fine." Aailaine took a deep breath to steady herself and gave Iasi the most defiant, alluring look she could muster. "But-but I'm... much better with you holding me."

"Is that so?" he chuckled, pulling her close again. Their bodies were very close, and she could almost feel his bare chest through her shirt. He gently lifted his hand to her face, and gently pushed back some of her hair of her neck. She took in a sharp breath as he lowered his face to the skin he exposed, laying a soft kiss there. Aailaine's breath came out shaky and Iasi sighed.

"You were also reading Yraly's books while I was gone. I swear that spindly..." Iasi remarked as he released her, running his hand through his hair as he took a step back. Aailaine slowly nodded, a blush spreading across her face. They both stood silently, neither looking at the other. After a moment, Iasi carefully sat on the ground and Aailaine followed his example. He seemed to be in deep thought and she worried that her actions had upset him.

"Ia-"

"Do my compliments bother you that much?" he interjected, looking at her. She looked away from him, her blush deepening. She traced circles in the dirt as she contemplated her answer.

"No. I mean, yes, but not in a bad way." Aailaine started to wish that she could disappear into the ground. "It's just that I'm not used to hearing things like that, and I didn't know how to respond to them, so-"

"You asked Yraly, of all people. I love her, but she is not the most tactful. And neither are those books of hers." Iasi sighed and Aailaine nodded. She began to wonder whether it was possible to use the amulet to just disappear when he sighed, leaning back on his hands.

"Well, you don't have to respond with such, um, suggestive comments. Those books are meant for...um...seduction, not really flirting." The werecat seemed to ponder his words before continuing as Aailaine covered her mouth with her hands. She had never considered that to be the purpose of the books. "I doubt that seduction was your intended purpose. You could just say thank you, or nothing at all. You could also just ask me to keep my compliments to myself."

"No!" she exclaimed, and then quickly drew her knees to her chest, surprised by her own outburst. "I mean, thank you and I'm sorry for being so weird about them. And not just telling you how I felt."

"You're welcome, Aia and there's nothing to apologize for." Aailaine nodded, refusing to meet his gaze. She heard him sigh again as he stood, making his way back over to his side of their little camp. She chanced a look up as he curled up on the ground again, his back to her.

"Sleep well, Aia." His voice came out quiet and Aailaine's spirits sunk even further. Not only had her little experiment failed, it seemed that she had completely misunderstood the implications of what she was saying. Aailaine drew her knees to her chest and dropped her head down between them.

"*Ritye*," Aailaine muttered, scolding herself softly. She should've asked Yraly to explain the books to her, rather than jumping in assuming she understood. She looked up into the sky and noticed the clouds that were starting to cover the dim stars. "Now he probably thinks I'm stupid for not knowing how to take a compliment like a normal person."

"I'd never think you're stupid." She looked up at him, but Iasi hadn't moved. Only his ears and tail twitched, slightly moving across the ground. "I think it's cute that you felt you needed to respond to my compliments in a specific way. So, don't beat yourself up over it, Aia. Think of something pleasant and get some more sleep."

"Okay. Um, thank you, Iasi." Aailaine grabbed her amulet as she laid back down, closing her eyes. The amulet seemed warm and comforting in her grip and was pulsing steadily, almost resembling her heartbeat. Aailaine felt something cold touch her face and saw snow falling slowly and softly from the sky. It melted almost immediately as it touched the warm ground, but just the sight of the white ice brought a smile to her face.

As the steady rhythm of her amulet and soft touch of the snow lulled her back to sleep, she heard Iasi's voice, but she couldn't make out what he said. She tried for a moment to return to consciousness but fell under the spell of the first snow and slept soundly.

Chapter 30

"So this, this is Yoltri?" Aailaine wondered in awe and Iasi nodded, leading her through the last few trees. The trees and vines had seemed to lose interest in Aailaine since the night of the new moon, and their journey through the forest had fewer interruptions. However, Iasi had also limited his conversation with her to only answering her questions and it made her sad. Despite him saying he found her confusion cute, it was obvious that what she had done bothered him in some way and she wasn't sure what to say to reconcile with him.

"The elves prefer to live simply." Iasi shrugged but Aailaine thought the town itself looked graceful. The small, sphere-like buildings were enchanting, with their pine wood rooftops and elm wood walls. The most outstanding feature of the town was an enormous tree growing in the middle, towering over the top of the other trees. It had tiny, blunt-tipped leaves, which were mint green and its large blooming flowers, which were white, light red and dark pink, seemed unreal. The petals blew from the tree to where Iasi and Aailaine stood and the many elves stopped their business to look at the pair.

"C'mon." Iasi placed his hand on her shoulder and slowly pushed her into the town. The elves parted, giving them a wide path to walk down and Aailaine found herself staring at their clothing. It was colorful and distinct, and she began to notice that some of the men were wearing robes similar to the women. The other males wore short or long-sleeved shirts with large buttons down the front and black pants. She also noticed some spindly among, seeming almost like children next to the graceful elves. Unlike Yraly and Sillyph, who made an effort to hide their legs and abdomens, these spindly had their robes altered to reveal their spider-like attributes.

"*Keoi*, Iasi. It is wonderful to see you return." Aailaine looked up to see a single elf walking toward them. His skin was a pale green and his long, deep blue hair was in a high ponytail, blowing in the strong cold wind. His narrow eyes were a sky blue and he stood towering over her. His flowered red and yellow robe had long, wide sleeves and a slight opening at the neck. It seemed to split down the sides near his feet and he wore plain yellow pants underneath. Around his waist was a red sash, and he walked in a strange kind of sandal. He moved so gracefully that it seemed to Aailaine like he was gliding, despite the soft clack she heard. "Who is this you bring with you?"

"Her name is Aailaine Danend. She was invited to come to Hirie." Iasi bowed his head and Aailaine followed suit before looking up to meet his gaze of the elf. He stared at her with his narrow eyes and she began to fidget. "I was hoping you could help her find out where she was needed, Erolith."

"You need look no further." Erolith knelt in front of her and touched his head to the ground, bowing to her. "Welcome to Yoltri, *Ki i Orassul*."

Aailaine looked around as all the elves surrounding them bowed to her. She turned to look at Iasi and rather than looking surprised, he merely smiled and nodded. Before she could question why, Erolith stood and offered her his slender hand. She carefully took his and nodding his head to Iasi, Erolith began to lead Aailaine toward the large tree at the center of the town. Iasi followed behind them and the multitude of elves followed behind him. Their robes created a sea of colors behind her and Aailaine found herself in awe as she kept glancing back. Once near the tree, Erolith released her and continued through the open plaza, drawing closer to the tree.

"Velatha, *Fogeako* is among us." Aailaine watched in wonder as the trunk of the tree twisted and two glowing, colorful eyes looked at her. The tree seemed to have trouble seeing her and leaned forward, causing a sea of flowers to fall around them.

< Hmmm. > The tree's voice echoed through Aailaine's mind and left her feeling dizzy. Iasi quickly moved behind her and wrapping his arms around her waist, caught her before she fell. He slowly stood her up and kept one of his arms around her to steady her. <So this is the one who has stirred the forest. The trees have been very talkative lately and it has taken all my power to keep them calm.>

"I-I'm sorry," Aailaine stammered, struggling to stand on her own. When Sirix had spoken to her, all she heard were the thoughts the dragon had been pushing to her. The tree's thoughts seemed to be heavy and full of memories and Aailaine could barely hear the tree's words over the torrent of memories that tried to fill her head. "I can barely understand you."

"Then I shall use a medium." A young female elf with orange hair and eyes walked up from the tree, standing next to Erolith. Her robe was jet black with bright stars, as if she were wearing the night itself and it contrasted greatly with her golden skin. The tree turned to the werecat holding up the young girl and hummed with delight.

This time when the tree spoke, rather than thoughts filling her mind, her words came from the elf. "I see that you have sought me out yet again, Iasi."

"I was merely a guide for her, Velatha." Iasi bowed, gripping Aailaine tighter. The elf and the tree laughed, causing another cascade of flowers. The girl then walked up to Aailaine and gently touched her braid.

"It does indeed seem that *Fogeako* has again come to A'sthy." Now that she no longer felt dizzy, Aailaine looked straight past the elf girl to the tree, who leaned back to her original position.

"Again?" she queried, confused. "Who, who was the first?"

"Your mother was the first, for if she had not faced her destiny with a strong will, you would have never been born." Velatha addressed her question and continued speaking. "You are here for the artifact that must be taken to Exla, are you not?"

"I-I am." Aailaine softly proclaimed, pulling herself from Iasi's grip, who let her go easily. The elf pointed off to their left and Aailaine looked to see the peaks of faraway mountains. She turned to look at the orange haired elf, who continued looking and pointing in the direction of the mountains.

"That is Anceo." Velatha spoke, leaning closer to Aailaine than before and she felt that she could almost touch the tree's face. "What you seek lies there. Anceo is protected by a powerful barrier, preventing all from entering."

"Then, how will I get there?" Aailaine wondered. Velatha shook her large body, causing some of her branches to fall. Some of the branches had still blooming flowers on them and it was these that the female elf gathered, presenting them to the young girl.

"My blossoms are special: they imbued with the powerful magic that Orassul granted me and have the power to enter the barrier." Velatha revealed, encouraging Aailaine to choose a branch. She carefully looked over the bundle and chose the branch with several white flowers on it. "Be strong, *Ki i Orassul*. You still have many trials before you will see the silvery sands of Exla."

"Thank you, I...I'll do my best," She affirmed, looking up to the tree. The tree's eyes almost seemed to smile at her and the elf walked back up to Erolith and disappeared, almost as if she had never existed. Erolith, pleased with the proceedings, walked back over to Iasi and Aailaine.

"You may stay with us until you are ready." As Erolith started to lead them away, Velatha called after them.

< Look after her, Iasi. Stay true to yourself through this dark time and you will see light again.> Aailaine watched as Iasi turned around and walked back up the tree. He leaned against her, rubbing her bark and it seemed to Aailaine as if he was trying to hug her. He was too far away for her to hear what he said, but she could almost feel Velatha's good will toward him. As no words drifted through her mind, she assumed Velatha's words were for him alone.

After a while, he released the giant tree and made his way back to Aailaine and Erolith. Upon Iasi rejoining them, the male elf led them through the crowd, which watched after Aailaine with awe. She still felt uneasy under all the attention and folded her hands in front of her, staring at the ground. The grass underneath her shoes felt more like moss than the grass that littered the plains or the forest floor. She considered asking Iasi about it, but when she looked up to him, he seemed sullen. His usually cheerful eyes were crestfallen, and he seemed preoccupied with his own thoughts.

"Here." Erolith's voice pulled Aailaine from her scrutiny of Iasi and she looked at the small dwelling. It was different from the other houses as its roof was the only painted one, with the sun on one side and moon on the other. Erolith bowed and left the pair to themselves without another word.

"After you." Iasi opened the door and allowed Aailaine to walk into the dwelling. She stepped into the central area, which had four chairs in a circle with a simple rug in the middle. Behind the circle of chairs was a medium-length table with six chairs and a green table runner running down its length. The kitchen was simple; it had a few cabinets and an oven, as well as a Pahri, a gnome-made device used for storing food.

Aailaine stepped into the dwelling and noticed a small wash room off to her left. It had a toilet and a basic wash closet, which she doubted had gnome plumbing. Further into the dwelling she found three bedrooms and a larger wash room between the one to her left and in front of her. She walked into the largest bedroom to find it was decorated simply. It only had a large bed, a nightstand and a chest for furniture and two colorful wooden mats hanging on the walls.

Aailaine carefully undid her sheath and quiver and leaning it against the chest, sat on the bed. The mattress felt unusual and sounded like it was filled with leaves, but still felt soft and comfortable when she laid down on it. She placed the flower branch on the pillows and closed her eyes.

"You can bathe whenever you like. I'll fill the basin for you." She sat up to see Iasi leaning in the doorway, his face still woeful. She sighed deeply, casting her gaze down to the wooden floor. "Is something wrong?"

"That's what I should be asking you." she mused, stroking her thumb with her other hand. She looked up at him and he was looking at the floor, refusing to meet her gaze. After a while, he attempted to smile.

"I'm fine," he boasted, but Aailaine could see that it wasn't true. She slowly stood and made her way over to him. Grasping the amulet in one hand, she touched his bare chest with the other, willing the light to flow. It flowed down her arm like water and disappeared into Iasi's skin. The werecat closed his eyes, breathing deeply as the light flowed into him. Aailaine concentrated on pleasant thoughts, hoping that her good intention could flow with the light.

"You can stop now, Aia." Iasi carefully moved her hand from his chest and the flow stopped, slowly fading from view. Once the light disappeared, a wave of dizziness came over her and she started to stagger. Iasi reached to grab her, but she waved him away.

"I'm fine." She shook her head to clear the spinning and smiled up at him as she regained her equilibrium. "Are you better now?"

"Yea, I feel a lot better now," he admitted, running his hand through his hair. "Thanks."

"No problem, Iasi," Aailaine whispered, and the couple stood in silence. She racked her mind for something to say as the silence dragged on. She didn't want to him to leave, but she wasn't sure what else to do. "So, um, which room are you taking?"

"The one on the other side of the wash closet." Iasi shrugged. "I put the food from the pack into the Pahri, and I left the pack in the sitting room."

"Oh, okay." She looked down at the floor again as they heard a gentle knock on the door. Iasi left the doorway to answer it and Aailaine released her breath, relieved. She slowly followed Iasi out into the sitting room just as he closed the door. He turned around to reveal two sets of robes in his hands.

"Erolith is giving us these to wear while we stay here. It'll give us a chance to wash our travelling clothes and refresh our clothing." Aailaine nodded as he handed her a silver bundle. He kept the ruby one for himself and rubbed his bare chest. "I'm going to go change now, it's getting a bit too cold for me to stay shirtless."

She waited until he disappeared into his room before returning to her own and closing the door. She laid out the gift on her bed and slid out of her travelling clothes, piling them neatly before facing the robe. It had long sleeves that opened above her elbows and swallowed her hands. As she started to put it on she noticed that it had a lower neckline compared to the robe Erolith had worn, but a simple shirt was provided to cover her chest. The belt was white with yellow suns dancing along the fabric and she noticed that the sleeves were trimmed with the same white material. It had seemed too long for her, but when she slipped into the outfit, it barely skirted the ground. A soft knock at her door drew her from her thoughts.

"Aia? Are you decent?"

"Yes, come in." She turned as Iasi came into the room. Rather than a robe, Iasi was wearing a ruby shirt that fastened diagonally down the front with sleeves that stopped at wrists. He wore jet black pants and his sleeves and collar were trimmed with black as well. The entire shirt was marked with faint gold markings that shimmered as he moved. Iasi looked down at himself.

"To be honest, it's a bit too much material for me, but I don't mind wearing it, considering the weather." Iasi smiled, looking back up at Aailaine. "There was a message as well. Erolith would like you to feast with the town tonight. Yoltri has the longest living elves, as this is where the magic of the forest is thickest. For obvious reasons."

"*Oiihead*," Aailaine remarked, thinking of Velatha. She didn't notice her use of Eroir until after she said it and worried, she chanced a glance at Iasi. It didn't seem like he noticed and if he did, he was choosing to ignore it. "What about you?"

"Well, I wasn't really invited, this is all about you. But I will go if it will make you feel better." Iasi shrugged. "I doubt Erolith will mind."

"Then please, come with me," Aailaine pleaded, looking down at the floor as she slid her hands into the sleeves of the robe. "I would feel more comfortable if you were there."

"Thank you for desiring my company, *Fogeako*." Iasi grinned and left her doorway. As he turned, she noticed the giant tree etched in gold stitching on the back of the shirt. She followed him, and he sat in one of the chairs, stretching out before attempting to take a nap.

"It doesn't bother you right?" she whispered, moving to stand in front of him. "I'm...sorry I didn't tell you. I..."

"It doesn't change anything." Iasi commented, not opening his eyes. "To me, you're still same beautiful woman I've been helping and travelling with. Now you just have an important title to go with it."

"Thank you, Iasi." Aailaine smiled at his assertion and started to return to her room.

"I'll come get you when it's time, so feel free to lie down." Iasi's voice came over the chair and Aailaine nodded, even though he couldn't see her. She continued into her room and closing the door, laid down on the bed again. The soft crinkle of the filling seemed musical to the young woman and she rolled onto her side to hear the sweets sounds again. She glanced at the flower branch and stroked the silvery white petals. Closing her eyes, she whispered a silent prayer as she held the amulet close to her chest.

"Orassul, please continue to watch over me. I will save this world, no matter what it takes."

Tolsan

Where the War begins

Chapter 31

Hvidr stood in the middle of the street, shifting uncomfortably as she waited. Many dwarves stopped to chat with her and she always politely entertained their banter. As soon as they passed on however, she would begin to fidget again. She hated being in the open space of the caverns and longed to be back at her desk, surrounded by her papers and baskets.

When Elmeye had finally contacted Hvidr, the she-dwarf was relieved to hear that they had found Soseh. In the weeks leading to the Covern, Hvidr had been little more than a nervous mess, although she maintained her stoic outward appearance, as Rfkr had taught her. However, she was not as pleased to learn that she was now the bait, since Soseh would now recognize Sirix in human form.

"*Ritye,* Rfkr, just how much trouble did you leave me?" Hvidr complained, wishing she had her hammer on her person. However, being a member of the Shadow Brigade, she couldn't openly brandish her weapon in the streets of Mathydar without cause. Although the Viwl still held the greatest mistrust of the Nivim, it was only through the Shadow Brigade that she was allowed to live in the city. Hvidr had originally chose Mathydar to be closer to Rfkr but soon found she loved the simple life it offered her. The Shadow Brigade gave her the best of both and she had enjoyed it to its fullest.

"Hvidr!" She quickly looked up as a young dwarf made his way through the dense crowd toward her. His violet colored eyes were excited as he ran, and his short crimson curls bounced around his baby face. Novrec was supposed to have been the newest member to the Shadow Brigade from Yoltnir, but the minute they met, Hvidr had known something was wrong. His face was too childish, his attitude too innocent, and he reminded her of a Stryn recruit, not a seasoned trainee from her clan. After revealing her suspicions, Elmeye and Sirix found another Novrec living among the Viwl. That Novrec admitted to having been born to the Nivim but having no desire to become a warrior, was training to become a Hongekako. That's when the women realized Hvidr's Novrec had a high chance of being Soseh.

"Novrec." Hvidr nodded as he stood in front of her, bending over to catch his breath. As soon as he had recovered, he began to glance around.

"Where's everyone else?"

"Already at the meeting place. I agreed to wait here for you." Hvidr rolled her eyes and started to walk away. Novrec hurried to keep up with her. "Honestly, Novrec, if you can't be punctual-"

"I'll get better, I promise. I did pass my Trials after all." Novrec beamed, and Hvidr fought the urge to punch him as he followed her. If this Novrec was truly the werecat Rfkr had been afraid of, she failed to understand his fear. Elmeye had said he would be too clever to choose a dwarven disguise, and yet their best lead on him was a dwarf. Either this werecat wasn't as clever as Elmeye and Rfkr thought, or he was underestimating Hvidr.

She led the false dwarf through the busy streets of Mathydar. With the Covern mere hours from starting, dwarves and deep-dwellers alike were flooding into the streets, waiting to hear what the result would be. The day of Covern was a holiday from work and school, so many school children were also running around the city.

As they walked through the many caverns and crowded tunnels, Novrec entertained himself by whistling and adjusting the pack around his waist, irritating Hvidr every time he touched it.

Since werecats can't get rid of their tails when they change, Elmeye mentioned that Soseh had an obvious tell; he would wear packs around his waist or many layers of clothing to stash his tail in. Every time Novrec touched the pouch, Hvidr wanted to rip it from him and reveal his true identity to everyone around them. However, in order to not endanger herself or Elmeye's plan, she squashed her emotions and instead focused on their destination.

Finally stepping out of the tunnel, Hvidr stepped into a large empty cavern, devoid of buildings or crevices. In the center waited the rest of the Shadow Brigade and they hailed Hvidr as she and Novrec approached.

"*Fukoie i kea, Tang.*" A built man greeted them, his armor gleaming brightly. He was the only member present to be wearing his full Nivim armor, although many other members of her clan were wearing scattered pieces. Hvidr lifted her tunic to reveal her breastplate, and Novrec revealed his armored glove. Satisfied, the man nodded as Novrec moved to converse with the rest of group before pulling Hvidr aside.

"Our clan stands ready in the tunnels outside the city should the worst happen and the Stryn members are in position throughout the city." he whispered, his eyes locked on the false Novrec. "*Fa koduo ngo*? That Novrec is..."

"*Oiihead*, and you'll see once the trap is sprung," Hvidr whispered back before standing in front of the group. Clearing her -

throat, she waited for the talking to die down and for everyone to face her. Trying her best to avoid looking at Novrec, she began her speech.

"*Tang, Fukoie.* Many of you know that the Covern is one of the most important events that happen here in the Tolsan and with the threats of the Shadows, we can never be too vigilant." Hvidr commanded the attention of all those present and she hoped that the enchantress and dragon were present in their disguises. "However, you may wonder why only the Nivim members of our Brigade are present. That is because we have a traitor in our company."

Whispers began to spread throughout the small gathering at Hvidr's accusation. Novrec's eyes widened and he shifted uncomfortably as everyone around him spoke. Hvidr raised her hand to silence them and looked to their leader, who gave her his consent to continue.

"Don't fret, for the traitor is already found." Hvidr watched Novrec visibly relax. She closed her eyes and breathed deeply, hoping that everyone had gotten word of the trap. She opened her eyes and stared directly at the pretentious werecat. "Now it is time to render our judgment."

Faster than Hvidr could follow, one of the dwarves leapt at Novrec, growing bigger as they moved. Despite his previous awkward demeanor, Novrec swiftly avoided the attack and once the dust cleared, Novrec was gone. In his place stood an overly dressed werecat facing a tall, scaly woman. The rest of the Shadow Brigade turned to face the stranger, their weapons readied in their hands. Hvidr graciously accepted as she was handed her hammer, loving the weight of the heavy weapon.

"It seems my plan was almost perfect," Soseh sighed, coyly leaning away from Sirix and calmly fixing his platinum hair. Hvidr watched curiously; Elmeye had said the plan was to force Soseh to reveal himself and Sirix would fight him with the Shadow Brigade, ensuring he didn't escape. However, despite her rage, the dragon woman merely slammed her tail against the ground, making no move to attack.

"What is it, Sirix, afraid to fight me with all these little insects around?" Soseh taunted, and Sirix launched at him, but it was obvious that she didn't mean to hurt him. Soseh laughed as he avoided the attack, easily sliding under her. "You had much more passion when we met in Dochel. Do I need to squash one to make you fight me?"

Soseh turned his hand toward Hvidr, a staff materializing in his hand. The tip of the staff began to drip with red magic as he aimed the spell directly at the she-dwarf and Hvidr gripped her hammer tightly. Elmeye wouldn't let Soseh kill her and she knew this, but it didn't stop her heart from beating wildly as he pointed the death spell at her.

"Perhaps killing this one will make you see reason." Just as he was about to release the spell, one of the hooded dwarves ran up to Soseh and grabbed his right leg. Soseh quickly fired the spell at them instead, but it fizzled and died before touching the little person. Soseh looked shocked when the dwarf's hood fell back, revealing a set of yellow eyes and long white hair. She smiled at him broadly, squeezing his leg tighter.

"Goodbye, Soseh."

"Defend!" The words had barely left Hvidr's mouth when the blast of magic hit her, and she stood behind her hammer to soften the blow. The other dwarves planted their shields in front of them, forming a wall that helped to block the explosion. In all the cycles she had known her, Hvidr never knew Elmeye was capable of such strong magic. The enchantress had made it well known that she despised the casting of spells, and preferred enchantments to using magic. However, the sheer force of her spell required the highest skill of casting, and she had done it without speaking the words.

Once the dust began to settle, Hvidr stood and chanced to look where the two spellcasters had been standing. Elmeye stood alone, her cloak billowing around her as she stood in front of a large puddle of blood. The look on her face was pure bliss and for the first time, Hvidr saw the little woman smile with pure joy.

"It's done," Elmeye sighed, and turned to face Hvidr and her fellows. "Hurry back to the Threrayrt, the Covern will start in mere minutes and you should be there protecting it. I trust the Stryn are capable, but they still need your support."

"Thank you for aiding us." Sirix bowed to the group, and the bulky man moved next to Hvidr, placing his hand on her shoulder.

"Thank you for helping rid of us of this threat to our peace." he bowed deeply to the pair. "On behalf of my entire clan, and Rfkr's memory, if you need our help again, we will come to your aid."

"How touching."

Hvidr's blood ran cold as everyone looked up to see Soseh hovering near the roof of the cavern. His right leg was gone, but the stump was no longer bleeding. He was breathing heavily, and it was obvious that it was taking all of his power to remain in the air.

"Elmeye, I never expected to see you again, seeing as how I'm pretty sure killed you." he hissed, his ears flat against his head as his tail expanded. He spat blood in her direction, which she easily side-stepped. From her cloak flew three death spells, but Soseh easily avoided these, landing on the ground near the entrance. He almost fell over from his lack of balance, but quickly resorted to using his tail to support himself.

The leader of the Brigade saw this an opportunity and letting out a cry, ran toward him and swung his blade at the werecat. However, his blade struck empty stone and Hvidr looked in horror to see the werecat firing a spell at him point-blank.

"No!" Hvidr ran to strike the werecat with her hammer, desperate to stop him. Soseh quickly turned and fired the spell at her and she realized she couldn't avoid it. At that moment, Hvidr was lifted off the ground and thrown back as Sirix took the full force of the magic. The dragon woman was forced to step back but was otherwise mostly unharmed.

"I guess we are both too quick to count our victories before they are realized." Soseh glared as the dragon woman brought her tail down on him and he was forced to roll away. As soon as he stood, Elmeye was on top of him, attempting to strike him with magic. This he avoided as well, launching himself into the air and toward the opposite side of the cavern. Once he landed, he drew his left leg into the air, completely supporting his weight on his tail. "However, I will still win this."

Just then, an explosion shook the walls, causing the ground to shake beneath them. Hvidr swayed, trying to keep her balance as the tremor continued, fearing an earthquake was beginning. However, the tremor subsided, and she could hear faint screams coming from down the passageway.

"The Covern *will* fall, even if I have to destroy this entire city to do it." Soseh laughed as Shadows poured through the tunnel and rushed to attack the company. The dwarves sprang into action and engaged the intruders, making short work of the small group that had come through. Soseh was now fading from slight, becoming more and more transparent as he slowly teleported away.

"NO!" screamed Elmeye and she flew toward him, only to pass through him and connect with the stone wall behind him. Soseh laughed again as he disappeared, his laugh echoing long after his departure. Mixed with the sounds of the screaming, it was a haunting sound and one Hvidr knew she would never forget.

"Hvidr!" Sirix ran over to the dwarf troupe, a troubled look on her face. "The Shadows have likely entered every corner of the city. We have to protect the Threrayrt and the Covern."

"Our clan is here this time; they were waiting outside the city to prepare for the worst. We must join them." The bulky dwarf interrupted Hvidr, quickly moving to address the dragon woman. "We must warn them-"

"Done." Sirix closed her eyes for a moment and Hvidr thought she saw her glow. However, it quickly faded, and she turned to face Elmeye.

"We will protect the Covern. Elmeye!" Sirix yelled for the little enchantress but Elmeye was still standing where Soseh had disappeared, her fists balled in anger. Her long white hair hid her face from view and when she finally looked up, her yellow eyes were the deepest black Hvidr had ever seen.

"Let's go, Sirix. It'll be faster if I ride you." Elmeye ran and jumped onto Sirix's back as she shifted. Sirix growled in her dragon form but made no effort to throw Elmeye off.

"We will let our clan know not to attack you, Sirix," Hvidr assured her and her companions nodded. Elmeye merely grunted as Sirix flew out of the cavern, her long body barely fitting through the narrow tunnel. As Hvidr and her company followed behind, she couldn't help but wonder how many they would lose this time.

Chapter 32

As Sirix flew through the large caverns and narrow corridors, her snout was filled with the smell of fire and blood that seemed to fill every crevice of the city. Mathydar was a killing ground once again and the Shadows had the upper hand. Despite the Nivim and Shadow Brigade being prepared for the attack, the Shadows had spawned throughout all of the city at once and with most of the experienced Brigade members helping her and Elmeye, the invaders quickly tore through the few defenders that remained.

Sirix released a torrent of white flame from her belly as a group of Shadows attempted to trap her in a tunnel and from her back, Elmeye was constantly casting spell after spell. While she hated having the sorceress ride her, she agreed that it would be quicker than moving separately and the girl was doing her best to thin out any Shadows they passed.

Soon they reached the main cavern of Mathydar and Sirix was immediately met with plumes of smoke and the overwhelming stench of death. Upon entering, Sirix quickly morphed to her human form as Elmeye leapt from her back and for a moment the pair was dumbstruck by what they saw.

In front of them, the entire cavern was filled with smoke and Sirix could faintly make out the tongues of orange flames through the grey. She saw the shapes of people running, attempting to reach the safety of their homes as the Shadows maliciously hunted them, cutting down everyone in their path. She also saw Daywalkers among them, dwarves and humans who were helping the dark beings slay their own kind.

Elmeye was the first to wake from her stupor and quickly ran into the smoke calling over her shoulder as she went. "I'll put the fires out and clear the air of this smoke before everyone suffocates. Hurry to the Covern, make sure they're safe!"

"*Oiihead*!" Sirix called and she ran off in the other direction, producing her staff from her white robe. She knocked away a short Shadow that was chasing a girl through the smoke and held off the creature as the girl scrambled to run away. The extra limbs of the spindly Shadow reached out after the girl, but Sirix quickly shattered these with a twirl of her staff and knocked the Shadow's head against a nearby wall.

As it turned to a puddle of black and faded, Sirix continued on, killing Shadows and Daywalkers alike, saving whomever she could. However, more often than not, she would find a Shadow lording over its recent kill and the rage inside her would cause her fire to rise from her belly, despite her human mouth not being able to handle it and soon her mouth ached from the burns.

Suddenly, Sirix felt a gust of fresh air and noticed that the thick smoke was finally thinning. She assumed the sorceress was having some luck putting out the fires and soon the colorful dome of the Threrayrt came into view.

The gem sphere was still hanging from the roof of the cavern in perfect condition, with no sign of a scratch or damage. A group of Shadows merely stood underneath it, as if waiting, and Sirix slowed, confused. The stairs to the gem room were clearly visible and there was nothing preventing the Shadows from entering. However, they made no move to enter or to scale the wall to knock it from the ceiling.

Hiding in a dark alley, Sirix watched the proceedings carefully. She wasn't sure if the Covern leaders were inside the Threrayrt or not, and she didn't want to risk their lives if they were. Their innate desire to kill and the surrounding chaos should've driven them to destroy the gem, which served as a symbol of peace between dwarves and Deep Dwellers. If they were ignoring it, Irdrin was telling them to, which did not bode well for the leaders inside.

"We wait." She heard a single Shadow speak, although she couldn't tell which from the group it was. "We wait until *She* appears. And then we crush her."

"Crush her." The others echoed and she knew that "She" meant her. The Shadows were waiting for her to fly in to save the Covern, only to crush her beneath the weight of the Threrayrt, killing both her and the leaders. Sirix smiled; once again, the secret of her human form was working to her advantage. She slowly made her way around the Shadows toward the stairs that would allow her into the gem room. She watched through the thinning smoke as a group of Nivim warriors ran to attack the standing Shadows, only to be overwhelmed by a group that stood near the outside.

Sirix slowly made her way up the stairs, careful not to draw the attention of the Shadows that waited for her to appear out of the sky. As soon as she was safe from their view, she ran the rest of the way into the gem. Upon entering, she quickly ducked under the swing of the dwarf's axe and avoided the thrust of another, landing on the table in the middle of the meeting room.

"Sirix! By god, woman, what are you doing here?" The leader of Viwl clan quickly motioned for the warriors to stop their attack and Sirix gingerly stepped down from the table. She carefully looked around the room and saw all three dwarven SkiRyldes as well as the three Deep Dweller Mayors. "And by Orassul, what is happening out there?!"

"Sirix?! Kleia's Vuiej?" The Stryn SkiRyldes Srkyeni looked at her with disbelief. "I thought she was a dragon."

"The Shadows are attacking Mathydar with the intention of leveling it. Their main goal is to destroy this room, along with the six of you." Sirix ignored the leader's questioning and heard curses rise from all six leaders. Dhonir, who was the first to calm down, commanded her warriors to watch the entrance, spear and axe ready.

"What of my clan? Has anyone sent word?"

"Thanks to the Shadow Brigade, who was warned of the possible attack, your clan was waiting outside the city. They began fighting back as soon as the Shadows appeared." Sirix revealed, and the SkiRyldes breathed a sigh of relief and turned her smile toward the other leaders. "However, I know not how the battle fares. An... acquaintance of mine is helping to put out fires and save those who can be saved, but my main concern is saving you six."

"Two attacks in one season, what is happening?" The mayor of Mathydar demanded, his hand slamming into the table. "Why are the Shadows suddenly becoming more active?"

"It's been a thousand years." Viregda whispered, everyone looking to her. Her voice was quiet and quivered slightly as she spoke. "I was going to mentions this, but the Void finally touches the edge of these mountains. Some of my Hongekako confirmed it, when

- 254 -

they tried to reach the western ridge. It will reach Slalan by summer; maybe that's what he was waiting for all this time."

"How will we escape?" squeaked one of the Mayors, clearly afraid for his life. "The Shadows, they will overrun the city and the Tolsan!"

"*Ika!*" Dhonir argued, beating her fist proudly against her breastplate. "My clan will not allow this city to fall. The Shadows will not have Tolsan; this is *our* home! We held these mountains long before Irdrin appeared and we *will not* lose them!"

"Agreed." Srkyeni spoke, standing next to his fellow dwarf. "We may not be trained like the Nivim, but this is our stone. If it is time to take the fight to the Void, then we stand with Nivim."

"*Oiihead,*" Viregda softly joined her companions and the mayors, after sharing a look, nodded in agreement. "We may not always agree, but Tolsan is our home. We have held our ground for over a thousand cycles against the Shadows; we won't lose now."

Just then the Threrayrt shook, swaying back and forth slightly, knocking everyone but Sirix to the floor. Sirix looked up to the ceiling to see a crack forming, slowly spreading down the sides of the room. Sirix sharply looked down to the six leaders and growled.

"We move. NOW!" She moved quickly to stand the three dwarves and three humans as the room shook again, the cracks becoming larger and spreading faster. Allowing the two Nivim Warriors to bring up the rear, Sirix quickly lead her cares from the collapsing room, slowing as they reached the bottom of the stairs.

Motioning for them to stop and remain silent, Sirix carefully crept down the stairs and peered into the street. The large group of Shadows remained under the Threrayrt even as it began to break and fall on top of them, killing a large number of them. Sirix looked up to see a green mo'qire, afraid from being trapped in the cavern, trying to dig its way back out, its tail smacking the side of the Threrayrt sharply and breaking the gem's supports.

Growling, Sirix quickly launched herself into the sky and threw herself against the frightened dragon. The mo'qire screeched at her and tried to bite her as she pushed it away from the Threrayrt. The Shadows beneath moved instantaneously with her movements and nearly seven werecats shifted into akhby as well, moving toward her and the frightened mo'qire.

Preparing to defend itself, the mo'qire screeched as it attacked the nearest Shadow, wrapping its long body around its neck. However, the legless dragon was no match for the Shadows and they quickly killed it, ripping the poor beast to shreds before facing Sirix.

Sirix, however had already begun to attack the Shadows on the ground, who were making their way to the stairs where the Covern hid. She incinerated them in a torrent of flame, making short work of the Shadows on the ground and careful to avoid flying into the already collapsing Threrayrt. She twisted to face the Akhby shadows, just as all seven dove at her. She moved quickly to dodge them, but in her effort to avoid breaking the Threrayrt, she couldn't avoid all of them.

Sirix was pummeled into the ground as three of the Shadows slammed into her and a torrent of blood sprayed from her snout. She found it impossible to move as she watched the gem room sway over her, the Shadows now determined to finish her off. Sirix willed her body to move and slowly she began to rise from the ground. However, she knew that she had broken too many bones to avoid the

Threrayrt once it fell, and for a moment, Sirix resigned herself to death.

Time slowed for the dragon as she watched the Shadows destroy the last of the supports and the room began to break apart, the pieces falling toward her like rain. Sirix closed her eyes, waiting for the inevitable impact.

It never came. Sirix opened her eyes to the pieces of the Threrayrt suspended in mid-air. She looked as the Shadows flew away toward a distance rooftop, only to be obliterated by a flash of white light. Sirix saw what she took to be Elmeye standing on a rooftop with some Viwl Hongekako. She heard their melodic voices as they sang the gem back together, using the strength of their will and Elmeye's magic to restore the shattered gem to its previous form.

Sirix's sight began to fade as the young girl walked up to her, Hongekako and the Shadow Brigade in tow. With her blurred vision, the enchantress seemed smaller than usual and her voice sounded far away. Sirix couldn't understand what Elmeye was trying to say and gave in to the blackness.

Chapter 33

Elmeye wandered the empty streets with a heavy heart. Survivors of the attack were attempting to gather the dead bodies, loved ones trying to find those they had lost in the initial confusion. She knew the Hongekako would be busy preparing many crypts for the dwarven dead, and the deep-dwellers would have to ask the Viwl for help to account for their own.

It had been almost a week since Soseh tried to destroy the Covern and Mathydar, and the city still had yet to recover. After the attack, the six leaders mutually agreed that the deep-dwellers and dwarves could no longer sit idly by and ignore the Shadows. They all agreed to attend the Meet in Exthay in order to ask the other races for help in an all-out war against the Shadows, deciding to finally take the fight directly to the Void.

Sirix also had yet to wake up. After Elmeye and the Hongekako stopped the Threrayrt from crushing her the dragon passed out, unable to transform back into her human form due to her injuries. Unsure what to do, the dwarves moved her into the deep-dweller commune, the only building large enough to house her dragon form. Elmeye had tried to heal Sirix's wounds the best she could, but she were unsure of how to properly treat her and without a Teieimoko, she had no one to ask.

Elmeye was dragged from her thoughts as she came upon a little girl, not much taller than her, crying in the middle of the street and clutching a dead woman's body. Some nearby deep-dwellers were trying to pry the little girl away, but the girl fought them, refusing to release the body. Elmeye, her heart heavy, walked up slowly and touched the girl's shoulder. The girl turned her snot-covered face to the enchantress and seeing someone who appeared her age, spoke quickly her.

"Mommy, Mom's not moving, and I can't find Dad!" she wailed, more tears and snot flowing from her face. "I can't leave Mommy until I find him. She told me to stay with one of them always!"

"Little one," Elmeye cooed, and the girl realized that Elmeye was not a child and backed away from her, holding onto the body's hand tightly. "Your mother can no longer help you. Go with these people and they will help you find your father."

"But Mommy said..."

"Your mother wants you to be with your father. These people will help you." Elmeye promised, meeting the girls gaze. She watched as the girl glanced between her and the body, and fresh tears flowed down her cheeks as she slowly released her mother's hand. When the rescuers moved her this time, she let them and followed them as they led her away.

Elmeye walked closer to the body and felt her heart sink even further as she looked over the woman's dead body. Reaching toward the body, lying face down on the ground, was a man's body, his muddy hair sporting strands the same color as the girl's. Elmeye glanced after the little girl, who disappeared as the rescuers took her inside a home crevice.

Elmeye quickly hurried through the streets, stopping to help if she could but otherwise allowing the deep-dwellers and dwarves to continue their efforts. Every death pierced her heart as if she had killed them herself and she tightened her fists in frustration. She had killed them all; in failing to finally kill Soseh, all the deaths were on her head.

She arrived at the deep-dweller Commune and pushed open the heavy doors. She started to make her way to the door leading to the back of the building when Hvidr came out, looking relieved at the sight of the enchantress.

"Figured you'd be back soon. Sirix finally woke up, and she's been asking for you." Elmeye followed the dwarf as they walked back to the room where they had placed Sirix's body. She was still in her dragon form, but her eyes had opened, and she lifted her head as the pair walked into the room.

<Elmeye...> Sirix's voice flowed weakly through Elmeye's mind, as if it might fade with the slightest breeze.

"Thought for a moment you had given up, Sirix." Elmeye smiled weakly at the dragon, sitting on the floor in front of her. "Don't you have a mission to accomplish?"

<Soseh...escaped,> Sirix groaned, closing her eyes as she laid her head back down. Elmeye looked at the ground, tracing the designs in the floor with her small hands. <Aailaine...not...safe...>

"Nowhere is safe." Elmeye cursed, slapping her hand against the stone. Hvidr stood silently beside her, her eyes glancing around for trouble. "Until that *shooke* is dead at my feet, he will continue to be my plague on this world."

Sirix remained silent and continued to breathe heavily, the conversation obviously draining her. Elmeye waited patiently, not wanting to push the dragon. Soseh, after all, was her problem and Sirix, she was just another one of his victims.

<*The Covern?*>

"Safe. Although a war is about to begin." Elmeye sighed, leaning back on her hands. "They want to attend the Meet to ask the plains races for support in their war. A messenger has already been sent."

<*The Void...it touches Tolsan...*> Sirix revealed, and both Elmeye and Hvidr stared at her with disbelief. <*Viregda...she confirmed it...it will reach Slalan soon...*>

"*Ika...*" Hvidr, whispered, clutching her shirt tightly. "No wonder Irdrin is desperate to take the mountains. If we tell the other races..."

"Everyone will easily join the war." Elmeye finished. "Add in that Aailaine is on her way to awaken Orassul, and you're guaranteed to unite everyone to fight him. People were willing to ignore the Void when it seemed so distant, but now it's on our doorstep."

<*I...must...go...then...*> Sirix attempted to move, but Hvidr carefully pushed the dragon down. <*I must...*>

"The Meet isn't for another season, Sirix." Elmeye watched as Hvidr tried to ease Sirix back onto the mat. "Besides, you can barely move, let alone make it to Exthay."

<*Slalan...*>

"I'm sure Viregda has already made plans to move her city, and both of you have a debt to repay before you can leave Mathydar." Hvidr hinted, looking between them both as Sirix gave up and settled on her mat once more. "The Covern also *asked* for your help rebuilding Mathydar, and I will make sure you do so. Once you're well enough to."

Sirix finally conceded, closing her eyes slowly. *<Like father, like...>*

"Daughter." Elmeye finished as Sirix's voice faded off, and the dragon's gentle snore filled the room as she fell asleep. Hvidr gave Elmeye an exasperated look. Elmeye shrugged and offered the dwarf the seat next to her. Hvidr took it and ran a hand through her hair.

"He would've been pissed, you know. Missing such a big fight against the Shadows." Hvidr sighed and chuckled to herself. "He must be cursing in his crypt. Old man never knew when to stop fighting..."

"I heard he fought to protect Aailaine, even though he didn't have his sword." Elmeye sighed and Hvidr looked away as tears poured from her eyes. Elmeye lightly rubbed her back as Hvidr leaned into her hands.

"He...wasn't even in Mathydar. The Viwl, some of their Hongekako had been killed on the way to Mathydar and somehow, he knew. He just knew it was the Shadows. Now I wonder if he knew about the Void." Hvidr brought her hands to her face, trying to hold back her tears. "When he found me, he...was already hurt so badly and he yelled for me to find Aailaine. After all these years, he came looking for me first, to make sure I was okay."

"Aailaine, does she remember you?"

"No, she has no idea I'm Rfkr's daughter. When I returned, I thought she might, but I guess she was too young. Most have no clue actually." Hvidr continued to cry in her hands. "My mother died right after I was born, and he sent me away to train as a Nivim warrior once Kleia gave him Aailaine. He didn't like it when I came back to

Mathydar, but no one realized it anyway. Guess we don't have much of a resemblance."

"Rebuilding the city will take quite some time," Elmeye remarked, hoping to change the subject. The dwarf sighed again, wiping her eyes before dropping her hands to her lap. "There's a lot we can't fix, like all the lives that were lost. But, I'll make sure we do all we can."

"Will you help with Slalan?" Hvidr queried, nodding her head to the sleeping dragon. "Sirix seems determined to help with that as well."

Elmeye turned an annoyed gaze to the dragon. "I would rather get straight back to finding Soseh, but I doubt Sirix will give me much of a choice."

"So, you're staying with her, then?" Hvidr wondered, setting her gaze on Elmeye's companion. Elmeye shrugged and looked up toward the dark ceiling.

"Probably. She's still my best bait for finding Soseh and I have to keep her alive somehow; I can't let all of them die. Kleia's and Rfkr's death already weighs heavily on me." Elmeye smiled sadly and glanced over to Hvidr. "Speaking of which, this is the last job, okay? You did me a huge favor and I almost caused your home to be destroyed. So, no more from me."

"I'm getting too old anyway. I'll probably be dead before your next favor. But, thank you." Hvidr looked almost relieved and placed her hand on the enchantress' shoulder. Elmeye gently placed her hand on top and the two small women sat together, listening to Sirix's soft snores.

Yasmina Iro

Hirie

Where peace is also fading

Chapter 34

Iasi sat among Velatha's branches, collecting the pink and red flowers. Some of the elven girls had asked him to collect them and while he knew they had ulterior motives, he decided to do it anyway. It gave him time to think and he enjoyed spending time with Velatha, who was humming sweetly. His shirt today was a deep blue and sleeveless despite the cold, with the image of a mo'qire breathing fire on his back.

Hearing male laughter, Iasi looked down to see Aailaine walking with one of the elven males. He was showing her the village and nearby forest and Iasi started to frown. They had been in Yoltri for about two weeks, and the young elven male often insisted on "showing her the town." Aailaine always accepted, much to Iasi's disappointment and while admitting she had already seen everything, she saw his invitations as a chance to become friends. From the way the male elf tried to put his arm around her, Iasi knew they were invitations to other things and his frown deepened.

After their interaction on their way to Yoltri, it became painfully obvious that Aailaine was new to sexual advances and ignored any signs of such. She was so deprived of companionship that she immediately latched on to anyone who showed her kindness, and Iasi hated the way the elf was taking advantage of her. Iasi had distanced himself from her to avoid the same temptations; he couldn't deny how much he wanted to embrace her. Although, he also wasn't sure if it was his own impulses that drove him to be closer to her. Irdrin's dark whispers were growing louder, and he wasn't sure how much longer he could ignore them.

<What is it, little one? > Velatha shook the branch he was sitting on to get his attention. Iasi sighed and resumed picking flowers, adding them to his baskets. Velatha turned to look and spied Aailaine and the elf. < Ah, I see. You are jealous. >

"*Kodad inghuonggo*, Velatha," Iasi growled, trying to concentrate on the flowers as he heard more laughter. "I am her guide, nothing more. I am worried about her, not jealous."

< You are a horrible liar. > Velatha giggled as she moved the flowers away from him and lifted the branch, encouraged him to climb higher. Iasi sighed and climbed through her branches. < You are at least attracted to her, and you cannot deny that. What is her name again?>

"Aailaine, Aailaine Danend."

< Ah, a Plainsfolk surname. Smart choice. > Velatha commented and Iasi paused, giving her a strange look. The great tree merely closed her eyes and urged him to keep going. < Do you know what her name means? >

"It sounds spindly, but no, I have no idea." Iasi confessed, finally reaching the top of Velatha's branches. "What am I doing up here?"

< You need to be directly in the center. > Velatha cooed and the werecat sighed, hoping for more of an answer. He disliked it when Velatha chose to be a "mysterious, wise, old tree" but she always did things for his benefit. He wasn't quite sure why she liked him so much, but he was glad she did. < Her name means exalted. Fitting, don't you think? >

"Exalted and allure, huh…" Iasi thought, carefully trying to weave through Velatha's tight branches to reach the center of her canopy. The spaces were becoming extremely small and Iasi was finding it difficult to fit through. "Velatha, could you do something about these branches? I can hardly move."

< Shift if you need to, but if I do anything to aid you, it will fall. >

"I can't shift, I'll lose my clothes. What will fall?"

< You will see. > Iasi groaned at the tree's vague answer. He carefully shifted in a wevran and held his clothes in his tail. < Why must you choose such a disgusting form? >

"You said shift if I need to." Iasi shot back. So deep in her canopy, he saw no flowers and a sea of brown and mint floated in his vision. It reminded him of the sea and even in his lizard form, Iasi felt his stomach churn. Even though he was far from either sea, just thinking about being in them made him feel sick.

Finally reaching a bigger space, Iasi shifted back into his werecat form and carefully redressed. "Velatha, what am I up here for? I need to finish collecting flowers for those girls."

< I finished that for you. You're not interested in them anyway. You have *Earibuoko*.> the tree argued, moving her branch violently and Iasi slipped, falling onto his rear. Before he could stand, Velatha slanted the branch downwards and he began to slide down at an alarming speed.

"Velatha! I thought you said you couldn't move!"

< Do not worry, I have no intention of harming you. > The branch slowly curved horizontally, and Iasi came to a gentle stop in front of a large, white flower. It stood larger than him and its curled

petals had a hint of blue. The center reminded him of Aailaine's hair with its many colors but somehow always seeming light blue.

"What is this?" He spoke in awe, slowly walking up to the flower. He touched one of the petals and a shock ran through his entire body and he quickly pulled back.

< It's a flower Orassul left here with me. It is filled with a piece of Orassul's light. > Velatha hummed. < It's the source of my power. Be careful touching it. There should be some sort of container there; try and find it. >

Iasi glanced around for the container and found a small pot behind the giant blossom. He slowly picked it up, studying it in his hands. It seemed old and brittle, but he hit it, and besides making a strange hum, the pot showed no signs of breaking. Rather, as it continued to hum, the dirt and cracks began to fade until the pot looked brand new.

"How did this even get here?"

< Some elven girl left that at my roots many cycles ago. It contained the dirt from her sister's grave and she asked me to save her sister. > Velatha revealed, and the tree's orange haired avatar appeared before Iasi. < You know the girl's sister as my medium. I kept the pot, since I didn't know what else to do with it. >

Iasi shrugged as he looked it over. He supposed she wouldn't have any use for such a small container, as she had no worry about dying and none of her offspring would fit, since they were the trees that populated Hirie. "So, what do I need to do?"

< Touch it to Orassul's flower. Gather some of the light. > the tree instructed, and he did so, tipping the opening toward the flower. Once the two objects touched, water flowed from the flower to the

pot and Iasi watched it curiously. Despite its magical nature, the water seemed simple and plain to him and once the pot was filled, he brought it to his nose. It had no scent like normal water and he looked around with a chagrined expression.

< Try drinking it before you judge it. > Velatha urged, and the werecat sighed. He took a small sip of the water and let out a yelp of surprise. Despite its normal appearance, the water's taste was unimaginable. It tasted like clear rain from plains, the sweet bite of honeymead and the sour bitterness of beer. < That water is Orassul's Joy. Everything it enjoyed about this world, that water tastes like. That was the Creator's gift to me; everything that truly made them happy in the world.>

"Why are you giving this to me?" Iasi looked at the water with wonder as he placed the lid on the pot. Velatha laughed, shaking the branches he was standing on.

< It's not for you; it's for Aailaine. She may share it with you, but it will help her awaken to her powers. > Velatha opened up her branches to make a path outside and Iasi found himself next to the elves' baskets, now teeming with the red and pink flowers. The sun had already begun its descent over the tops of the trees. < She may not like water but let her know this water is different. >

"I will," Iasi agreed, grabbing the baskets and jumping from Velatha's branches. She hummed with delight as she patted his head, leaving a small white flower in his hair. Iasi purred, rubbing against her branch before heading off to find the girls.

Upon his arrival, they flitted to him like moths to a flame and he tried to resist the urge to roll his eyes. Normally, he indulged their flirting, even spending time with the girls. Today, however, their actions only served to annoy him.

He carefully handed each girl her basket and danced away as quickly as he could. They made an effort to follow him, but he quickly shifted into a snake and avoided their gaze as they ran past him. He picked up the jar and clothing with his tail and he slithered his way to the home he and Aailaine were borrowing. As he reached the final crossroad, he returned to his werecat form and he began to dress. Just he finished and began to step out of the trees, he stopped to see Aailaine and the elf in front of the dwelling. He stayed hidden, listening to their conversation.

"I'll see you around Vulred, I suppose." Aailaine nodded to the male elf, who took her hand and kissed it. She had her hair up in a tri-bun with an orange comb, similar to how the girls wore their hair, and Iasi assumed they had convinced her to try it. Her dress today was vermillion, with orange flower petals dancing around her. Her sash was a brilliant orange and trailed the ground behind her.

"Can I not convince you otherwise, my dear *Fogeako*?" the blue-haired elf pulled her close, wrapping his arm around her waist. It took all of Iasi's willpower to keep from emerging and pushing him off her, but he remained hidden. Aailaine quickly pushed him away for her and kept her hands between the two of them, an angry look on her face.

"*Fa fea ed eahtu orambuorgu.*" The air around them felt heavy with her anger as she spoke, and Iasi was surprised. He was sure the magic in the air and her use of Eroir was part of it, but it had almost felt like she was casting a spell. "I said, I'll see you around. Don't make me change my mind."

"Well, I say different, *Earibuoko.*" Vulred grabbed her dress and pulled her against him, forcing his mouth on hers. At this, Iasi's anger took over him. Before he realized it, he had moved between them and threw the elf off her, almost losing the jar of Orassul's Joy, which he still held tightly in his tail.

"Don't you ever touch her again, *heiirmeia.*" Iasi hissed, his ears back and flat against his head and his tail inflated. He felt like beating the elf into the ground, but resisted, not wanting to upset Aailaine, who stood behind him with her hands to her mouth. The elf stood, dusting off his robes before staring at Iasi defiantly.

"And what makes you think you have the right to say that? It's not like she's yours. You don't have anything to offer her." Vulred spat, staring at Iasi defiantly. His words cut Iasi, but he maintained his glare. "At least I have something."

"No, she's not mine. She belongs to no one and I believe she told you no." Iasi stood up to the elf, looking straight him in the eye. He rose to his full height, holding the jar tight in his tail. His voice dropped deeper as he continued speaking. "Now, I believe Aailaine said she'd see you around. Don't make me ensure that never happens."

At this Vulred's eyes widened as he understood Iasi's implied meaning and he looked away, contemplating his options. With a grunt, he finally turned away and made his way back into the village, his sandals clacking defiantly. Relaxing, Iasi turned to speak to Aailaine, only to find himself alone and the door to their home open.

As he walked in, he heard Aailaine crying in her room and with a heavy chest made his way to her door. Hesitating, he knocked slowly and carefully.

"Aia? *Or kodad...or kodad uab?*"

"*Goad bia...*" Her soft words burrowed into him like hot knives and he turned away, moving the jar from his tail to his hands.

"Okay, I will." He placed the jar next to the door. "The jar contains a gift from Velatha. I'm leaving it by the door."

He waited to see if she would reply but heard nothing. Sighing with a heavy heart, he dragged himself away from her door and collapsed into one of the sitting chairs. Iasi gazed into the woven rug, tracing the threads with his eyes. The pattern was mesmerizing, enough to make most people forget their troubles and worries. Try as he might, however, he couldn't stop thinking about the scene in front of their borrowed home.

"I should've intervened when he first grabbed her. I should've insisted she stop seeing him." Iasi felt a tight unpleasant knot in his stomach and chest as he groaned, curling up into the chair. The flower Velatha had placed in his hair fell from him and sat on the floor. Iasi stared at the white stain and found himself thinking back to the male elf. His whole body began to shake with anger and jealousy.

"I will find that *heiirmeia*." His eyes became irritated and Iasi quickly removed his contacts, throwing them to the ground. His red eyes glowed brightly in contrast to the Darkness that flowed across his skin. Iasi curled his fist, feeling extremely powerful, like he could do anything. Kill anyone. "He will pay for forcing himself on Aia. I, I will..."

"Iasi?" Aailaine lit one of the lamps and Iasi flinched as the light touched him. The Darkness quickly fled, filling the dark corner of the room. He watched it spread and then disappear under the door, looking for another victim to claim. Aailaine sat in the chair across from him, pulling her feet onto the seat. Iasi immediately looked away from her, not wanting her to see the dark thoughts on his face, or that he had removed the contacts. Even without the Darkness cloaking him, his anger for what the elf had done and his own inaction fueled the Darkness growing inside of him.

"I'm sorry." Her voice came out as no more than a whisper and sounded tearful. He glanced up to see silent tears rolling down Aailaine's face as she stared at the floor. Iasi's anger reached its boiling point and jumping from his chair, he knelt in front of Aailaine. "I-I'm sorry that I made you angry."

"I'm not angry at you, Aia." Iasi wiped the tears from her face and hugged her. "I could never be angry at you for something like that. That is never your fault."

"If I had been more forceful with him..."

"Stop it." He quickly hushed her and stood, walking toward the door. "I'm going to get that *heiirmeia*."

"*Ika*!" Aailaine quickly jumped up and threw her arms around Iasi, stopping him from moving. He tried to break free of her, but she held on tightly, sobbing into his back. "Please, Iasi, don't."

"Why?" Iasi barely recognized the voice that came out of his mouth. It was deep and gruff, filled with darker things. "He forced himself onto you, he should pay for touching you. He should di-"

"DON'T SAY THAT!" Aailaine screamed, hitting her fists into his back. Her pounding seemed to wake him, and Iasi shook his head as if to clear it. He slowly turned around as she fell to her knees, sobbing into her long sleeves. He quickly sat beside her and pulled her into his lap, holding her close. She leaned against his chest, wrapping her arms around him and sobbing into his shirt.

"What he did was horrible, but he doesn't deserve to die for it." Aailaine sobbed, burying her face in his chest as he gently stroked her hair. He kissed her head tenderly, lingering in the beautiful scent, hoping it would calm the Darkness that raged inside him. "Please, Iasi, don't do anything."

"I-I can't do that," Iasi growled, gripping her tighter, then relaxing his grip. "I have to do something."

"*Fohto*, Iasi, don't hurt him." Aailaine begged, looking up at him. Her usual silver eyes were stained with red and all kinds of fluids ran from her eyes and nose. Iasi sighed as he looked down at her and he felt his chest ache with emotion. He merely pressed her head against his chest again.

"Fine, what-what if I just tell Erolith what he did?" he compromised, rocking her gently. "He might be whipped or banished, but they won't kill him."

"Okay." Aailaine whispered, her sobbing slowing. Iasi continued to rock her, humming softly. He held the woman tightly in his arms and while he respected Aailaine's feelings, a deep, Dark part of him still wanted to kill Vulred.

Chapter 35

Iasi adjusted the pack on his back as he stood in the sitting room, waiting for Aailaine to return. He had told Erolith what the male elf had done, and the leader had banished him to be at the mercy of the forest and its inhabitants. If Velatha's anger meant anything, he probably didn't last long.

"I'm almost ready." Aailaine quickly walked into the small kitchen and grabbed some bottles before heading back to her room. For the two weeks they had spent in Yoltri, Aailaine had brewed the rice wine she loved. Iasi had set up the barrel in her room to allow it to ferment and she was refilling the bottles that had originally carried the wine, as well as filling extra bottles that the elves had given her.

He sighed heavily, setting the bag back down on the floor and sitting in one of the chairs. The elves had also given them provisions for the trip to Anceo, and even though they would pass the city of Likha, Iasi preferred to avoid stopping. The only downside to the elven provisions was the lack of meat and they had eaten the last of the teyom meat before they arrived.

"It'll work out," Iasi muttered to himself, shifting in the chair so he could watch the door to Aailaine's room. "After all, she has a bow and I hate hunting in the forest outside of season, but I'm sure Velatha will understand."

Remembering the old tree, Iasi's ears and tail perked up and he quickly stood. He yelled some words quickly at Aailaine about Velatha and hurried out of the home, running through the snow to the center of town. Velatha was waiting for him, watching him with a warm smile as he quickly hopped up into her branches, knocking down some of the white fluff.

< I was wondering if you were going to leave without saying goodbye. > Velatha used to her branches to return the werecat's hug. < Are you two almost ready? >

"Almost, she's packing up the rice wine she made."

< Ah, the smibi. > Velatha nodded and Iasi gave her a weird look. Her leaves and branches came down in a shower as she laughed. < I know many things, Iasi. Very little escapes my sight. >

< Like your state. > The tree's normal light and happy voice became serious and Iasi looked away, plopping down on the branch. She stroked his cheek lightly, leaving a red flower in his hair.

"It was so stupid, Velatha. I should've been more careful." Iasi wanted to punch himself, but he knew that the tree wouldn't let him. "I knew better, but I did it anyway. I just had to."

< Your cause was just, little one. Do not blame yourself for having a good heart. > Velatha placed another flower in his hair, one of the lighter pink ones. < Many would not have done what you did because of fear and would have left them to their fate. >

"I just wish it hadn't happen. If only they had listened..." Iasi sighed, rubbing Velatha's branch gently. The tree spirit moved her branch so that she could see him, and he avoided her gaze, watching where his hand was rubbing her bark. Every time he visited her, he expected her bark to be rough and break off like most trees, but it was always soft like a sponge. He now wondered if the cause was the giant flower he had found in her center.

Yasmina Iro

< I felt your anger Iasi. > Velatha shook her branch to force him to look up. What he saw in her eyes wasn't anger or pity, but a great amount of concern. < I almost sent my children after you, until I realized that it was you. >

"I'm sorry Velatha. I try so hard to control the feelings the Darkness gives rise to, but..." Iasi blurted, and then stopped himself, realizing it was pointless. "That night was difficult. You were right, I am jealous, but I'm also scared. What if, I only feel the way I do because of the Darkness?"

<I doubt that, Iasi. After all, the Darkness would drive you to kill her, not embrace her.> Velatha assured him, but Iasi couldn't help but doubt her. There were times when he felt the desire to kill her, but the urges were rare. <Your care for her and her light will continue to preserve you.>

"I know," Iasi admitted, looking at his hands. "If not for the light from her amulet, I think I would've lost myself a long time ago."

<Continue to be her strength but watch your anger. > Velatha brought him close to her eyes and he was forced to look into one of them. Her eyes swam between a multitude of colors, just as Aailaine's hair could not be considered one color.   < From what I remember, it can take a lot, but your anger can be terrible. The Darkness will only enhance this and quicken your change. She can't afford to lose you yet. Neither can Chadirra. >

"I...I know, Velatha." Iasi hugged her face warmly. He avoided touching her eye, not sure if it would bring her pain. "I promise. I do have a question."

< Anything that I can answer. >

"What was Orassul like? Was it male or female?" Velatha remained silent, presumably in thought. Iasi waited patiently, swinging from her branches. He had made sure to sit high enough so he could see the dwelling and occasionally glanced over to see if Aailaine had come out. He had told her to look for him in Velatha, but he worried about how much she heard from her room.

< Orassul was like no being that had ever walked this world. I can't even describe how amazing it felt to be around the Creator. It chose what it wanted to be, although I believe it's natural appearance was similar to humans. > Velatha hummed with delight. < I think that's why Orassul created humans. A being to match its form. >

"Hmm." Iasi looked up again to see Aailaine outside of the building and scanning Velatha for him. He quickly stood up and waved to her and her face lit up when she spotted him. He motioned that he was coming back, and she nodded, heading back inside. He jumped down from Velatha's branches and turned to face the tree once more. "I have to go."

<Wait. > Velatha reached up into her canopy and pulled down a new outfit similar to the one he usually wore, dumping more snow onto the werecat. Iasi was still wearing the shirt Erolith had given him and had considered wearing it until they left Hirie, but he graciously accepted the tree's gift. The new outfit was almost completely identical to his old one; the only noticeable difference to him was the gold bands that now wrapped diagonally across the shirt and shrug. As he examined the contents, he noticed that the shrug she had given him was longer than his other one, providing more warmth.

< I know you lost your shirt when you were fighting day servants of the Shadows. > Velatha smiled warmly at him as he brushed the snow off his new clothes; even though she had no mouth, he could always tell when she was smiling. < I hope my gift serves you well. Erolith's shirt is not bad clothing to fight in, but more importantly, it's not what you are used to and will not flow with your body. >

"Thanks, I will wear it with pride." Iasi bowed one last time and made his way back to the home. He found Erolith standing outside and mentally groaned. He wanted to change as soon as possible, but it seemed Erolith would not let him pass easily.

"Iasi, I am glad I was able to catch you before you left." Iasi sighed internally as Erolith hailed him and he considered not slowing down. Erolith stood between him and the door, however, and he would have to purposely go around. "I have a gift for *Fogeako*."

"She's inside. I can go get her." Iasi stopped next to elf, hoping that Erolith would agree. Instead the male elf handed him a large package, lying it on top of the clothes he already carried.

"I'd rather not inconvenience her. Please give it to her in my stead." With that, Erolith walked away briskly and Iasi sighed. He already held up their progress by visiting Velatha and now with Erolith's present, he found it impossible to open the door. He considering kicking the door but didn't want to risk scratching the wood. He finally settled on using his elbow to lightly tap the door, hoping Aailaine was in the sitting room.

He waited for a moment, but he didn't hear anything from inside the dwelling. He tried taping again and failed to get any response.

Sighing and carefully adjusting the contents in his arms, he lightly kicked the door a few times. He backed up slightly and kicked the door a little harder just as Aailaine opened it. The force of him kicking the door and her opening it at the same time caused him to teeter back, about to lose his balance. His tail, however, quickly caught him and he managed to stand back up, still balancing Erolith's gift.

"Iasi! I'm so sorry, are you ok?"

"I'm fine. But can you take this package? It's for you." Iasi's arms sighed with relief as Aailaine removed the heavy gift and took it inside the dwelling. The werecat quickly excused himself and went to his room, quickly unbuttoning the shirt. He took this as a moment to check his boots for damage, but the dark leather had no scratches or scuffs. He quickly dressed in the new outfit Velatha provided, enjoying the old tree's gift. He felt touched that Velatha felt the need to replace his shirt for him and provide him with a warmer shawl. Usually he would've changed shrugs, but he had left his winter shrug with the Chekari.

He shifted into an ozkok, testing the new outfit's durability. Iasi was pleased to find that the new outfit was indeed made from Clilar, a strange plant that only grew in the Redan desert. The plant somehow allowed for their shape-shifting abilities, shaping with them as they rolled between forms and never tearing.

"Iasi?" Aailaine knocked and carefully opened his door as he morphed back into his natural form. Iasi pulled his hair back as he stood, enjoying his new, warm clothing. When he glanced at Aailaine, she was giving him a strange look.

"What?"

"You don't have ears," she remarked, and Iasi flicked the cat-like ears on the top of his head.

"These are my ears. I don't have ears like you, but yes I have ears."

"Then, how would you look if you were human?" she pondered aloud and Iasi sighed. He preferred to either stay in his natural form or change into a creature. But he slowly shrunk in height, his short black curls becoming long blond straight locks and his ears disappearing back into his head. He flashed bright brown eyes at Aailaine and pulled back his hair to show off his ears.

"Ethnically, I'd be a Goldsman if I were human." Iasi rubbed his bronze skin. "That's why I'm so tan even as a werecat. My sister was born in Hirie, so her skin is kind of a light green."

"So werecats take on characteristics of the place they were born?" Iasi nodded, shifting back into his form. Aailaine pondered this for a moment before speaking again. "What about family traits?"

"We have them," Iasi laughed, walking back out to the sitting room to grab the pack. Whatever gift Erolith had gotten Aailaine remained a mystery, for Iasi saw no sign of the gift except the discarded paper that had contained it. He shouldered the heavy bag and nodded toward the door. Aailaine glanced around for a moment and satisfied, stepped out. Iasi locked the dwelling and continued speaking as he walked out behind her. "If you look at me and my sister, you'll see the similarities. Although I have tan skin and she has green skin, we have a similar face and body shape and black hair. That we gained from our parents."

"Oh."

Iasi could tell from her answer that she didn't really understand. Instead, he carefully slid his hand into hers and Aailaine stopped, looking down at their hands. For a moment, Iasi's thoughts raced back to the incident with Vulred and thought she might pull away. Instead she gripped his hand tightly and continued walking. A strange warmth filled Iasi from his chest even though no light was flowing between them.

They continued to walk hand in hand until they reached the edge of Yoltri, where Iasi released her to move the branches out of the way. After she passed him and he took his place behind her, he found himself thinking about the nice sensation of her hand in his. He tried to shake these thoughts from his head and he swore he heard Velatha's laughter echo through his mind.

He turned one last time to look at the great tree and smiled as some of her blossoms flowed on the gentle winter wind and blew past them. As he plucked one from the air, he looked to see Aailaine watching him. He carefully placed the red flower next to her ear and smiled at her.

She slowly plucked a white blossom as it flowed past them and placed it in Iasi's hair as he bowed his head to let her. She also took this chance to kiss his cheek again, surprising the werecat. This kiss was much more gentle that the one in Pasyl, but Iasi felt the same warmth and giddiness spread through his body.

As he followed behind Aailaine, he couldn't help but hold his hand to his chest, wanting to hold on to this happy feeling and praying it was indeed his own.

Chapter 36

Aailaine took a large breath in, looking deep into the fire. It had been two days since they left Yoltri and Iasi had been pushing them to make it through the forest quickly. After meeting Velatha, the trees and vines had stopped reaching after them as often, which made travel easier, but Iasi still seemed worried about being in the forest. They often stopped because Aailaine couldn't push herself anymore, which always frustrated the werecat. Aailaine had asked why, but he always ignored the question and kept pushing her to keep going.

Slowly, Aailaine's gaze drifted to her sheath, where it lay on the ground. Reaching for her bow, Aailaine carefully slid it out of the quiver and stroked the glowing runes. She wasn't sure what they meant, as she knew nothing of enchanting, but they seemed to always glow when she touched them. If she readied an arrow for release, it almost felt like the runes were giving her strength to fire her shot with a steady hand.

She pulled at the bowstring, loving the slight bend of the upper and lower limbs. Picking up an arrow from the quiver, she stood, notching the arrow. She touched the soft green fletching to her lips and lightly kissed them. The plant-like tip wriggled, blunting itself and Aailaine looked at it with a soft expression. During her morning practices, she appreciated the apparent sentience of the arrows; it saved her from always losing them as rather than embedding themselves, they merely bounced off harmlessly.

Relaxing, she un-notched the arrow and replaced both it and her bow in the quiver and drew her blade. After the incident outside Yoltri, Aailaine tried to remember to practice with the sword, although she forgot to most days. She readied the blade, standing as Iasi had taught her.

"Relax," she reminded herself, taking in steady breaths until she felt tranquil. She completed the first play; always play with the steel. She tossed the blade back and forth between her hands, rolling her wrist to twist the blade. She waited until her invisible attacker came at her and switched the blade to her right hand, blocking them with ease. She tried to feel the sword as an extension of herself, rather than a foreign object.

"Mind a partner?" Aailaine opened her eyes as Iasi reappeared, slight stains on his shrug. In each of his hands were two brown Starechf, their heads gone and the blood dripping from their feathered bodies onto the ground. He took off the shrug and after removing his blades, laid the birds' bodies on it. "Caught dinner."

"I see." Aailaine shrugged, twirling the blade in her hand. "I don't mind, but I'm still not that good."

"Well, then I'm perfect practice. I'd be lying if I said I haven't gotten rusty." Iasi readied himself, taking in deep breaths before assuming the proper stance. "I should practice more often too. So, come at me when you're ready."

Aailaine adjusted the grip in her hand, holding the blade so it pointed at Iasi. "I won't be easy on you."

"Neither will I. Just don't shock me." Iasi grinned before coming at her from the left. Aailaine quickly switched hands and blocked his attack. He followed by swinging up on her right and

Aailaine used her free hand to stop him again. Stepping forward, she locked her left leg behind him and pushed her shoulder into him.

Iasi fell back and quickly rolled, facing Aailaine. He raised an eyebrow and slowly stood, beckoning her to come at him. She gripped the handle tightly, giving it a quick jerk to insure no energy flowed. She came at him from the left, waiting until the last minute before switching the blade and going around his guard. She lightly slashed his exposed midsection before rolling to avoid his second blade.

"I thought you said you weren't good." Iasi carefully stroked where she cut him and whispered some words, causing the scratch to disappear. Aailaine shrugged, tossing the blade between her hands.

"I didn't think I would be, compared to you." She slashed the air with the blade, flashing him a challenging smile. "I guess you have gotten rusty."

Iasi returned the gesture with a devilish grin, wasting no time in lunging at her. The sounds of their blades clinking echoed throughout the dark forest and Aailaine felt her resolve waning. Her taunt had pushed Iasi to try harder and she found herself being backed into a corner. It was harder for her to continue attacking with Iasi's two blades; he would easily block her with one and attack with his second.

< I need to get that second blade away from him.> Aailaine thought as she backed away from the werecat, trying to think of a way to penetrate his defense. Iasi played with his blades, almost juggling them between his hands. Her eyes widened in surprise as she thought of something, and her mouth broadened into a big smile.

Aailaine came at him again, moving to slash at his exposed midsection. Iasi blocked her with ease and he was clearly disappointed. She smirked as she continued forward, sliding on the snow behind him and grabbing his other hand. She twisted his wrist, forcing him to drop his other blade and he grunted in pain.

"Still disappointed?" she whispered, moving her blade to under his neck. A shiver ran through his body and his breath quickened. For a moment, Aailaine thought he was hurt and pulled back. She released his wrist, only to have him turn around and place his blade at her throat.

"Always remember-"

"To follow through." Aailaine's voice joined his as he released her, pulling his blade back and picking up the one she forced him to drop. She felt slightly ashamed, having let him fool her with his show of pain. She stabbed the blade into the ground, sighing heavily as she sunk into the wet snow.

She felt Iasi's hand as he slowly touched her chin and lifted her head up to meet his eyes. She gazed into his crimson eyes, tracing the details with her own. She could almost see her chrome eyes reflected in his sea of red and instead of fear, she felt intrigue. Aailaine's eyes drifted over his face quickly, watching the way the firelight danced over his skin.

"You did well. Don't be frustrated with yourself." Iasi smiled at her and she had to shake her head to clear it. "We should spar more often, to give you a better sense of timing."

"Y-Yea..." Aailaine's voice came out shaky and unsteady, and Iasi frowned, looking at her concerned. He knelt in front of her and moved his hand to her forehead. Her thoughts jumped to the rough kiss Vulred had forced on her; it had defied everything she had wanted her first kiss to be and looking at Iasi's alluring eyes, she couldn't help but want him to kiss her instead.

"Are you okay? Is something wrong?"

"Something..." she repeated, still looking into his eyes with an absent look. Without thinking, she quickly leaned in and pressed her lips against his. Iasi immediately pulled back and backed away, turning to face away from her. Aailaine felt disappointed by his actions and brought her knees to her chest.

"I don't know...sorry," she uttered, putting her face into her knees. She stood to walk to her side of the camp when he turned around, clutching her arm harshly. She stared him, surprised at the agonized look on his face. He glanced away for a moment, gripping her more gently before pulling her closer. He pressed her face into his chest, hugging her tightly and she carefully put her arms around him.

"Iasi?" she quavered, her voice trembling as he pulled her face up toward his again. He leaned his face down and Aailaine felt her heartbeat quicken. He paused, his lips seconds away from hers and she could feel his breath on her upper lip. She saw the fear and worry in his eyes and closed her own, breathing deeply.

"Aia...Aailaine..." his voice was shaky and unsure as he whispered her name and Aailaine's heart jumped into her chest in anticipation.

"Please." Their lips were so close that she could feel the air from her mouth against her own lips, and she shuddered, gripping Iasi more. It seemed that her soft word was all he needed, because he softly and gently slanted his lips across hers. The kiss felt warm and soft and she felt a tingling feeling her chest. It was strange, but not unpleasant and his thumb stroked her cheek lightly.

Her lips parted slightly and his grip around her waist tightened as he matched her. Aailaine found herself tightening her arms around him, trying to pull him closer. Iasi slowly pulled back from her, his cat ears out to the side and he looked away. She found herself unable to speak and just clung to him awkwardly, not sure if she should let go or not.

"Aia," Iasi's soft words drew her attention back to him and she gazed deeply into his eyes again. She became vaguely aware that his tail was stroking her leg, but his glowing carmine eyes captivated her.

"Yes?" she breathed, leaning her face close to his again. She wanted to feel his lips against hers again. Iasi's gentle press against her lips was everything Vulred's kiss hadn't been and she found herself wanting more. She wasn't sure what that "more" was, but she wanted it.

"I think, we should eat." Iasi turned to look at the Starechf, where they still laid on his short shrug. Slowly and lingeringly, he released her and walked over to the dead fowls and started to clean the birds using his blade. Aailaine slowly lowered herself onto the ground and simply watched him as he prepared their meal. Their kiss was still first and foremost in her mind, but she couldn't deny her hunger. The werecat carefully cleaned and carved some of the meat into bite sized pieces, taking the rest and salting them before wrapping them in Aailaine's wax paper.

"There," Iasi remarked, using a few cooking rods to angle the meat over the fire. After adding a few more sticks to the blaze, he sat next to Aailaine, not looking at her. He kept his gaze on the fire and

Aailaine started drawing circles in the dirt. They sat awkwardly, and it seemed neither of them knew what to say.

"Iasi?"

"Yes Aia?" He turned to look at her and she could feel his gaze as she continued to draw random shapes in the dirt. Her next question was stuck in her throat and she wasn't sure she wanted to ask it or how to correctly ask.

"What...what am I to you?" Iasi turned away from her again, and she sighed deeply. Aailaine watched as he carefully reached to grab one of her hands and gripped it tightly. She looked up at him and he still had his eyes looking away from her, a slight smile on his face.

"You're...more than a friend to me, Aia. I've never been this long with someone I didn't consider family. I'm still trying to figure out myself, exactly what that means." He met her gaze for a moment to look away again, a slight blush coming to his face. Aailaine stared at him and he looked to meet her gaze again. "You're blushing."

"I am?" she gasped, quickly moving her hands to her cheeks and looking away. Her cheeks felt slightly warm under her hands, but when she removed her hands, her face didn't feel hot. She put her hands to her cheeks again and turned to look at Iasi, smiling slightly. "Sorry."

"It's fine." He stroked the back of her hand with his. He slowly let his hand fall from hers and leaned forward to check on the meat. He hummed with satisfaction, removing a few of the rods. "It's done enough for me, but you might want to let it cook longer."

"Okay." Aailaine moved closer to the fire, keeping a close eye on the skewers that remained. Iasi moved to a dark corner of their camp and ate his meat with his back to Aailaine. As she waited for her meal to finish cooking, she found herself thinking about the moment that had passed between them.

Chapter 37

Iasi stretched in the warm midday sun, glancing back down to look at Aailaine. She was sitting on one of the tree roots, taking a well-deserved break. He looked up from the tree branches he sat in and the Anceo mountains loomed over him. He felt a shiver run up his spine, which he tried to ignore. He nimbly made his way back down from the canopy, careful to not knock down any snow before landing softly next to Aailaine. She looked up at him and smiled.

"Well?"

"We're almost there. If we wanted to, we could make it to Anceo today." He shrugged. He had been pushing them to make it to the edge of Hirie, but only because he didn't want to stay any longer than they had to. The trees could feel the Darkness growing inside of him and instinctively reached out to him. It took all of Velatha's strength to consistently pull back on her children and Iasi hated being a burden to her.

"Then let's keep going." She smiled, standing as she adjusted her quiver. Iasi nodded, allowing her to take the lead while he followed behind. Since the attack of the dwarves, no other Daywalkers had attacked them, despite the three weeks they had spent in Hirie. This troubled the werecat greatly and he insisted on following behind Aailaine. Daywalkers were known for being persistent and their lack of activity bothered him.

"Hey Iasi," Aailaine glanced back over her shoulder at him and he looked up to meet her gaze. He jerked his head to the side and she leaned slightly, avoiding a branch. "Have you ever been in Anceo?"

"No. Like Velatha said, there's a barrier."

"But she's always putting her flowers in your hair." Aailaine nodded to the flower branch where it stuck out of the pack, the white blossoms still as vibrant as the day she received them. Iasi shrugged, motioning for her to watch the path. "You never thought of trying?"

"It would be a lie if I said I hadn't. I always tried it as a child." Iasi plucked one of the blossoms from the branch, sticking it next to his ear. "Chadirra would always catch me trying to sneak off and that would be the end of it. I'd be strictly watched until we left Hirie."

"It sucks to be contained like that, doesn't it?" her voice drifted away, and Iasi watched her curiously. She was looking up at the trees and her face was neither sad nor happy, but somewhere in-between. "I like being outside and seeing all there is to see."

"You're not from Dochel, are you?" Aailaine slowly stopped, casting her gaze down. She seemed to be thinking, and Iasi waited, his tail twitching. She slowly looked up at him and seemed to be searching his face for something. He tried his best to keep his expression neutral, not wanting to give himself away. Something about her story had bothered him from the moment he met her and now, knowing she was the *Fogeako*, he finally felt safe to ask her about it.

"You don't believe I'm from Dochel?"

"No. You're always asking questions to things you should know." Iasi shrugged. "I'm no expert, but life in the plains is difficult.

But you didn't know anything about the first day of the week and the new moon and still seem lost about a lot of common things."

"I'm...not from Dochel, but you have to swear you'll never tell another living soul." Aailaine's face became serious and she intensely stared at him. Iasi was taken aback by her expression but nodded curtly, determined to get his answer. She walked back to him and leaned close to his ear.

"I'm from the Tolsan." Her voice was so soft he barely heard her. He gave her a confused look when she pulled away.

"Really? I thought only dwarves and fairies lived there."

"Some humans do as well. Although, they look nothing like me," Aailaine admitted, looking at the ground with a crestfallen expression. "Not one of them would ever let me forget it."

"Don't let it bother you anymore, Aia." He lifted her face up gently and smiled kindly at her. "Let whatever happened there stay there. You are in a new place now. Don't let the past keep you from enjoying the present."

"Yea." She tried to smile, but it escaped her. Iasi lightly kissed her forehead and released her. A true smile slowly spread across her face and she started walking again. He noticed that she seemed to like the little kisses he gave her and he enjoyed giving them. Iasi had never spent so much time away from his family and even of the short times he had been away, he was always by himself. His nights with lovers or customers would be just that and he would be gone the next day. Iasi always distanced himself from falling for anyone, to avoid the pain that would come with the eventual departure. Chadirra really hated that part of his job, but she never made him give it up.

"Something on your mind, Iasi?" Aailaine pulled Iasi from his thoughts and he smiled softly.

"Just thinking about my sister. She has never liked my job, but she supported me anyway." He smiled warmly and laughed softly. "She just always wanted me to be happy."

"Your sister sounds like a good person," Aailaine remarked, holding a branch out of his way while he ducked under it. He nodded, beaming.

"She is. She wouldn't coat the truth with lies just to make it sound better and supported everyone through what they wanted to do." Iasi sighed, remembering the burden he had been to her. "Everyone viewed my sister as their mother, even the ones that were older than her. That's just how she is."

"That must have been hard on her, to have to raise you by herself." Aailaine apologized, but Iasi shook his head and flipped her braid to her other shoulder.

"I'd imagine. She was only twelve cycles when she had to start taking care of me and I was a handful. But she just has that same kind and understanding nature toward everyone and is mature beyond her age." Iasi shielded his eyes as they finally stepped out of the forest. The Anceo mountains stood proud and tall above them and they looked like any other mountain range. He reached up as the flower in his hair vibrated and both Aailaine and he watched in awe as the flower flew out from his hair and turned into a small creature, like none he had ever seen.

She had small insect-like wings and was no bigger than Iasi's hand. Her hair was snow white, like the flower that she came from.

Her bare skin was a strange yellow, almost the color of honey and she never stayed still, constantly moving side to side.

"Hello, Iasi and Aailaine." Her voice was light and airy, like she might blow away at any moment. "My name is Ouscum. I am Velatha's flowers given life by the barrier here. I am to guide you to the artifact you seek. As we pass through these mountains, I will slowly fade away, as all flowers must do."

"Then, what should we do?" Aailaine fretted, glancing up at Iasi. With sudden realization, he pulled the branch off and looked at the other flowers. Ouscum carefully landed on the branch and stroked the other blossoms.

"You must pick another blossom. I am all but none. These flowers will not wilt as long as they remain on this branch." Ouscum smiled and nodded before flying in the air again. "I may not appear the same, just as no two flowers are alike, but trust that I am the same Ouscum as always."

"Alright, Ouscum," Iasi agreed, and he watched as Aailaine slowly nodded. Ouscum seemed content and began to fly in front of them, leading them to the Anceo. Aailaine reached out and gripped Iasi's hand tightly. He glanced down and saw her staring after the flower creature, a deadpan look on her face. He squeezed her hand and started leading them forward.

Ouscum paused as she waited for them to catch up. "We don't have much time. We must keep moving."

"We know. We're coming." Iasi felt as if something had pierced his very being when he stepped into the barrier and he gripped his chest with his free hand. He saw Aailaine do the same and he paused, not wanting to see her in pain. "Ouscum, the barrier."

Shroud-Legends of A'sthy

"You must walk through the pain, as I can only open a path. The barrier will resist, and the pain will continue until we reach the other side." The flower being didn't stop moving forward, motioning for them to follow. Iasi considered walking back to Hirie when he started to be pulled forward. Still gripping her chest, Aailaine started walking after Ouscum, determined to fight through the pain. The agonized look on her face broke him and he quickly scooped her up into his arms. He walked briskly to catch up to Ouscum and he fought through the pain in his chest.

To Iasi, it felt like the barrier was rejecting him and a strong wind was pushing him back. He fought against it, even as he felt that his spirit would be torn from his body. He collapsed to one knee, holding Aailaine tightly against him. Ouscum stopped, landing on the young woman's chest.

"Iasi, we must keep going. The barrier will kill you if you stay too long." Ouscum looked at him with sad eyes and Iasi nodded, a determined look on his face.

"I-I'm...I'm following." Iasi forced himself to stand and adjusted the girl in his arms. He gently touched her amulet and focused on it until the force on him lessened. Aailaine's agony shifted to a glazed look and her breathing slowed. Worry driving him, he walked as quickly as he could, keeping his head down to protect Aailaine.

"We're through." Just as the flower being spoke, Iasi felt the weight pass and he looked up to find himself surrounded by stone. Soft lamps lit the narrow hallway and Iasi stared at them in wonder. Aailaine coughed, bringing his attention back to her. He carefully let her onto the ground and stroked her cheek. She slowly opened her eyes and glanced around.

"Are we...in Anceo...?" Her voice was barely a whisper and she sat up quickly upon seeing the lamps. "El-Elddess? How are there Elddess lamps here?!"

"Tolsan is not the only area with Elddess, Aailaine." Ouscum revealed, flying between them. Her white hair was starting to turn yellow near the ends and her honey skin was turning a dirty brown. "We don't have much time. We can rest for a while, but once I am reborn we must get going."

"Agreed, but we do need to rest," Iasi wheezed, sitting down next to Aailaine. Ouscum landed on the floor and wobbled a moment, before collapsing on the ground. It hurt him to watch her slowly die, but Iasi understood there was nothing he could do. He merely held Aailaine in his lap and silently prayed to Orassul that her strength would return.

Yasmina Iro

Anceo
A place lost to Time

Chapter 38

"Ouscum, what exactly is this artefact?" Iasi adjusted the pack on his back as they continued to follow the flower pixie. Ouscum had already died and been reborn three times and each time she simply repeated that they needed to hurry. They seemed to have a long way to go and she didn't last more than an hour each time she was reborn. They only had ten flowers left, which meant they needed to find the artefact in the next three hours, or they'd be trapped. The path through the Anceo was littered with so many offshoots and branches that Iasi was already lost.

"I'm not quite sure what it is, just where it is." Ouscum admitted, flying backwards. Her hair was slowly breaking off, just as it had done previously. Iasi was tempted to pluck off another blossom but didn't want to waste any of their remaining time. "Do not worry. We will reach it as long as we do not stop."

Iasi gripped Aailaine tighter as he pulled her forward. She was in obvious need of a break, as was he, but he knew Ouscum wouldn't allow one. Her breath was heavy, and she was visibly pushing herself. He offered to carry her several times, but she kept refusing him, saying she didn't want to be a burden.

Releasing her briefly, he pulled out the jar with Orassul's Joy that Velatha had given him. He had forgotten about it after the incident with Vulred and he now remembered the precious gift. She looked at the pot in his hands with interest.

"What's that?" she piped, her interest waning when he took off the lid. "Oh, it's just water."

"It's no ordinary water. Velatha gave it to me for you." he remarked, pushing it toward her. She accepted it and gave it a disdainful look. "Just try it, Aia."

Aailaine gave it another jeering look but brought the jar to her lips and drank a tiny bit of the water. Remembering the experience he had, Iasi quickly caught the jar as she dropped it, replacing its lid as Aailaine stopped walking. Her eyes glazed over, and she was no longer with them.

"Aia?" He waved his hand in front of her face and his heart skipped a beat. He turned to call out to Ouscum but the pixie was already next to him.

"She'll rejoin us in a moment, but we must keep going," Ouscum sighed, running her hand through her yellowing hair. "Pick her up, I suppose, and follow me."

Iasi carefully scooped Aailaine up and she let him, only moving to wrap her arms around his neck. He shook her to see if she was aware yet, but Aailaine's gaze was set straight and she stared at nothing. With a heavy sigh, he passed the time by counting the lamps, intrigued by the soft glow. Aailaine had explained that the Elddess was actually a liquid that could be found in pockets. The liquid had to be harnessed in a special manner because once it came in contact with air, it immediately evaporated and burned. In the Tolsan, it was carefully harnessed and placed into the lamps, which only allowed drops of the liquid to be exposed at a time, allowing for continuous light. One drop could burn for days, so the lamps had a long lifespan before they needed to be replaced.

"Elddess..." Iasi whispered, regarding the lamps with awe as they walked past them. It was a wonder that only Orassul could create and it filled with him with amazement. His daze was broken when he heard Ouscum gasp and he watched as the pixie died for the fourth time, curling up on the ground before crumbling into nothingness. He carefully set Aailaine down, making sure she was comfortable before reaching for the branch. He picked another of the white blossoms and watched as it slowly morphed into Ouscum again.

"Time is of the essence." Iasi was surprised that this Ouscum was male, with short white hair and a deep voice. Just like the previous incarnations, this one wore no clothes and quickly started leading them. The werecat gently shook Aailaine, and she groaned, blinking her eyes as she came to. He smiled with relief and helped her to stand.

"Iasi...? What happened?" Aailaine held her head and gave him a questioning look. He gripped her hand tightly and started walking with her again. "I felt, amazing. Happy."

"The water you drank is called Orassul's Joy. It contains the memories of everything Orassul loved about A'sthy." Iasi quoted, repeating Velatha's words. "Every sip will taste different and give you different experiences."

"Hmm," Aailaine hummed thoughtfully, looking up at the stone ceiling. Iasi wanted to ask her about her experience but withheld his questioning. She still seemed dazed and tired from her ordeal and he didn't want to cause more stress for her.

"We are...almost there," Ouscum wheezed and Iasi launched forward to catch the little flower pixie. His hair was already yellowing, and he seemed ready to crumble. He forced a weak smile. "I don't...last as long in these male forms."

Iasi took slight offense to Ouscum's statement but bit his tongue. He plucked a flower and kept it in his hair next to his ear. Ouscum nodded and tried to fly, only to have Aailaine reach out and catch him. The pixie sighed and gave up, pointing silently in the direction they needed to walk. The werecat had to swallow back his fear as their path became more and more confusing, with them turning and changing direction more often. He unconsciously gripped Aailaine's hand tighter, trying to fight down his paranoia.

"Iasi?" He glanced down as she released his hand and turned his face to hers. He kept his eyes away from her, trying to hide his worry. She stroked his cheek and lightly kissed his lips, causing his heart to leap to his throat. She gave him a reassuring smile and started walking again. The Ouscum in her hand withered away and Iasi felt a rustle in his hair. He looked up as Ouscum leaned down into his face, a large smile on her face.

"We're almost there! Let's go, we must hurry." With that Ouscum took off, flying down the tunnels. The pair shared a look and quickly ran to catch up to the flower being. The pixie was flying faster than normal and it took all of their energy to keep up with how fast she was weaving through the tunnels.

"We're here!" Ouscum turned one last corner and Iasi slid behind her. He stopped dead in his tracks and stared with awe as Aailaine came up behind him. On a huge pedestal towered a giant ring, a pure white light flowing in and around it. The top of the ring appeared as if it had exploded outward and dripped before freezing.

The bluish-green surface seemed unlike any stone or metal Iasi had ever seen and the explosion looked similar to water.

"So...beautiful..." Iasi glanced down as Aailaine glided past him, her eyes fixated on the artefact. Her feet barely touched the floor and it almost seemed as if the ring was pulling her in. The bluish-green glow outlined her silver eyes perfectly and a sense of worry filled him when the light weaving in and out of the ring started to gather around her. He reached out to touch her as she slowly walked toward the ring, but Ouscum flew in front of his hand.

"Don't touch her," the flower being hissed, her usual smile replaced with a frown. "If you do, she won't receive the message she needs. Also, pure light like this will kill you."

"Kill me..." he echoed, watching as Aailaine reached up to touch the lowest dripping of the ring, the light river now flowing around her. As soon as her skin touched its surface, the river imploded for a moment, and then caused the room to become enveloped in a bright light. Iasi quickly threw his hands up to shield his eyes from the light but found that it wasn't painful. Rather, he felt warmth flowing through him, reminding him of the cleansing light that flowed from Aailaine's amulet. He looked up to find her and instead saw a being he didn't recognize. Its hair was snow white and its skin was alabaster, resembling a doll. The robe that clung to its skin like water was made up of a million colors of the rainbow and shimmered in the white light. The being turned to look at him and its rainbow eyes regarded him with sadness.

"Iasi..." When it spoke, Iasi felt an overwhelming sadness fill him, as if every sad and regretful feeling that had ever been felt was being forced into him. He clutched his chest, the feeling causing a heavy pain. Its eyes regarded him with remorse as the light faded and he could see Aailaine again.

"Iasi?!" She quickly walked over to him and he gave her a pained smile as the weight faded from his chest.

"Well, did you get it?"

"No, that...wasn't the real one." Aailaine admitted, casting her gaze down. "It was only a clue. There's another clue, but we...need to go back to the Dochel."

"Back to the plains, huh?" Iasi surmised, running his hand through his hair. She nodded, still looking away from him. He opened his mouth to speak again, when Ouscum quickly flew between them, clearly about to whither again. Her wings were beating frantically, and she flitted to and fro.

"Daywalkers are here! We, we need to get moving. I don't have mu-" Her body crumbled before their eyes and Iasi quickly pulled off another flower. The male Ouscum seemed to keep the frantic nature, for as soon as he formed, he flew off toward the entrance of the chamber.

"We, we have to go!" he called to them and Iasi quickly morphed into a keory. He motioned for Aailaine to climb on his back and waited patiently for her to settle herself and the bag.

Once she was ready, he nimbly began after Ouscum. As they ran through the twilight mountain, Iasi couldn't shake the feeling that it was somehow his fault they had been found. As he quickly turned another corner, he found that Ouscum had withered and he prompted Aailaine with his tail to pluck another flower.

She carefully pulled off another blossom and Ouscum transformed, becoming male again. Instead of running off, he pointed toward the wall and pressed himself against it. Iasi followed his example, backing up so Aailaine was underneath the Elddess lamp. In front of them passed a shapeless mass of Darkness, the liquid simply flowing over the ground. Iasi closed his eyes as it turned, hoping it wouldn't notice him.

"Has it found him yet? It's a pain to keep destroying these lamps." Iasi kept his eyes closed as two sets of footsteps joined with the Darkness. From the way they walked, he recognized them to be elves and his heart sank. No race was safe from the darkness in their hearts, much less the Darkness around them.

"Not yet. Just keep doing it. You know the Darkness can't pass them." Iasi's eyes snapped open as Aailaine gripped his thick fur tighter, pressing her face into his back. He cast his gaze up as Vulred walked into his vision and the werecat felt his rage boiling up inside him. At the hint of his negative emotions, the Darkness quickly rushed down the tunnel toward him and he threw Aailaine off, running to meet the Darkness as he shifted.

"IASI!!!!" He heard her scream his name as he and the Darkness collided, the black substance flowing over and inside of him. He let it, his rage blocking his reason and fueling his carelessness. He glanced back to her, his skin and clothing as black as night and his red eyes glowing as the contacts fell from his eyes.

"I-I'm fine." He tried to smile but found himself smirking instead. His voice was not his own as he fought to ignore the voice in his mind telling him to attack Aailaine. "I'm going to lead them away. Follow Ouscum and get out of here."

With that, Iasi slid in front of the two elves, his gaze fixated on the blue-haired male. His own rage overpowered the suggestive whispers of the Darkness and Iasi smiled viciously.

"Let's play cat and mouse," he threatened, licking his lips as the two elves ran away from him in terror. The Darkness rolled off his skin and caught Vulred's companion by the ankle. The elf tried to free himself but the werecat was on him in an instant. Iasi grabbed the elf by the throat, crushing his windpipe as the elf struggled in his grip. "You be the mice."

"P-Please don't," the elf gasped, trying to free himself from Iasi's grip. This only caused him to squeeze harder and with a loud 'crack!' the elf stopped moving. Iasi's grin widened as he tossed away the dead body and started after his true target.

"And I'll be the cat."

Chapter 39

Aailaine stepped out into the hazy dawn, cradling Ouscum against her chest. One flower remained, which she had placed in her hair to ensure a female form. The female Ouscum in her hand flew from her and turned to face the Anceo, a concerned look on her face. Aailaine turned to look at the mountain as well, filled with worry for Iasi as the day slowly became brighter. The mass of Darkness covered him as soon as Vulred came into view and she knew that it had sensed Iasi's anger.

"Iasi," she whined, dropping to her knees with the pack still in her arms. She wanted to go back into the mountain, but she wasn't sure that with all the mountains twist and turns she'd be able to find him. Ouscum landed on the black leather, gently touching her face. "Will he be able to find his way out? The maze, doesn't he need you to guide him?"

"He should be fine. The spell on the mountain was lifted when you touched the artefact, but I kept it up to confuse the Daywalkers. That's why I died faster than when we were going in." Ouscum admitted, casting her gaze down. "Now that we're out, the spell should be completely lifted. The question is, will he be the same when he comes out?"

"He will." Aailaine assured the pixie, although in her heart she wasn't as sure. She had hoped that they would never see the male elf after he had been banished from Yoltri, but for him to appear in Anceo and to be a Daywalker was beyond her expectations. She knew

Iasi had never forgiven him for forcing himself on her and she was sure that he would kill the elf this time. With the Darkness covering him, it would be near impossible for him to fight that feeling.

"He'll be fine, he has to be." she reasoned as she rocked back and forth, cradling the bag in her arms. The jar of Orassul's Joy fell out of the pack and Aailaine glanced at the container. She carefully picked it up and took off the lid, smelling the water. It previously had no scent, but now it smelled sweeter than honey and at the same time, as bitter as sadness.

She took a small sip and closed her eyes as she felt the cold winter wind blow across her face, the soft touch of a spindly's kiss on her cheek and the sweet taste of honeymead run down her throat. The simple joys lessened her worry and she hummed with delight. She barely glanced up as Ouscum passed away and the new one vibrated in her hair. The tiny pixie climbed down to Aailaine's shoulder and stroked her cheek with her tiny hand.

"I'm sure he'll-" Just as the flower pixie began to speak, the duo felt a rush of wind come out of the mountain and looked up to see a dark shape slowly coming toward them. Preparing for the worst, Aailaine quickly drew her bow and notched an arrow, aiming for the slow-moving shape. If it saw her, it gave no indication, walking at the same pace. She felt her heartbeat speed up with fear and she tightened her hold on the grip.

"A... Aia..." she slowly lowered the bow as the dark shape revealed itself to be Iasi. He was completely draped in Darkness and it flowed over him, tightening its grip on his long shawl. He continued walking out into the soft morning light and let out a scream of pain when the sunlight touched him. He stopped walking forward but didn't retreat back into the mountain. The Darkness on him started to flee for a moment, revealing his tan skin before clinging to him again. Iasi let another anguished cry but refused to return to the shadow of the mountains.

"Iasi!" She dropped the bow and ran up to him and he took a small step back, growling. His ears flattened, and his tail was puffy, appearing twice its normal size. She slowly stopped, only an arm's reach away from him. "Iasi?"

"STA- stay away from me, Aia." he groaned, visibly in pain and trying to restrain himself. His arm lurched forward, almost grabbing her clothing and he stopped it with his other hand, holding it against his chest. Aailaine watched in horror as the Darkness began to evaporate and Iasi fell to his knees, trying to contain the pain. "This Darkness, it...it wants me to kill you, and I...can't do that. It won't let go, even with the sunlight. Just...leave."

"No!" Aailaine crossed the short distance between them and threw her arms around the werecat. The moment her hands touched the Darkness it swarmed to cover her, and Aailaine lost her sight. She found herself lost in a sea of black and a deep fear rose within her. She had always been afraid of pure darkness, ever since she was young. The soft light of the Elddess lamps helped to appease her fear although she never went into unlit parts of the Tolsan.

Lost and confused, she began to thrash around, reaching for something when she felt a hand in hers. Thinking it to be Iasi, she pulled herself toward the hand, only to have it release her and grab her throat. She quickly pushed the hand off her and ran away from it, only to find more hands touching her and reaching out to her. They pulled and tore at her clothing and she stumbled, falling down onto the ground she couldn't see.

"Iasi! Iasi, help me!" Aailaine curled up on the ground and she could feel the hands searching for her in the dark. She felt something tugging at the back of her mind, as if someone was trying to remind her of something. She needed a source of light, anything that produce enough light to scare away the Darkness and the hands that sought to kill her.

< The amulet! > Remembering the trinket, she quickly grasped it and concentrated with all her might. She squeezed it until her fingers began to hurt and then squeezed it even harder. She jumped as one of the hands touched her and the rest joined, clinging to her. Their fingernails dug into her body and she thought she heard words, but she couldn't understand what they said. She tried her best to ignore the pain and keep her thoughts on the amulet and its light, tracing the dragon with her fingers. < Please, give me light! >

As if summoned, a single beam of light seemed to glow inside Aailaine's hands, and she moved her hands to see that it was her own hands producing the glow. The unseen hands screamed as they released her, and Aailaine breathed in the fresh air as the Darkness around her evaporated. She looked to see Iasi on his knees, still covered by the Darkness. He seemed to be slowly evaporating with the liquid and Aailaine quickly embraced him again. This time, the glow from her hands expanded, and consumed them within the bright light.

When the light faded, Iasi had collapsed onto the ground and no trace of the Darkness remained on his skin or on the ground about them. She gently touched his chest and found him breathing, although he seemed to be asleep. With the Darkness coating him, Aailaine had failed to notice the bloodstains on his clothes and her heart filled with immense sadness. She knew from the lack of wounds that the blood couldn't be his and she had a good guess to whom it belonged.

"He's probably worn out from his ordeals." Ouscum offered, the pixie slowly fading for the last time. Aailaine caught the flower being in her hand, and Ouscum hugged her thumb. She felt a twinge of sadness and regret in her chest, knowing that it was the pixie's fate but not being able to do anything.

"Is there nothing I can do to save you?"

"I do not need to be saved, as I was never truly alive in the first place," Ouscum smiled, hugging her tighter. "Although it makes me happy that you feel the need to save me. You truly are *Fogeako*..."

With her last words, Ouscum crumbled away into dust, never to be reborn again. Aailaine sat alone, Iasi asleep on the ground as the sun rose high into the sky. She glanced down at her amulet and was worried when she noticed at slight crack in the sapphire. She carefully stood and picked up her bow and pack from where they lay and moved them closer to the werecat's sleeping form. She pulled out one of her white gems, but the sapphire remained dormant.

Confused, Aailaine replaced the gem and pulled out an eri, and tried to enjoy the chilly winter morning.

Chapter 40

Iasi awoke suddenly and was surprised to find it dark. He slowly sat up and checked his surroundings. There was a small fire blazing to his left and although he didn't see her, there were signs that Aailaine had been there. He turned to his right and saw the Anceo Mountains, appearing tall and ominous in the night. The half-moon was still behind them and framed the giants with its soft glow.

He moved as if to stand and noticed he wasn't wearing his shirt and his short shrug graced his shoulders. He quickly glanced around for his winter clothing but didn't see them lying around the camp. Iasi grunted as he stood, his body still aching. The Darkness had driven him to ignore pain, even as the elf had stabbed him repeatedly. The wounds immediately healed, and he continued to carefully carve into Vulred's flesh...

"No," Iasi muttered, trying to shake the dark images from his mind. While he had wanted to kill the elf, the slow painful torture the Darkness had driven him to left him disturbed and he felt a shiver run up his spine. He moved closer to the fire and sat back down, unsure of what to do.

"Oh, you're awake." He looked up as Aailaine returned to their camp, her arms filled with various vegetables. She carefully placed them on the ground, and walked over to him, handing him his shawl and shirt. He accepted them, and they felt damp in his arms. "I went to wash the blood off them, sorry if they're not dry completely."

"That's fine, thank you." Iasi quickly slipped the shirt back on and smiled at her warmly. She sighed with relief and moved to the carrots, turnips and onions she had gathered. He watched her curiously as she pulled out some of the Starechf and the wooden skewers. She carefully unwrapped some of the meat and started to layer the meat and vegetables on the rods. "What are you doing?"

"I thought it would be interesting, you know, to try it." Aailaine shrugged and continued to make six vegetable and meat skewers. She added some of the wooden rods to the flame before angling the meat over it. "It's something more than just one or the other."

"Sure," Iasi frowned. He didn't like vegetables much, so he wasn't sure how he felt about them being cooked with the meat without being in a stew. He tried to mask his disappointment as Aailaine sat next to him on the ground. "So, is this...it?"

Aailaine gave him a horrified look and he felt like he had said something wrong. Her eyes widened with fear and she quickly turned away from him.

"I mean, I suppose, if you need to leave, I guess, you can." she stammered, barely hiding her fear and disappointment. "I mean, you have your family, and all."

"Don't misunderstand." Iasi took her hand and brought it to his chest, causing her to turn and face him. Tears were starting to roll down her cheek and he began to feel bad for his words. "If you want me here, I will stay with you no matter how long you need me. I just...thought after that..."

< You would hate me. > he thought to himself, unable to meet her gaze. "I just wasn't sure if you still wanted or even needed my help."

"I do." She nodded quickly, gripping his hand tightly. He slowly looked at her, and her soft look nearly caused his heart to burst. He turned away from and leaned close to the fire, checking their meal. The meat seemed to need a little longer, so Iasi left them alone. Aailaine took this chance to speak again. "I need to get to Mixoh."

"Well that's a challenge." Iasi sighed, leaning back on his hands. "But I'll get us there."

"Thank you," Aailaine agreed and for a while the pair sat in an awkward silence. Iasi wanted to apologize for what had happened in the Anceo, but he wasn't sure how to approach it or if he should say anything at all. He glanced over at Aailaine, where she sat with her knees to her chest, her eyes on the fire. She slowly reached into the pack next to her and grabbed something before motioning for Iasi's hand.

Slowly, she carefully dropped a pair on contacts into his hand and he couldn't hide his surprise.

"Where...where did you get these?" he asked softly as he placed them in his eyes. He was sure the ones from the mountains had been lost once they fell from his eyes. Aailaine shrugged and pulled out a small container from the pack, containing several pairs of contacts in various colors.

"I bought extra while we were in Pasyl. More blue for you and some for me." Aailaine admitted. "After what happened on our way there, I figured it wouldn't hurt to have extra in case something happened again.. Also, I may need to hide my eyes as well, as time goes on."

She carefully picked up one of the rods and sniffed the meat. She gingerly took a bite and hummed with delight. She picked up another stick and handed it to Iasi.

"Here." He carefully accepted the stick and he couldn't deny that it smelled delicious. He took a small bite and examined the taste as he chewed and swallowed the Starechf and vegetable medley. He had to admit it tasted better than having to eat the vegetables by themselves, but he still preferred his meals with more meat. He quickly finished off the skewer and picked up another.

"So, does it taste good?" Aailaine was playing with the empty stick in her hands nervously. Iasi nodded as he started on the second stick.

"It's good, Aia. Definitely a winner." She visibly glowed and reached for her other two skewers. Iasi quickly finished his own meal and looked up at the night sky. The half-moon had finally passed over the peaks of the Anceo, and he enjoyed its soft glow. He heard a soft sliding noise and looked back down to see Aailaine lay her head in his lap. He lightly tapped her head, giggling softly at her childish behavior.

"You shouldn't lay down after eating or your stomach will hurt when you wake up."

"Mhmm. Don't care." she purred, rubbing her head in his lap. He sighed, laying his hand on her shoulder as she fell asleep. He rubbed her shoulder gently, mesmerized by her ever-changing hair. He lightly stroked it and watched as the colors rippled in the soft firelight.

He looked back up to the moon and watched as it slowly began its journey across the sky. Even as the fire slowly died, and the moon disappeared past the trees, Iasi sat awake with Aailaine sleeping in his lap. He knew that he wanted to protect her always, even if it meant giving into the deepest Darkness.

Appendix

Language in A'sthy

Eroir

The Ancient Language of A'sthy, Eroir is considered to be the language of Orassul. Dwarves and elves uses Eroir more heavily while younger races tend to speak only common. Eroir is also the language used to guide magic and is taught to enchanters and wizards. Sorcerers may avoid using Eroir altogether.

Eroir used in this Book*:

ang/aŋ/
    det. same
angger/aŋˈgɛɾ/
    v. want
ashe/aˈɛɛ/
    conj. and
beirz/bɛˈiːrz/
    adv. sorry
bia/biˈa/
    adv. away
bo/bo/
    prep. over
dikang/diˈkaŋ/
    adv. long
e/ɛ/
    v. do
eahtu/ɛaçˈtu/
    adv. that
earibuo/ɛaribuˈo/
    v. shine
earmom/ɛarˈmom/
    nm. bird
ei/ɛˈi/
    nn. bitch
fa/fa/
    pron. you
hebu/hɛˈbu/
    adj. deep

fea/ɸɛa/
    neg. never
feahtum /ɸɛaçˈtum/
    prep. with
fear/fɛaɾ/
    v. will
fei/fɛi
    pron. you
fingge/fiŋˈgɛ/
    nn. morning
fogea/fɔˈgɛa/
    v. save, rescue
fohto/ɸoçˈto/
    v. please
fuko/fuˈko/
    nm. warrior
fuo/fuo/
    adv. well
gazu/gaˈzu/
    v. watch
gibdeo/gibˈdɛo/
    v. take
goa/gɔˈa/
    v. go
guofi/guoˈfiː/
    adj. stupid
ngea/ŋɛa/
    adv. there

heia/hˈɛia/
nf. problem
heiirmeia/hɛirˈmɛia/
nm. asshole
hez/hɛz/
nm. girl
hongekako/çoŋɛˈkako/
nf. stoneshaper
i/i/
prep. of, the
ide/iˈdɛ/
v. come
ika/iˈka/
neg. not
interj. no
ikade/iːkaˈdɛ/
v. sleep
n4. sleep
ikta/iːkˈta/
v. live
inghuonggo/iŋhuoŋˈgɔ/
adj. quiet
kea/kɛˈa/
nf. shade, shadow
kei/kɛi/
det. what
keoi/kˈɛoiː/
interj. hello
ki/kiː/
nn. day, light
kod/kɔd/
v. be
meiuoko/mˈɛiuoko/
nm. vintner
muir/muˈiz/
v. obey
nao/ɴaˈɔ/
v. thank

ngo/ŋo/
adj. sure
nuif/ɴuˈif/
nf. nymph
odo/ɔˈdɔ/
adj. happy
oiihead/ɔiːiːˈhɛad/
interj. yes
oka/oˈka/
v. have
or/oɾ/
pron. her, him, it
orambuorgu/ɔrambuorˈgu/
adv. again

rea/rɛa/
pron. I

ritye/riːtʼyɛ/
n. damn
rizi/riːˈzi/
v. rise
sheeideong/ɕɛɛiˈdɛoŋ/
adv. quickly
tang/taŋ/
interj. welcome
teieimoko/tˈɛiɛimɔko /
nm. rider
uab/uˈab/
adv. ok
uoduoshe/uoduoˈɕɛ/
nm. evening
ura/uˈɾa/
adj. young
washck/waˈɕk/
nn. master
yelaneri/yɛˈaɴɛˈriː/
nn. universe

* Verbs are not conjugated in this dictionary

Creatures in A'sthy

Mo'qire- Mountain dragons. Similar to a lindworm, they have only two front legs with long claws for digging. They dig their way through the mountain rock hunting for jewels to eat. Dwarves will sometimes use Mo'qire tunnels as shortcuts through the mountains.

Yeitre- Mountain wolves. They are the size of a bear and have thick coats of fur. Races outside the Tolsan consider it's fur valuable, since dwarves refuse to hunt them and any clothing made using the fur is rare.

Siraya- Rabbits-like creatures with short antennae. Being found in almost every region, these creatures come in various breeds and color. They are very skittish and family oriented, meaning that finding a den can lead to a very lucrative catch.

Ozkok- Desert dragons. Resembling snakes with wings, these dragons often prey on dune siraya, following the creature back to its den before sliding its way in. Their bites are extremely venomous, and if one is bit in the middle of the desert, death is certain.

Akhby- Plains dragons. Sporting long horns that curled forward for females, backward for males, they have a long serpentine body with clubbed tails. These dragons are most likely the most intelligent, being the only dragons capable of speech. Akhby can communicate telepathically with other akhby and races, making them a popular choice for Vuiej.

Totiriel- Large mountain rams with sharp horns. Along with jewels and various stones, the wool from these rams is a stable export from the Tolsan. However, hunting these creatures can be dangerous, as despite their herbivore nature, they are known to rush anything they presume to be a threat.

Teyom- Wild boars that roam around the plains. They have no horns with short snouts and stubby legs and are quite easy to hunt and kill. They can often be found near troll farms, drinking the irrigation water or trying to get the crops.

Wevran – Eight-legged lizards that are common in Hirie and Dochel. Come in a variety of colors and are considered a treat by trolls and elves. These reptiles can be quite large, with some breeds growing to 30 cm in length.

Wonir- Forest wolves. Much more docile than their mountain and plain counterparts, these wolves live peacefully with the elves, staying away from their cities and often running away from elven hunting parties.

Starechf – Chicken-like birds. They are quick to take flight when startled, but otherwise are relatively stupid. They are easy to kill and considered a staple meat in Hirie and Redan.

Keory- Wildcats that roams the mountains at night. They roam in packs, making them a deadly foe if faced alone. They primarily hunt totiriel, but are known to kill yeitre as well.

Dairn- Large hounds that roam in Dochel. These hounds are extremely dangerous and impossible to tame, despite being capable of speech like akhby. They are well known to raid troll farms for their livestock, and don't hesitate to attack those who try to stop them. Their bites are infectious and most would rather take the lost than try to fend it off.

Yineru- Three-legged sheep. They are quite docile and are sometimes kept as pets. They do not produce wool but are a staple livestock in troll farms.

Author Bio

When it comes to travelling, Yasmina Iro knows a thing or two about putting on the mileage. She can often be found exploring the world, travelling to learn about new cultures and experience our beautiful planet. From her home base in the U.S., she enjoys creating new worlds and cultures for her readers to explore with her. When not exploring A'sthy or Earth, Yasmina can be found decorating beautiful cakes in her kitchen while caring for her blooming family.

Made in the USA
Columbia, SC
12 June 2018